Nature Studies in Australia

This edition published 2026
by Living Book Press

Copyright © Living Book Press, 2026

ISBN: 978-1-76183-247-5 (hardcover)
         978-1-76183-245-1 (softcover)

First published in 1903.

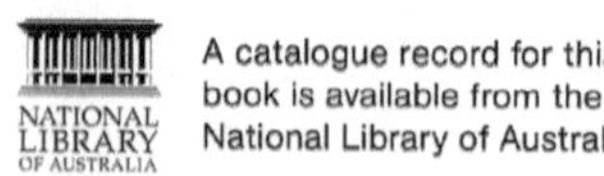
A catalogue record for this book is available from the National Library of Australia

Nature Studies in Australia

by

WILLIAM GILLIES

Contents

"The lives of many men and women are passed in a succession of petty anxieties about themselves, and gleaning of minute interests and mean pleasures in their immediate circle, because they are never taught to make any effort to live beyond it; or to know anything of the wonderful world in which their lives are lived."

—RUSKIN

RED-CAPPED ROBIN SHOWING
ITS RED FRONTAL MARK.

FLAME-BREASTED ROBIN SHOWING
A SMALL WHITE FRONTAL MARK.

SCARLET-BREASTED ROBIN SHOWING
A LARGE WHITE FRONTAL MARK.

RECOGNITION MARKS OF ROBINS

(ROBINS OF ONE SPECIES KNOW THOSE OF ANOTHER BY THESE MARKS).

PREFACE

THE new world-wide movement towards Nature study owes much to the Cornell University, New York State. The Cornell conception of Nature study is that "it is seeing the things which one looks at, and the drawing of proper conclusions from what one sees." This little book is an attempt to help the reader to do this. It is also an attempt to awaken delight and wonder in the presence of Nature. The interest in living things which is born with every child was often killed by the old methods of presenting knowledge. Technical language was used, which made things that were really familiar look strange and forbidding. Anatomy and physiology were introduced at a stage when the child is interested solely in outside appearances; the single robe of Nature was torn into separate parts called Sciences, which seemed to have no connection; and a jumble of facts was presented, under the name of Natural History, culled from every part of the world except from the child's own surroundings. Delight in the beauty and wonder of life was not drawn out; and, indeed, the whole course of study was often subordinated to the needs of students who were preparing for a medical course. Little wonder that the child's interest was soon killed.

The scrappy object lessons of the past will need to be given up. The teacher must feel the unity of Nature, and treat each object as part of an organic whole. The world is not divided into thought-tight compartments. It is natural for the child to look on the world as one; and it is mischievous to check this natural feeling by presenting one part of Nature as if it had no connection with another. The good teacher of Nature study will try to foreshadow for the child that unity of Nature which the mature man finally arrives at. Study of the separate sciences will come in due time, when the child becomes the student.

It is essential, too, that a school course of Nature study should be systematic. Much harm has been done in the past by loose, desultory Nature teaching, and also by the idea that, when children are taken into garden or field, they can do good work without systematic guidance and strict discipline. The brightest Nature teaching will fail unless there goes with it a method as severe and a discipline as strict as in teaching arithmetic.

In dealing with types of life, from the earth-worm to the bird, we have carefully followed the natural order from lower to higher forms, except in one case—that of the birds. We have opened the course with the birds, because, in nine cases out of ten, a child begins his voluntary Nature studies with the observation of birds. Birds arrest his attention even more than flowers; and many a man looks back to the bird-music of his childhood as that which first awakened his soul. In the winter time, too, when the flowers are gone, the birds are still present. These beautiful creatures of the air are always with us, in town or country, in summer or winter; and no part of Nature study, therefore, gives such large and immediate reward as the study of birds.

It is the gift of God to every child that it can love all that is beautiful; but this faculty, like every other, has to be cultivated. So long as this faculty lies uncultivated, the statesman will labour in vain to put content into the heart of the people. Keeping this in mind, we have frequently given the poet's view of Nature. We cannot forget that the poet managed to interest men in Nature long before the naturalist got the ear of the people. Our ideas of birds and beasts and flowers are largely those of Chaucer and Cowper, of Burns and Wordsworth. We have to remember, too, that the poet's word is the last word, when we are seeking for the meaning of the facts and laws ascertained by the naturalist.

There is still another reason for presenting the poet's view of Nature: it is in this way that the faculty of imagination can best be trained. To do original work in Nature study it is necessary to have, not only a good eye and a clear mind, but a quickened imagination. Tyndall has told us how much he owed in his original investigations to his power of making clear mind-pictures of processes which can be seen only by the eye of faith; and he acknowledged a deep obligation to Tennyson's poems for developing this faculty of imagination. The trained imagination, in truth, is the natural extension of our powers of seeing. If, in the past, we have been narrow in our views; if we have failed to see the true inwardness of things, it is largely because we have not been trained to use this inner eye. The imagination has, therefore, been appealed to in various ways.

Much of the book has been written in the open air; it is hoped that many will read it out of doors. We have had too much indoor study of outdoor life.

We are pleased to acknowledge our indebtedness for many figures to Mr. John Gould's *Birds of Australia*. The remaining plates not acknowledged are by the authors' camera. Valuable help has also been received from the *Victorian Naturalist* and from *The Emu*, the journal of the Ornithologists' Union of Australasia; also from the admirable collection of specimens arranged in the National Museum under the direction of the Honorary Director, Professor W. Baldwin Spencer, and his assistants.

February, 1903.

INTRODUCTION

"NATURE study is learning those things in Nature that are best worth knowing, to the end of doing those things that make life most worth living." This quotation from Professor Hodge's *Nature Study and Life* expresses admirably the aim and purpose of Nature study, and rightly emphasises the fact that education is to be judged by its results in character, and by the expression of that character in life, rather than by any mere acquisition of knowledge, however useful or interesting. It is significant that, as soon as this truth began to influence educational practice, as soon as teachers began to feel the unreality and dead formalism of so much of school education, there should have arisen the cry—"Back to natural methods! Back to the study of Nature herself! Let our children front facts, let them deal with realities, and not with half-comprehended symbols. Let them learn to form judgments for themselves rather than blindly accept the ready-made opinions of other minds. Let them acquire habits of close observation and the added power of reflection upon the facts observed, so that what is studied becomes theirs in very truth, and must out in character and deed. Let us aim at producing men who shall be personalities, and not mere hollow-sounding shells echoing what is spoken into them." If these are the ideals towards which we are feeling our way, no better fundamental study for the elementary school can be found than the study of Nature, whose realities, go where he will, the teacher cannot escape, and whose abundant store lies waiting round every school-house. The charm of it lies in the fact that we deal with living things in action. Every healthy child is attracted and held by the wonder and beauty of natural life. The varied movement, the glowing colour, the strong pulsating life-current, the evidence of purposeful activity, the loveliness and the mystery of it all cannot fail to interest him vitally; and, given eager interest, what cannot the teacher do? How, otherwise than by the stimulus of eager interest in Nature study, can we explain the marvel of the child's phenomenal progress in knowledge and in power of expression during the first five years of life, before we receive him into the school?

Nature study answers satisfactorily to every test the educator may apply. Are we concerned with the intellectual aspect of mental training chiefly, then no subject can give more interesting and effective exercise in close and sustained observation, in comparison and generalization, in collecting and systematising truths, and in working out the causes and results of observed facts. But, best of all, no subject satisfies so thoroughly the emotional and æsthetic necessities so strong in the child's nature, or brings him into a better mental attitude towards his Creator's work. Faulty education too often makes light of these most potent factors for good or ill, and turns out a man who is—

> *"A reasoning, self-sufficing thing,*
> *An intellectual all-in-all."*

We want more appeal in our teaching to the fine things, the enduring things, of life. These, whether found in literature or other form of art, have their roots in Nature study.

One of the soundest maxims of teaching practice is: *"Strive to form a body of school interests by utilising the outdoor, the* **LIFE** *interests of the child.*" The day is not far distant when the facts observed in the Nature study will form the greater part of the subject-matter of all those elementary school subjects, such as reading, composition, and drawing, which are meant to develop power of expressing thought. "Let a fellow sing of the little things he cares about," says Kipling; and, if we want to cultivate the power of full and satisfactory expression, we must see to it that the impression has been clear and adequate. But an idea depends for its meaning and fullness upon the strength of its relationship to what is already in the mind, and the great mass of a young child's ideas are ideas gained from observation of Nature. It is only when impression and expression constantly act and react upon one another that the best results are achieved in either. Too many men are crippled on account of want of harmony between these in school life. Stimulating, thought-provoking impressions should precede and control expression; and, correspondingly, the desire to express a thought adequately will produce more satisfactory impressions. Given perfect response between impression and expression, and the truth of the saying "Education is not a preparation for life; it is life" becomes apparent. With this perfect response, what might not be possible in education! But we want fine impressions which will bring us out on our best side. An ever-present aim in training young children should be to give them an early interest in fine things, and then to be ever on the watch to utilize this interest in their general training. That child is little to be envied who has not been allowed to satisfy his nature by keeping pet animals, who has not been encouraged to plant a seed and wonder at the mystery of its growth, who has been allowed to grow blind and deaf to "all the mighty world of eye and ear," and to whom the procession of the seasons calls up no "time of the singing of birds" or "season of mists and mellow fruitfulness," but merely a few diagrams of ellipses on a school blackboard and a few facts of mathematical geography. There is still too much of the teaching that touches real life nowhere and allows the scholar to think justifiably that school tasks are merely some conventional stuff which must be held for examination purposes, but which may be jettisoned as soon as the hateful school period is over. Contrast with this a teaching which is as real and as rational as the life outside, which makes constant appeal to this life, which insists upon first-hand impressions, and which gives power of expression in order to satisfy a real need. This is the education which is "life itself."

So far, I have emphasised only the disciplinary value of Nature study; and it cannot be doubted that a sensitive child trained in a stimulating way would not only have received valuable and strengthening mental exercise, but would have approached much nearer to that harmony with his environment which is the aim of all education. He should have the power of responding to the wealth of stimulus pouring in upon him from every side, he should have a fine background against which to set his thoughts, he should have a wealth of suggestion to occupy such odd moments as he can devote to "leisurely delights and sauntering thoughts," he should have a heart to sympathize with every mood of Nature, and a determination—

> *"Never to blend his pleasure or his pride*
> *With sorrow of the meanest thing that feels."*

And through all he should see clearly that natural beauty is not all, but that one should look through Nature up to Nature's God. But, besides all this, Nature study can claim the highest economic value. This is especially true in Australia, where so much of our national prosperity depends directly upon our natural resources. Knowledge of, or ignorance of, a few facts of Nature may mean the difference of millions of pounds to us. A single insect pest may lay waste the national harvest, a fungous disease may blight a national industry, a noxious weed ignorantly introduced may mean the expenditure of thousands to keep it in check. That we realize this is shown by our legislation, wherein we prescribe courses of action designed to keep such evils in check. But no such laws can be efficiently administered until the community as a whole understands more fully what it is that must be guarded against. It is useless to expect the trained orchardist to keep his orchard clean when every cottage garden in his vicinity is a breeding ground for the pests against which he is battling. Nature study in the elementary school cannot deal with the economic side to any great extent, but it can and ought to direct attention to a class of facts now ignored by fairly well educated men. It will undoubtedly give a great stimulus to the study of the beneficent and the injurious agencies in Nature. In the future, we may hope that the youth who is just leaving school shall no longer feel his fingers straying towards a stone whenever he sees an innocent bird, that his first impulse will not be to plant his heel on every creeping thing that crosses his path, and that the sickly rose-bush in his cottage garden will not be left to struggle unaided against mildew or aphis. At present there is still a disposition to regard the penalties inflicted upon our ignorance or our carelessness as inscrutable mysteries, or as plagues sent to chastise national wrong-doing. They are chastisements, but not in the sense popularly attributed.

Nature study as a school subject is comparatively new in Australia, and it requires most careful handling in its inception. It is so fatally easy to run off the right rails on to the wrong rails. Nature study is so bound up with science that the mistake is often made of confounding it with systematic botany, or zoology, or entomology. These sciences may undoubtedly be treated just as interestingly as Nature study, but they are not elementary school subjects; and, in their elaborate classifications, the study of the living creature often becomes subordinated to other ends, so that the work becomes an affair of dried specimens and diagrams rather than of life in action.

Again, it must not be forgotten that it is for its reaction upon our own development, upon our own practical needs, upon our own lives, that we study the life-history of Nature. The grand result aimed at is to relate Nature-knowledge to ourselves, to show how it helps us materially, how it may brighten our lives and enkindle our thoughts. John Burroughs, one of the truest and most sympathetic writers upon Nature subjects, puts the case admirably: "If I name every bird in my walk, describe its colour and ways, &c., give a lot of facts and details about the bird, it is doubtful if my reader is interested. But if I relate the bird in some way to human life, to my own life—show what it is to me, and what it is in the landscape and the season, then do I give my reader a live bird and not a labelled specimen." This added human interest is the most difficult factor for the average writer or teacher. Among our Australian authors, Mr. Donald Macdonald appears to me to have this gift in a high degree. His Nature articles should be studied by teachers.

No teaching can be of the highest rank unless it is stimulating and suggestive. It opens up fields for research, and at the same time implants the eager desire to seek. Any teacher can be a collector and imparter of facts. A better teacher goes further and reaches the relationship existing between the facts. The best teacher, however, does all this and, in the doing, prompts the exclamation—How fine! I never thought of that before! Wonderful! These last are the teachers who will make Nature study the subject of all others destined to work a beneficent revolution in our school practice—the change from unreality to reality, and a determination to make school education not merely a poor preparation for a life ten years ahead, but an active agent in producing a full and abounding interest in life in each present year.

This book makes no pretence to outline any systematic course of Nature study. It is a reader designed to interest the senior boys and girls of elementary schools, and I heartily commend it to the goodwill of teachers as embodying the essential aims of genuine Nature work. They will find it not only instructive but full of suggestion, and withal most inspiring. The authors have the keenest sympathy with their subject, and their human-heartedness is felt throughout. Nature does not yield her secrets to the unsympathetic. The thoughts "that often-times lie deep" come "thanks to the human heart by which we live." Let me commend to readers the aim set forth in the chapter on *Method in Nature Study:*—"The fact, the meaning of the fact, and the wonder and beauty of the fact—these are the three elements in every full observation of nature."

I began with a quotation from Professor Hodge's valuable "Nature Study and Life." I may appropriately end with an application, from the same book, of a beautiful saying, which sets forth what I believe to be the real position of Nature study rightly introduced into elementary schools:—"I am come that they might have life, and that they might have it more abundantly.[1]"

FRANK TATE.

31st January, 1903.

---

[1]   John 10:10

CHAPTER I.
The Return of the Birds.

My friend Mr. Gray was coming to spend a few weeks with me at my home in the country. It was a fine afternoon in September when I waited for him at the railway station.

Mr. Gray, a remote descendant of the poet Gray, was a city man. We sometimes called him the poet; for, while he was keenly alive to the beauty of Nature in its general aspects, he was not yet conscious of the charm of knowing the face of Nature in detail. We would quarrel in a good-natured way about this, and I had gleefully laid my plans to make the poet into a naturalist.

On our way from the station we saw a gathering of house-swallows on the roof of the school-house. There was much twittering and restless movement.

"Look at the travellers," I said, "just arrived from Queensland!" "Ah!" said Mr. Gray, "the bird that chases the summer o'er the earth." "And what is all the talk about?"

"Who knows? They may be comparing notes of travel and adventure, or making plans for the summer. The younger birds may be busy wooing; for most of them nest in this month."

Crossing the river, we stopped to look at the swallows that were catching flies below the bridge. Besides the house-swallow, with its rust-red throat, there was the fairy martin, white-bellied and touched with white above the tail.

House-Swallows.

We stood for some minutes enjoying their graceful flight, and then we scrambled down to the water-edge to see the nests of the fairy martin. There they were, under the bridge, a colony of thirty nests, from three to seven inches apart! I had known the colony for years.

"The birds came back from the north last week," I explained, "and started at once to get the old nests in order. They work in the cool of the morning, or, as now, in the cool of the evening."

Watching closely, we saw that about half a dozen birds had been told off for each nest needing repair. The nests were bottle-shaped and made of mud. "The bottle-swallow is the name the bird goes by among the farmers here."

With a long stick I broke off the neck of one of the finished nests, and, almost at once, the whole colony of martins set about repairing the damage. In less than a quarter of an hour hundreds of mud-pellets had been carried up and the neck restored.

When the ordinary work had been resumed, we noticed that the six birds that were working at one of the nests were all bringing grass or feathers to line it.

A sparrow, on its way to a neighbouring farm, perched for a minute on a beam of the bridge. The martins seemed to be disturbed.

"Are they afraid of him?" asked Mr. Gray. "Yes," I replied, "the fairy martin is a gentle bird, and is easily bullied by sparrow or kingfisher, or even by the little diamond bird. The kingfisher is fond of young martins, and will break off the neck of the bottle bit by bit till it reaches the nest."

"Last year," I went on, "I found a sparrow in possession of a nest just completed. The whole colony joined in an effort to eject him. Failing in this, they plastered him in!"

We found that the eggs of this swallow vary somewhat in colour, some being white, while in others the white is spotted with tawny brown.

Fairy Martins.

Mr. Gray would hardly believe that we had been half an hour at the bridge. "Yes," I said, "the day is too short for the naturalist or the poet who insists on seeing Nature with his own eyes." "For the poet?" said Mr. Gray, inquiringly.

"Yes," I replied; "Browning would sit quite still in a wood for an hour, and the birds would hop about his feet. Tennyson would spend an afternoon in watching how the lark rose into

WHITE-SHAFTED FANTAIL.

the air and dropped to the ground. Nature will not give up her secrets to the man in a hurry."

Skirting the river, I heard the call of the white-shafted fantail. "Here," I said, "is another bird that has come back from the north. The farmer has few better friends than this little flycatcher." While we waited to see the bird, Mr. Gray said: "What sights these travelling birds must see in their long journeys!" "I doubt," I replied, "whether they have much to see. Much of their travelling is done during the night, and they fly so high above the earth that, even in the daytime, little or nothing can be seen of the lands passed over." "Then," said Mr. Gray, "how do they find their way—these travellers without compass? I should like to hear more of all this." "Then you shall," I replied; "we'll talk it over this evening." Mr. Gray had risen to the bait at once.

The fantail now came into sight, flying near the ground, and with the wavy, erratic flight peculiar to the bird. It was white of throat, with buff breast, and with white shafts marking the tail. The pretty fanlike tail was longer than the wing, and was never at rest.

"What graceful poses!" said the poet, "and how trustful it is!" "Yes," I replied, "I've known it to try to settle on the gun of a man who sought to shoot it." "Shoot it!" cried Mr. Gray, "the beautiful, friendly bird! The day after tomorrow there may be no fantails on our creeks; and life, for the Australian, will be less worth living. If those who come after us are bitter about it, and call us barbarians, can we blame them?"

I heartily agreed with him, but added: "I'm not afraid: we are going to enlist every boy in the land as a protector of the bird." As we passed on, the fantail broke into its little song of gladness. "You hear, Mr. Gray, the bird is thanking you!"

We were crossing the home paddock when some ground-larks ran out of our way. This bird, which we ought to call the pipit, is a little larger than the sparrow, but lighter in colour and more slender in build. In the season, the pipit is almost as common in the field as the sparrow in the street.

"Here," I said, "is another of the birds that have just come

BLACK AND WHITE FANTAILS.

to spend the summer with us. Do you notice that it does not fly away, but runs before us or to the side?"

We followed up one of the birds quietly, and it kept running away for almost five minutes before it lost patience and took wing. Even then it flew for only a hundred yards, and then settled again to search for insects. "It seems to be devoted to earth-study," said Mr. Gray; "I can't feel much interest in a lark

Ground-Larks or Pipits.

that can't soar and sing." "Mr. Gray!" I cried, "you are wrong! I have a great respect for that bird; and, before you go to bed to-night, you will agree with me!"

CHAPTER II.
The Migration of Birds.

"The happy birds, that change their sky
To build and brood; that live their lives
From land to land."—*Tennyson.*

The evening fell chilly, and, as we drew up to the fire, Mr. Gray reminded me of my promise. "Well," I said, "I don't wonder that you are interested, for I know few things in Nature more fascinating than the mystery of the migration of birds. Poets, from Homer downward, have touched it with wonder, and naturalists have made guesses without number about it."

Till recently, ideas on the subject were still crude. Boswell knew all about it; for Dr. Johnson, in his usual breezy, dogmatic way, had said:—"Swallows certainly sleep all the winter. A number of them conglobulate together by flying round and round, and then, all in a heap, throw themselves under water and lie in the bed of a river."

Gilbert White, too, says that a Swedish naturalist, Linnæus, was persuaded that birds retired under water, and talked in his Calendar of Flora as familiarly of the swallows going under water in the autumn as he would of his fowls going to roost before sunset.

White's own belief wavered between this theory of hibernation and the theory of migration. An incident in a parish not far from Selborne had set him thinking. Some sportsmen killed a duck with a silver collar about its neck on which were engraved the arms of the King of Denmark.

Finally, being compelled for lack of information to leave the question open, White appealed to young men of fortune and leisure to give time and travel to the investigation of the subject. There are signs at this late day—a century and a half after it was penned—that his appeal will meet with some response. Much has been learned since White's day; but we are still groping our way to the heart of the matter.

The difficulties in the way of the student of migration are great. The birds, in most cases, fly so high that their movement overhead is unseen and unheard. Much of the ground, too, is covered during the night. Again, though in some cases the birds travel in companies, in many cases they slip away unseen in twos and threes, and even singly. Another feature that adds to the perplexity is that, in some cases, the young birds do not leave at the same date as the parent birds, and cannot therefore benefit by their experience.

"Have you any idea why they fly so high, and why they fly at night?" "It may be," I replied, "that flight is easier in the rarer air above. Possibly, too, the birds are safer from hawks at these heights. During night, also, they are freer from danger."

Then there is the question of food. There may be no food supply for long distances, even when passing overland; and so these barren tracts have to be crossed by night-and-day travel.

It is in a time of storm that the observer gets his best chance, for then the birds are driven down near to earth or sea. At such times of storm, numbers perish by contact with the windows of lighthouses, and it is to the better-educated lighthouse-keeper of the future that we must look for much of the information which we need.

That we know so much as we do is largely owing to the fine observations of Herr Gätke, of Heligoland, an island used as a resting-place by myriads of migratory birds.

Something has been learned also by telescopic observations directed by day towards the sun, and by night towards the moon. These observations show that the birds pass at heights of from one to five miles.

We come now to the question of how the bird finds its way to its goal. The two main concerns of a bird's life are to feed and to breed. We may suppose that the bird which today has to breed in one country and for half the year feed in another was able, at a remote time, to do both in the same place.

As a cold change of climate came on with the gradual approach of the ice age, the food supply for part of the year would fall off, and the more active birds would go afield to get more. These birds, invigorated by better food, would, on their return, displace the less enterprising birds which had remained in the old home. Thus, in time, the migrating bird would become the common type.

If, in imagination, we follow the sinking of land below the ocean level, we shall see how some of the birds were gradually forced, in following the old land track, to cross a stretch of sea growing imperceptibly wider. So gradual would this process of subsidence be, that, by the time the bird had to pass out of sight of land, *a sense of direction* may have been formed, enabling the bird, without any help from eye or nostril, to cross the ocean.

"But I suppose," said Mr. Gray, "that most of our Australian migratory birds do not need to fly oversea. Australia seems big enough to give them all the change they need."

"That is so," I replied. "There are a few exceptions of great interest, which I will tell you of again. All the birds we saw today migrate from one part of Australia to another."

I took the pipit for an example. On the approach of winter, the pipit leaves Victoria for the north. One detachment, on leaving the southern part of Victoria, flies across the Goulburn Valley, over the Riverina, and so into the back blocks of Queensland.

It will help us to understand the migratory instincts of the pipit if we look at the habits of the European pipit. Indeed, so little observation has been given to migration on our side of the equator, that it is necessary to go to the northern hemisphere for sound working ideas on the subject.

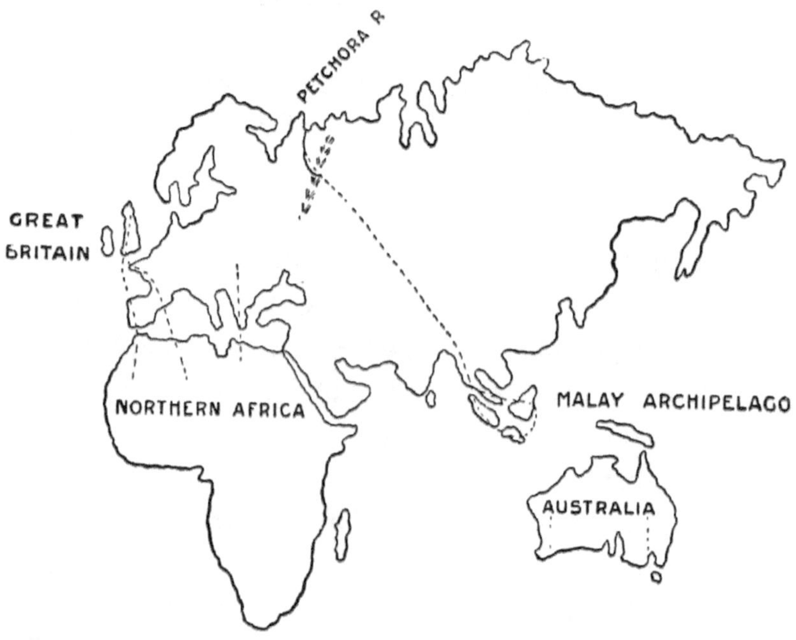

MIGRATION MAP — LARKS & PIPITS

(ROUTES OF FLIGHT MARKED IN DOTTED LINES.)

The European pipit, which in all essentials is the very bird we saw today, crosses the Mediterranean to winter in Africa. Thousands of the birds are sometimes washed ashore after a storm on the Mediterranean. It seems to be proved, indeed, that only a small proportion of the pipits that set out for Africa ever return to their homes in North Europe.

Of still greater interest is the pipit of North Russia, called the Petchora pipit. Starting in autumn from the banks of the Petchora it crosses the Ural Mountains, travels past the source of the Obi, and, skirting the Himalayas, finds its goal in the Malay Peninsula and the islands of the Indian Archipelago—a journey of 6,000 miles, performed in fourteen days.

What an undertaking for a little bird! Many die under the buffeting of the bitter winds of the Urals; others, beaten out of the ranks by the icy winds of the Siberian steppes, lose their way; hawks, familiar with their route, take toll as they pass, swooping down on them just as the hill-robbers of Asia descend upon the caravan routes. Some perish of hunger; and many, while crossing to the East Indian Islands, fall exhausted into the sea and are drowned.

It is only a remnant that reaches the Promised Land—the land promised to the young birds by the deep instinct which draws them forward.

But it is a land of plenty—rich in the seeds and fruits and insects that they love. Very thin and worn when they arrive, they soon recover strength; and, when the time comes for the return journey, they face it with unabated courage.

"What a brave little bird!" said Mr. Gray. "Well, I shall look at it tomorrow with new eyes!"

CHAPTER III

Migrating Birds That Leave Australia

BRONZE CUCKOOS.

"**I** should like now," said Mr. Gray, "to hear of the birds that leave Australia in their migration. It seems strange that a bird cannot find every range of food and heat within our bounds."

"You have to remember," I replied, "that, on our side of the equator also, there have been great changes of land and sea

SPINE-TAILED SWIFTS.

surface, and that we too have had a glacial epoch that altered climate. In all these migrations of birds one has to allow for love of the old home."

Taking first the birds that do not go far from Australia, we shall look at the bronze cuckoos. These birds spend our summer in Victoria, Tasmania, and South Australia. At the end of summer, the birds in Tasmania cross the Strait and join the Victorian birds. To these are added a South Australian contingent, which works its way along the timber skirting the coast of Victoria.

Then all the birds move northward through Queensland and come to a stop in New Guinea.

Of the movements of the bronze cuckoo of Western Australia we know less; but it seems certain that, while most of the birds move north to winter in the islands of the Malay Archipelago, some of them go no further north than the Northern Territory.

A greater traveller than the cuckoo is the swift. Here we have a bird that may breakfast in Australia and dine in Asia, its estimated speed being 150 miles an hour.

The swift does not arrive in Victoria till November or December—in some years, not till January; and it leaves us for Asia not later than March.

What bird-lover does not know the thrill of interest on seeing the first swift of the season! Passing like a winged bolt, in a few moments it is out of sight.

"Why in such a hurry?" asked Mr. Gray. "Because," I replied, "the swift gets his living in the upper air, and, as the flies are comparatively scarce at that height, he has had to cultivate speed in order to catch enough."

Almost constantly on the wing, the bird is rarely to be seen resting during the day, except in the breeding season. It comes to Australia, not to breed but to feed, and so we cannot wonder that we have no record of a swift having been seen to set foot on Victorian ground.

The European swift rests occasionally during the day on church towers or on the face of a cliff. On the ground itself it never alights, because its feet are so short and feeble, and its wings so long, that it cannot rise from the ground. From tower and cliff it can let itself fall into the air.

We are in need of further observations regarding our swift.

There are few birds of greater interest or that touch the imagination more. Probably it will be found that the bird rests on the sides of sea cliffs at lonely parts of the coast.

"Is it a swallow?" asked Mr. Gray. "No; with its long wings, forked tail, and wide mouth, it is very like a swallow; but it is of different descent altogether. It is related, strange to say, to the hummingbirds and nightjars, and has become like a swallow, because it gets its living in the same way."

As it is only in fine weather that flies seek the upper air, the swift leaves us at the end of summer. One band passes up the eastern side of Australia, and then by way of Torres Strait and the Malay Archipelago reaches China. Having passed far north toward the limits of the Chinese Empire, they breed, following the law that every bird, excepting tropical birds, breeds in the coldest part of its range.

Another band passes up the western side of Australia, and joins the others among the islands north of our continent.

"A wonderful traveller," said Mr. Gray. "Yes," I replied, "but I have to tell you of a bird that goes still further afield—the sandpiper."[2]

This bird—the Ulysses of birds—spends half the year with us and the other half in Siberia! This means a flight of about 10,000 miles, performed twice a year!

We know that the sandpiper is of arctic origin, because it breeds in North Siberia, and comes south only to feed.

Now, many northern birds go south for food, but, as a rule, remain in the northern hemisphere. The southern hemisphere, where seas are broad and land scarce, has few attractions for

2.   Sandpiper or sharp-tailed stint. This species is the most common of many that annually visit us.

SANDPIPERS.

wandering birds. The ancestors of the sandpiper, however, found their way south of the equator.

"Can you imagine how the bird came into these perilous seas?" cried Mr. Gray, greatly interested. "Possibly," I replied, "through some famine in its usual tropical haunts. Possibly, also, the birds were blown out of their course through a great storm, and so were brought on to New Guinea and Australia. Probably, however, the habit was formed at the time when there was unbroken land-connection between Asia and Australia."

The sandpiper, which nests within the basin of the Yenesei River, leaves for the south at the end of June, and in about fourteen days reaches Australia. It passes Lake Baikal, through Mongolia and China, and then by the Malay Archipelago into Australia.

Towards the end of our summer, the sandpipers go north again in little bands, not working their way gradually, as some birds do, but with impetuous flight.

MIGRATION MAP
OF THE
SANDPIPER

One day in late autumn the bird is running upon the sands of Hobson's Bay. Fourteen days later it may be seeking insects in the marshes of South Siberia, which is just waking to life after the winter rest. The birds arrive as the ice begins to melt, and they follow the thaw as it returns north, until they reach the tundras of Northern Siberia, which are now alive with the hum of insects and gay with flowers.

"You have told me," said Mr. Gray, "of arctic birds that come south for food. Are there any antarctic birds that travel north for food in the same way?"

"Well," I said, "we know at least one bird that goes south to breed—the double-banded or sand dottrel. There can be little doubt that at one time many birds that bred on the Antarctic continent came north for food; but the only trace that we have today of this movement is in the journeyings of this sand dottrel. Just as the sandpiper goes to the sub-arctic regions to breed, so the sand dottrel goes, in order to breed, to the south of New Zealand—that is to say, as far towards Antarctica as it can now get."

The sand dottrel, which has nested in northern New Zealand, flies north to New Guinea via Norfolk Island and the coast of Queensland.

The dottrels that nest further south, in Otago or Stewart Island, fly through Tasmania, and then, passing over the Australian Bight and round Cape Leeuwin, reach the western coast of Australia. Some call a halt at the coral island called Houtman Rocks, a perfect winter home. Others, no doubt, go further north.

It is a long flight, and one of much peril. Flying by night, the dottrels may, in stormy weather, miss Tasmania, and then, should they continue long enough to miss Cape Leeuwin, they cannot escape exhaustion and death.

CHAPTER IV
The Balance of Nature

PART I: FEATHERED POLICE

Next morning I found Mr. Gray looking at a swallow's nest under the eaves of the stable. The young had just been hatched out, and the parent birds were busy feeding them. As I came near, the male bird swept round the house with a billful of flies.

"These birds must have arrived early from the north," he said. "Yes," I replied, "a few birds come much earlier than the main body, and, indeed, some birds, in a mild winter, never leave us at all."

"I've been watching them for a quarter of an hour," he went on, timing their visits to the nest. "Five visits in fifteen minutes makes a total of twenty visits in the hour." "There are four young birds," I said, "so that each bird will be fed five times in an hour."

"A few swallows about a place must make a great difference in the number of flies," said Mr. Gray. "Undoubtedly," I replied. "When people pull down swallow-nests they suffer. The birds give a great return for any trouble they cause. And yet my neighbour, who takes great pains to have a good cat to keep down his mice, and a good dog to keep away tramps, won't have a swallow-nest about his place!"

"These birds have been nesting there for the last four years,

WOOD-SWALLOWS.

and we reckon them as part of the household, just like the collie and the cat. They cause a little trouble, but we grudge the attention they need no more than Rover's bone or Nancy's plate of milk.

"When the time of the mosquito comes, we are thankful to

have them, and their beauty and cheerful twitter are a never-ending pleasure."

Later in the day we called at the hut of a selector by the creek. It was a low, rich, sheltered patch of ground, and gnats were numerous. Artificial eaves had been attached to the wall on one side of the house, and of these eaves several pairs of swallows had taken advantage. The selector, an old man who had come to Australia in his youth, had been a sailor in a Russian ship.

"Yes," he said, in answer to a question by Mr. Gray, "they know something of flies in my country. The gnats swarm during the short summer, and, but for the swallows, some of the low parts in the north would not be fit to live in. This," pointing to the wall, "is how we welcome the swallows."

"I was much struck," said Mr. Gray, as we walked on, "with the fact that the flies in the upper air are kept down by the swifts. I begin to see that there is no chance about the movements of birds."

"That is so," I said. "Each bird has its own special skill, its own particular field, and no region is neglected. Field and wood, lower air, middle air, upper air, river and marsh and sea—they are all occupied."

"How easy, then," said Mr. Gray, "to disturb this close-fitting plan, when man interferes with gun, and trap, and poison!" "Yes," I replied, "we are learning that lesson at great cost. Here is an old man who can tell us something about it."

We were passing an orchard, and the owner was leaning on the gate. "Yes," he said, in answer to my inquiry, "the insects and birds, and beasts and plants, all seem to fit into one another like a fine bit of clockwork.

"In the early days I had an orchard near town, and, at that

SILVER-EYES.

time, we had the native birds all about us. We had our own
troubles from some of these; but we could grow splendid fruit.
One heard little of the codlin grub, or the scale insects, or the

tree borer, or the red spider, or the score of fungi that eat us up today.

"But as 'the bush' was pushed farther back, the old birds banished, and new birds brought into the colony, all that was changed. Every year seemed to bring a new pest, and now half our time has to go in fighting them. Look at this..."

He pointed to a peach tree which looked as if it had been blasted by fire. On looking closer, we found that the leaves had been attacked by the black peach aphis.

"After the black aphis has left the tree, a green aphis follows. I don't know which is worse."

Presently a silver-eye, beautiful in its dainty dress of grey-green, flew out of the top of a mulberry tree. "Ah!" said the grower, "the first silver-eye I've seen for days. They and the tits used to keep down the aphis."

As we passed among some apple trees, we broke down the large, strong web of a spider. "In the old days," said the grower, "these webs were common all through the orchard, but since the new birds came I rarely see a web. In these webs there were caught every year thousands of moths, which have now no check, except laborious and costly ones. Last year I reckon that the codlin moth made a difference of £100 in my pear and apple crop."

"I begin to see," said Mr. Gray as we turned away, "that the question is a highly complex one, and quite beyond the ordinary observer."

"You are right," I replied; "we need the best scientific knowledge to deal with the matter."

"Caw!" cried a crow from a red gum tree. "Ah!" I said, "there's a bird whose case is still under consideration. Is he a friend or

CROW.

a foe—a bird to be protected by law, or to be shot at sight as an outlaw?"

"I understood that he was a hateful bird," said Mr. Gray; "that he plucked up the corn, and ate fruit, and picked out the eyes of lambs. Even in his 'caw' there seems to be a heartless, hard note. I dislike to hear it."

"Yes, there is a strong case against him; but we have to hear the other side. The popular judgment about birds is most unreliable. You heard how the fruit-grower praised the silver-eye. Well, there are some growers who shoot that bird, because, in the fruit season, it does a little damage. They do not see that the good done outweighs the evil. So is it with many other birds."

CHAPTER V
The Balance of Nature

<u>PART II</u>

Walking in the garden next day, we stopped to look at a lemon tree which was showing, both in leaves and fruit, signs of sooty mould. "How it disfigures the tree!" said Mr. Gray. "Yes," I replied, "but it is a useful signal to the grower—a black flag calling him to action! In the early days, when honey-birds abounded, there was little or nothing of this." "What," asked Mr. Gray, "have honey-birds to do with sooty mould? Is this another instance of the balance in nature?" "Yes," I said, "and one of the most interesting."

First of all, we examined the scale-insects, which begin the trouble. They looked like dried-up or dead scales on the leaves, but, on crushing one or two with the thumb-nail, we saw at once that they were alive.

From each of these scale-insects there exudes a sweet, gummy substance, reminding one of the honey-dew deposited on leaves by certain kinds of aphis. All the leaves infested by the scale-insect were sticky with this honey-dew.

Now this honey-dew is a favourite food of a certain fungus, called the *Sooty Fungus*. The spores of this fungus, wind-

42

This bird is sometimes called, from the crescent-shaped white band on the neck, the Lunulated Honey-eater.

borne, fall on the sticky leaf and multiply rapidly. It is this fungus that gives the appearance of sooty mould.

"So then," said Mr. Gray, "there are really two kinds of

SPINE-BILLED HONEY-EATERS.

life at work on the leaf—the scale-insect and the fungus?" "Yes," I said, "but notice that while the scale-insect lives on the juices of the leaf, the fungus lives entirely on the honey-dew smeared over the surface. It does not tap the juices of the tree."

"Then the fungus does not hinder the tree's growth?" "Oh, yes, it does, and seriously. The pores by which the leaf receives gases and gives them out are choked up, and the tree suffers in health at once."

"I suppose," said Mr. Gray, "that the honey-eating birds used to keep the leaves free from this honey-dew?"

"Yes, they helped to clean the leaves of the 'dew; sometimes also of the scale-insects. Since the birds were driven away there is no check. Honey-eating birds, as a rule, are fruit destroyers, and growers have no good word to say for them. Here is something on the other side."

Some ants were running up and down the branch where the sooty mould was thickest. "Why," said Mr. Gray, "do the ants run up this branch, and not the others?" "Because," I replied, "the ant has a sweet tooth, and is fond of the honey-dew. The ant, however, does not destroy the scale-insects as the bird does. On the contrary, in some scale-infested plants, the ant guards the leaf against leaf-eating creatures, and thus, indirectly, protects the scale-insects."

"What a complex problem!" cried Mr. Gray. "And what a rebuke to the old jealousy and independence of the sciences! What use is the botanist here, unless he work with the entomologist, or what use are both unless they co-operate with the microscopist who studies fungi?"

"Yes," I said, "and you must add the student of birds; also the chemist, when we come to talk of remedies. Nature is one, and laughs at our little divisions of Nature study."

Later in the day, on passing a field of growing corn, we saw half a dozen crows gibbeted on poles. "This farmer," said Mr. Gray, "seems to have no doubt about the crow being an enemy."

"Undoubtedly he is right to frighten the crow off his fields," I replied; "but whether it would pay to get rid of the crow altogether is another question."

And then I spoke of the American investigation of the great crow problem. In response to a popular outcry against the crow, the Washington Government ordered an inquiry. Naturalists examined the stomachs of 1,000 crows. The observations were spread over ten years, and resulted in a verdict in favour of the crow.

It was found that the crow is fond of insects possessing a strong odour. Now, many insects, by help of a pungent smell, escape attack from the ordinary insect-eating birds. It is clear, then, that the crow kills many insects that the other birds pass over.

In an average year, over a quarter of the entire food of the crow consisted of insects; but in the years when locusts or other insects were abundant, the crow lived on little else.

It was found that, while he ate some fruit, birds' eggs, and young chickens, the percentage of such food was insignificant.

Investigations of a similar kind are needed in Australia; but, meantime, we have reason to think that our crow belongs to the same type as the American bird, and that here also the verdict will be in favour of the bird. Here, as in America, the crow is one of the most intelligent of birds.

"Well! you surprise me," said Mr. Gray; "I understood that the crow was a kind of bird-fiend."

"The great intelligence of the bird," I continued, "may help the grower to keep him off his fields. If the farmer, or,

WHITE IBISES.

better still, the farmers of a district, wage vigorous war on the bold crows that feed among the crops, the bulk of the birds may be made to understand that it will pay better to confine themselves to insects. But to proclaim a general war against the bird would be a grave mistake. It is no light matter to disturb the balance of nature."

Imagine an invasion of locusts in a land without crows! A devastating army, and no effective check! We might be placed in the ridiculous position of having to breed crows in order to re-establish an army of defence!

We have a very striking illustration of the value of feathered police in the services rendered to the farmer by the white ibis. Millions of crickets and grasshoppers are eaten during the season by these birds. Again, where a district frequented by the ibis is laid waste by an army of harvest caterpillars, the bird gathers from far and near in great numbers. It is remarkable how quickly news of this kind is passed on through the bird world. So thoroughly does the ibis deal with the caterpillars or their pupæ that, after such a visit, the farmers reckon on a few years of freedom from the pest.

CHAPTER VI

How Birds Talk and Sing

"Hear how the bushes echo!
By my life, these birds have joyful thoughts.
Think you they sing like poets, from the vanity of song?
Or have they any sense of what they sing?"—*Tennyson*

PART I

I was astir early next morning—a beautiful morning, such as only September can give—and found Mr. Gray already in the garden. He was peering among the bushes in the shrubbery, as if seeking something.

"I'm looking," he explained, "for the owners of a dozen songs and calls, but I make no progress." He looked at me in a delighted bewilderment. There were not so many birds as he imagined. The varied notes of two or three kinds of bird deceive the unpractised ear.

What a merry din the little glad creatures made! As a background to the nearer music, there came from a distant tree the flute-like notes of the magpie. The harsh chirp of the sparrows seemed softened, and even the caw of an early crow appeared to have lost its sinister quality on this divine morning.

The sweet, light, musical note of the silver-eye, one of the slightest of bird calls, was the first we disentangled from the

49

BLUE WRENS.

medley. As we passed under a pepper tree, we could see the dainty little bird busy among the pink berries.

From the same tree came a burst of little sharp notes, so close together that one despairs of reproducing them. Passion and force gave a rude rhythm to the strain. It was a blue wren in full wooing song. We could not see the bird; but I know that he was in his gay wedding-dress of blue and black.

Out of another bush came the song of a rival, shrill and eager. "See! There he is!" The little blue-black throat was swelling in an ecstasy of battle or affection. From more distant bushes came other wrens' songs.

On the grass, a brown bird with tilted tail was quietly seeking her breakfast. Was this the object of the tourney of song, this little careless creature? What a superb air of indifference, as she snaps at a small Plutella moth!

"Hear how the wren crowds and hurries the notes," said Mr. Gray. "It is like a child that runs in to tell you of a joyful surprise, the words tripping over one another in the eagerness to unburden its little fluttering spirit."

"There, I believe, you have the key," I replied. The blue wren is a bird of great vitality, and when the tide of life runs high in the spring, it can no more help the eager play of throat and wing than the lambs in yonder field can help gambolling, or than the children can help running and leaping to school on this fine morning. By the way, that blue wren nearest to us is giving only half of his full song. They often do that in the spring, repeating the first half over and over again as if too eager to finish. The bird is on the tiptoe of life."

"Does this bird," asked Mr. Gray, "like the nightingale, keep all its singing for two months in the year?" "No," I replied, "the blue wren breeds more than once; and through most of the summer you can hear the quick, eager strain. When the last brood has been hatched, the young have to be trained in song. As summer goes on, however, there is probably less intensity in the strain; and we may say that it is the spring wooing-song that has earned for the bird the name of the superb warbler."

In spring, his energy is electric; and there is something of the fiery passion in his love-making which Wordsworth objected to in the nightingale. The blue wren, too, is "a creature of a fiery heart;" and if we could watch him as he "sings darkling," we might perhaps see fire flash from the eye, as Tennyson saw it in the eye of the nightingale.

"You seem," said Mr. Gray, "to think of the bird's song as a wooing or marriage song. Does not the bird sing, at times, out of pure gladness?"

"I believe it does. Darwin was probably right in thinking that the bird gained its highest powers of song through the rivalry of courtship; but the powers thus heightened are, I believe, used for other kinds of expression."

"In short," said Mr. Gray, "you believe that high spirits in birds, as in man, find a natural expression in song?" "Yes, and we have to remember that its best song can be given only when, as in spring, the bird is in high condition. The full song is a great strain on the bird; and, indeed, one might suggest this as the reason for the nightingale's complete silence after the brood has been hatched."

"Like a great tenor," said Mr. Gray, "who is silent all day before the night of a great effort!"

We were watching the blue-black throat as it rose and fell. "If only," I said, "it had a larger throat, what a rich song it might have!"

"What has that to do with it?" said Mr. Gray.

"A bird varies his song," I replied, "by shortening or lengthening, contracting or widening the windpipe; but if the pipe be a short, narrow one, no skill of the bird can give depth to the note; just as no skill can bring fulness of sound from a short, narrow flute or a shortened oboe."

As we passed the fowl-yard, on our way to the fields, we stood to watch a fine Spanish cock, which was crowing lustily, its head high, and its wings half-expanded. Almost like an echo came a response from a distant farm. "How noisy, in pairing season, must be the woods where these birds are native!" said Mr. Gray.

"It is not noise to the hen's ear," I said. "Yonder hen-sparrows prefer the harsh chirp of the cock-sparrow to the finest of wood notes. Indeed, the fine, light music of the bush birds could not be heard in the noisy street and the busy stable-yard—the haunts of the sparrow."

Half a dozen sparrows had perched on the bushes overlooking the fowl-yard. It was near feeding time. "Chirrup, chirrup!" came the call of a cock-sparrow, proudly showing his black chest-mark.

A portly hen, with a dozen chickens in her train, was scratching at our feet. "Tyook, tyook, tyook," came her quick call as a grub came to light; and the chicks tumbled over one another in their eagerness. A hawk flew overhead, and a warning cry from the mother made the little birds seek cover.

"They seem," said Mr. Gray, as we walked on, "to have a language of their own for all the occasions of life." "Yes," I said; "if we knew the birds of the field and wood as well as we know the barn-door fowl, we should find that most birds can talk about all matters that concern them."

Here is an endless source of interest and investigation; for, even in old countries, the subject of birds' talk has not been fully examined. A bird that has been left behind by a family group will mount a tree and give a peculiar call—a bird's coo-ee—until, by an answering call, it learns the whereabouts of the others. Then there is the low note of pleasure as a tit-bit is discovered, the note being, in some cases, repeated at every peck.

More familiar to the ordinary ear are the high, quick notes of alarm. There are also child-notes from the young birds, and their feeble first attempts at song. Then there are the broken, half-finished songs of the old birds, practising for the spring song after the winter silence.

CHAPTER VII

How Birds Talk and Sing

PART II

As we walked towards the creek, we heard a caged thrush singing from the window of a cottage. "Poor bird!" cried Mr. Gray, "it is not his 'to bathe the wing in dewy light,' and yet he joins the morning chorus."

Half-musingly he continued: "There was once in London a poor woman from the North Countree, who stopped to hear a thrush that sang at the corner of Wood-street. In an instant she was in the dale of her childhood. The mist was trailing upwards from the trees on the mountain-side, and the murmur of the river mingled with the morning songs of the birds. Poor Susan! For a moment her heart was in heaven."[3]

As we pushed our way through the melaleuca scrub near the creek, a little bird—olive-green and with white throat—was singing. "The brown tit," I exclaimed. We stood quite still and enjoyed the song—surprisingly liquid and mellow for so small a bird. It sings in a varied pitch, but the voice is so light that one must be quite close to the bird to hear the finer turns.

Very different was the note of the white-browed scrub-tit. It sang unseen, though we could see by the movement of the

[3]   "The Reverie of Poor Susan" (Wordsworth).

leaves where the restless little bird was. Its notes were grating, but clear and decisive.

It was pleasant, after this harsh note, to hear the strain of a belated robin that sang from a fence. The scarlet-breasted robin has a set bar of about seven notes—sweet notes, but a trifle hard. One, however, is not critical on hearing this song in July—often the first bird-song to break the winter silence. Nor, indeed, could we be critical on this glorious September morning, as we watched the swell of the flaming breast, the red showing boldly against the green of the meadow beyond.

"What has become of all the robins one saw in the winter?" asked Mr. Gray. "That," I replied, "was, till lately, a puzzle to bird-students, but we now know that, early in the spring, the bird goes deep into the bush to breed. In this retirement, the summer is spent, and, as winter comes on, the birds come into the open again. This bird on the fence is unusually late."

As we rested on the brow of a hill, we heard the weird note of the bronze cuckoo, and, soon after, the mellow cry of the pallid cuckoo. This last, like most cuckoo calls, is a leisurely, meditative strain, every note being round and clear. *Whoo-oo-oo-oo-oo-oo* came the notes, in ascending scale—a pleasing, melodious call.

To Australians, this call is the voice of spring. It is not the call of the cuckoo of the poets of England. It is not the bird "that tells its name to all the hills;" but to us it is just as rich in associated memories—the soft blue of a spring sky and the golden line along the creek that marks the wattle-blossom.

"The cuckoo's call always speaks to me," said Mr. Gray, "of long-vanished Septembers, and of the silence that broods over a wide stretch of wood and plain. Are there no other cuckoos to challenge this bird in his call for a mate?"

PALLID CUCKOOS.

"I have never," I replied, "seen rival cuckoos fighting. They seem to have so arranged their areas of action as to map out all the cuckoo-region systematically. In imagination, you can pass from call to call all over this wide region of wood and pasture."

"Yes," said Mr. Gray, with a distant look, "I can hear the mellow note repeated from the Murray to the sea!" "Happy they," I replied, "who have the poet's ears!"

Again came the soft, yet pervasive call, as of a bodiless voice.

"Listen!" I said, "do you hear the answer?" A harsh, purring note came from a tree at hand, *r-r-r-r-r.* It was the cry of the hen-bird.

From a clump of trees came the whip-note of the thickhead; and, immediately after, the harsh, guttural noise of the red-wattle bird.

When we came to the river, we heard the liquid musical note of the butcher-bird. His wife was on the same tree, and they seemed to be talking together in great good-humour. In full, rich

Butcher-birds.

recitative, with many a jerk and trill, the male bird seemed to be chaffing his wife, who, in turn, was never wanting in retort.

"Who would have expected," said Mr. Gray, "to hear so fine a note from a butcher-bird?" "Why," I replied, "should he not speak out his gladness like another bird?"

No doubt he does what in a man would be cruel; but it is not cruel in the bird-world. He is born to hunt the blue wren, and the blue wren is born to baffle the pursuit. Both enjoy doing what they were born to do—what they are fitted to do by the drill of a thousand years. We must all die, and the blue wren that makes a false move in the game gives up its life without sense of wrong. Hunter and hunted enjoy their lives.

Contrary to the usual rule, the butcher-bird seems to sing at his best in the autumn. This may, indeed, be a delusion of the ear, due to the fact that the strain comes at a time when few other birds are in song.

Another point in which the butcher-bird has a way of his own is his habit of soliloquizing. Getting into a tree by himself, in the pensive autumn time, he seems to muse musically over the stirring summer time that has gone.

From a great root that overhung the stream came the song of the male, at first a light tinkling call, but breaking into a pleasing run of varied notes with a suggestion of melody. From a neighbouring bush a black-and-white fantail was calling, "Pretty creature! Sweet pretty creature!" (See page 19.)

It was high noon when we reached the farmhouse that we sought. From a clump of trees beside the yard came a strange purring sound, repeated several times. It was the call of the cuckoo-shrike.

CHAPTER VIII
How Birds Talk and Sing

PART III

In the evening, as we walked home beside the marsh, we heard the crackle of a spur-winged plover and the boom of a bittern, rising to seek its supper, harmonized pleasantly with the fading light and the deepening shadows.

As we entered the home meadow, we saw against the pink clouds of sunset the fluttering form of the bush-lark as he rose to sing his vesper song. Like our native song-lark, he does not rise in spiral ascent, but climbs straight up, singing as he goes.

"In yonder farmhouse," I said to Mr. Gray, "the farmer's wife is an Essex woman. She told me yesterday that during the night she had heard the skylark of England singing beautifully."

"A dream?" asked Mr. Gray.

"No; there is the bird! The bush-lark often sings at night."

As we neared home, we heard the oom, oom, oom of the frogmouth that nests in the tree on the hillside; and from the trees at the garden foot came the *boo-book* of the boobook owl. The day was over, and the night watches had been set.

During the evening, Mr. Gray said, "I should like to make a musical note of some of the songs we have heard today."

"I doubt," I said, "if you can set down such songs as that of

60

BUSH-LARKS.

BOOBOOK OWLS.

the blue wren or the bush-lark. Where there is some approach to melody, there is a better chance of success. Here is the song of the butcher-bird:

A stranger who had never heard the song would not be able to get the real sound from this score; but one who knew the strain well and sympathetically would find the musical transcription helpful as a reminder. A good imitation is possible only on a reed instrument; but, when I whistled the notes from the score, they called up at once a picture of the butcher-bird that sings on the gum-tree by the river.

Some bird-calls, too, can be noted in a way that helps the memory. Here is the call of the magpie-lark—the "peewee"—to its mate:

In birds that have a good singing throat, there is a long tube, with a small membrane far down the throat. This membrane, which is close to the lungs, vibrates as the bird, in singing, forces air through the windpipe, and the result is a sound of the kind we have from a reed instrument.

Good songsters have the ability, in unusual degree, to lengthen or shorten, contract or widen, the windpipe, and thus to give the variety of note which, in a reed instrument, is obtained by pressure of the lips on the mouthpiece or by stopping the holes with the fingers.

Hence it is that Beethoven, using the oboe and the like instruments, was able, in his "Pastoral Symphony," to give a beautiful suggestion of bird-notes.

But, however good the musical transcription, player, and instrument may be, the wild, fine, bird-like quality can be given only by one who plays with good memory of the song itself. Given a good ear and the familiarity of one who has heard the song from boyhood, the finest bird song may be reproduced by simple means.

John Burroughs, in his delightful narrative of a hunt for the nightingale, speaks of a man in Surrey who was able, by blowing through a blade of grass held between his hands, to give a good imitation of the nightingale's song!

In making a musical transcription of the bird songs and calls of Australia, there is work to be done of high interest. A good observer is needed, preferably a native of Australia, who has a good ear and a good knowledge of music. Well done, such work might show that we are not so poor in bird music as the early explorers imagined.

Some day, efforts will be made to enrich the bird music of our country, not by haphazard introductions, but by scientific distribution. This is much needed in some parts of Australia. In Western Australia, for example, the bird music is of poor quality. The magpie has lost his mellow note, and croaks like a crow; while the magpie-lark's call has also degenerated.

Bird music! How good it is for the growing soul! Music in the home is good; but who can say how good it is to have music all around the home!

"Yes," said Mr. Gray, thoughtfully, "it is not without reason that the fairest creations of man are fabled to have been built to music: without it, you can never draw out all the beauty that sleeps in a child's nature."

There was a bright moon that evening, and we could not rest in the house. As we walked past a bush where a blue wren nests, the bird began to sing.

Mr. Gray was startled. "Another night-singer?" he said. "Yes," I replied, "we have several birds that sing regularly in the night-time, and a few, like the blue wren, that sing occasionally." Among the birds that sing, or call, regularly are the black-and-white fantail, the bush-lark, the little grass-bird, and, finest of all, the reed-warbler. The call of the pallid cuckoo, too, is heard long after dark.

A thick cloud had passed over the moon, and no sound broke the silence. In a few minutes, there came a flood of moonlight, and with it another burst of song from the wren's bush. It was the same song as by day, but somewhat broken.

"What does it mean?" asked Mr. Gray.

"Probably," I replied, "a beam of light had struck him. At the time of mating, the ruling thought possesses the blue wren. No doubt he sings in his sleep, as a dog hunts in dream; and when anything wakes him—a flash of light or a fall of leaf or bark—he breaks into a song of challenge as soon as he opens his eyes. Napoleon used to speak of the rarity of 'two-o'clock-in-the-morning courage.' This little creature, like the nightingale, is ready with his challenge at any hour of the night."

We walked towards the swamp, and were fortunate in hearing the strange, uncanny note of the little grass-bird. It is a monotone, the call of a recluse, and speaks of lonely wastes and of mystery.

Several times we heard the quack of wild duck, but not till we were about to turn homewards did we hear the note of the reed-warbler. Again Mr. Gray was startled: this time by the rich,

THE REED-WARBLER.

musical strain. This bird also is shy and retiring, but less so than the little grass-bird, which shares the reeds with it. Perhaps that is why we find less of melancholy in the note of the warbler.

"Do you believe," asked Mr. Gray, as we walked home, "that the melancholy cry means a melancholy bird?" "Not at all," I replied; "our habit of reading our own feelings into the lives of the animals leads us often astray. They enjoy their lives."

"Then," said Mr. Gray, "Milton was wrong when he spoke of the nightingale as a melancholy bird?" "No," I replied, "because, as Coleridge points out, the description of the bird is given by a melancholy man, who, 'poor wretch! filled all things with himself, and made all gentle sounds tell back the tale of his own sorrow.'"

It is much closer to the truth to say that in nature there is nothing melancholy. Animals have their bad times; but the close observer and the modern physiologist give no support to the idea that animals have much suffering.

They have, however, enough shadow in their lives to give them the joy of contrast. On a sunny day, following some dark days in winter, you are sure to hear some birds singing out their faith that spring will come again.

"But, after all," said Mr. Gray, as we got back to the library, "*these* are the world's rare songbirds!" and he pointed to the "poets' row" on the shelves. "When the silence of winter falls upon the birds, we can be indoors with vernal Chaucer, whose fresh woods throb thick with merle and mavis all the year."

CHAPTER IX
How Birds Feed

<u>PART I</u>

"There seems," said Mr. Gray, next day, "to be need for a closer knowledge of the kinds of food that birds eat." "Yes," I said, "until we know much more than we do, we shall be working a good deal in the dark in deciding between friends and foes."

"Is not the beak of a bird a guide?" asked Mr. Gray. "Yes," I said, "that is a help; but the beaks of some birds are adapted for feeding of a very varied kind, and it is in these cases that we have most difficulty."

"Here," I continued, as a swallow swept past, "is a case where we have no difficulty. The mouth is wide and the bill soft. The swallow could not eat grains or hard-shelled insects if it wished, but the bill is beautifully adapted for fly-catching."

By this time we were passing through the home meadow, and Mr. Gray cried out: "Here is my friend the pipit. How does it feed?" I replied: "On seeds, grubs, and beetles; and you see that the slender bill is well fitted for exploring among the grass. But, see, yonder is a lark with a much shorter bill!"

The bird to which I pointed, the bush-lark, is one which is often mistaken for the pipit. Both kinds often feed together in the same field, but the strong, finch-like bill of the bush-lark

WHITE-THROATED TREE-CREEPERS.

shows that it is able to deal with larger seeds and harder beetles than the pipit.

"I see," said Mr. Gray; "what one leaves, the other eats. Nature seems never to be at a loss for a gleaner."

We had now come to the belt of trees at the meadow-foot, and I replied: "If you look at that gum-tree, you will see another case of the same kind." A tree-creeper was running up the trunk,

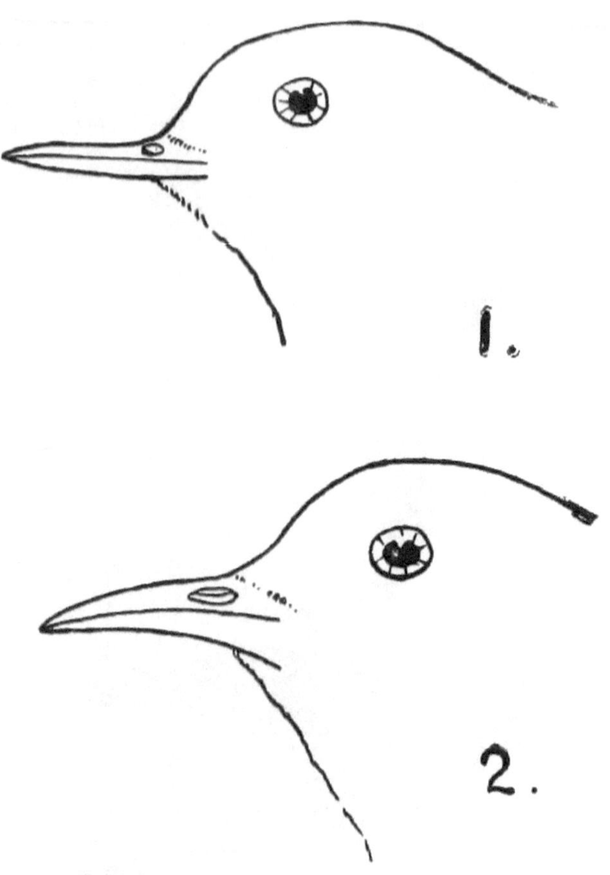

1. Head of Tree-runner. 2. Head of Tree-creeper.

peering into every crevice or roughness in the bark. At the same time, a tree-runner was coming down the trunk, peering into every crack and cranny. The tree-creeper missed no insect that could be seen by the upward glance, the tree-runner no insect that could be seen by the *downward* glance. "Is it a family arrangement," asked Mr. Gray, "a division of labour?" "No," I replied, "the birds are quite different. You are in luck to see them working at the same time." Here I drew roughly the bill of the tree-creeper—a bill of the ordinary type among insect-eating

BLACK-CAPPED TREE-RUNNERS.

birds. Then I drew the bill of the tree-runner—a most unusual bill, with a slight, but distinct, tilt.

"Neither bill," said Mr. Gray, "seems to be fitted for pecking the bark." "No," I replied, "the woodpecker's bill—strong, chisel-shaped—is quite a different bill; and, indeed, we seem to have no true woodpeckers in Australia. The birds we are looking at cannot hew wood or prise off bark. When they have picked

KESTRELS.

up all the insects that have come out for an airing or are only partially hidden, they fly off to another tree."

"They do not seem to be moving up or down in a straight line," said Mr. Gray. "No, they always move in a spiral progress. In that way they cover more ground, and are more likely to surprise the insects before they have time to retreat into their holes." It was a pretty sight, the spiral movements of the little, active birds—one upward and the other downward.

Towards noon we stopped to watch the evolutions of a nankeen kestrel in mid-air. "Is it engaged on business, or only playing?" asked Mr. Gray. "That," I replied, "is our insect-eating hawk. About this time of day insects fly high, and wherever the insects go, there you may find the nankeen kestrel."

"Has it the hawk-bill?" asked Mr. Gray. "Yes," I replied, "the bill is hooked, but it is short, and not so strong as in the ordinary hawk. The bird kills a blue wren or other small bird occasionally, but, on the whole, it is an insect-eater—a hawk that has fallen in the world—a poor relation of the true birds of prey."

Here we heard the rich note of the butcher-bird, and presently the bird flew across our path and perched on a young gum.

"There," I said, "is a bird of fiercer nature than the nankeen kestrel, though, at a distance, no one would guess it to be a bird of prey." With the help of the field-glass, we could see the stout bill with the hooked point. (See page 58.)

"He seems small to be a bird-killer," said Mr. Gray. "He is large enough," I replied, "to deal with the smaller birds, and, indeed, the silver-eyes, blue wrens, and tits fear him as much as a hawk." My friend, who was still looking through the glass, said: "I can't make out what he is doing." Taking the glass, I saw that the bird was using his strong bill on a blue wren which was fixed in a fork of the tree. The feet of the butcher-bird do not seem to be strong enough to hold a bird while he tears it; and so he fixes it in a tree fork.

"But," said Mr. Gray, "he had no bird in his claws when he flew past us." "No," I replied, "but he generally has a few birds and beetles in the larder. He chooses a place with a handy fork."

Sometimes, however, this shrike can deal with a bird without carrying it off to his shambles. Last summer, I found a butcher-bird pulling my canary, bit by bit, through the bars of the cage. The cage had been placed on the lawn to get the sun. I was too late to save the canary, but I shot the butcher-bird.

I hung the dead butcher-bird over the top of the mulberry tree. The silver-eye is very fond of mulberries, and, in ordinary years, takes heavy toll, but, with the butcher-bird on guard, not a silver-eye dared come near the tree. When the fruit season was over, I removed the dead shrike; and the silver-eyes came back to help me to keep the garden free from insects."

"You dealt with the silver-eye, then," said Mr. Gray, "as you would have the farmers deal with the crow?" "Exactly; we must study the ways of such birds until we learn to make them help us without taking too heavy a fee."

"Ruskin," said my friend, "used to tell gleefully that he had at last found a gardener who was willing to let the birds have the cherries—a small fee for their song." "Well, I think we can have the birds we want at a smaller fee than that, but the growers will need to make up their minds to pay some fee for good service."

CHAPTER X

How Birds Feed

PART II
BEAKS AND TONGUES

Next morning Mr. Gray found me standing over the cages of the pet cockatoo and the rosella parrot. "I suppose," said he, "that you give honey to the parrot sometimes?" "No," I replied, "the rosella is not a honey-eater. It lives, like the cockatoo, largely on nuts and hard-shelled seeds. You notice the strong, hard-biting bills of both birds."

I gave to each bird a few peanuts; and we admired the workmanlike way in which they got inside the shells. Then I tried them with a few hazel nuts. The cockatoo, with his powerful beak, made short work of his nuts, and the rosella cracked his also without much difficulty. Both birds were evidently able to deal with the many native seeds which have horny shells. As the parrot struggled with a nut, we looked closely at the tongue, and saw that it was not a brush-tongue, and therefore not adapted for honey-eating.

Later in the day a screaming flock of the musk lorikeet—the green 'keet—dashed past overhead. I turned to my case of birds and took out a specimen of this parrot to show the brush at the end of the tongue.

MUSK LORIKEETS.

This brush seems a rude instrument compared with the sucking tubes of the humming-bird; but anyone who has watched the bird at work on the honey-pots of the eucalypts knows that it is most effective. In a hot season, when the blossoms are plentiful, the bird revels in the work of honey-getting.

"A prince among birds!" cried Mr. Gray; "clothed in green and red, and fed on nectar!"

I led Mr. Gray to the lightwood tree at the garden-foot, and pointed to a nest of the wood-swallow. One of the birds soared into the air with the graceful sweep which wins for it the admiration of even the roughest men. It seemed to have no fear, and passed quite close to us.

Now, the tongue of this bird has what looks like a true brush. If we judged of the bird's food by its tongue, we should guess that the bird is a honey-eater. But as the bird is a fly-catcher, like other swallows, the brush must serve some other purpose, and this purpose has yet to be discovered.

Possibly the brush is of use in disturbing insects and making them take wing. "There seem to be plenty of interesting problems awaiting solution," said Mr. Gray. "Problems and interest without end," I replied.

"Here is a bird," said Mr. Gray, as we passed the duck pond, "which seems to revel in mud as the green 'keet in nectar!" Four ducks, all in a row, were fishing, with bills in mud and tails skyward. "What do they get down there?" asked Mr. Gray. "Pond-mud," I replied, "is rich in the eggs and larvæ of insects and also in seeds, and the duck has a sieve on tongue and bill for sifting out this food."

In the afternoon we walked in the field beside the river. On the damp flats the white ibis was at work. (See page 47.) With its long, curved bill it explores the roots of the grass where lie the wireworms and grubs of the cockchafer. Those worms and grubs, in eating the roots of the grass, do great damage to the pastures, and few farmers know how much they owe to the ibis, the herons, and similar birds.

We watched the ibis carefully, and saw how methodically it works. When it has eaten up or frightened into retirement all the insects in a patch, it moves to another part. Later in the day, it returns to the same patch and works over the area again. In this way a few birds on a farm may enable a dairyman to run an extra cow or two in each field.

"No wonder!" cried Mr. Gray, "that the ancient Egyptians worshipped the ibis and called it 'the father of the sickle.' I see now why we find the ibis so often on their walls and monuments." "And yet," I said, "there are farmers who will take their guests for a day's shooting of ibises and herons."

We were now passing through the great paddock that sloped up from the river. Here and there a white gum tree had been left. It was an ideal field for magpies, and we sat down on a log to watch a pair that were feeding near us. "Here," I said, "is another bird that goes systematically to work." The male bird of the pair was turning over dried cakes of manure and pieces of bark in search of insects. He would run up, tilt the bark over with his bill, seize the grub, and then run on to the next piece.

A little behind him, and to the side, was the female bird, which, bringing up the rear, saw that nothing was missed. They worked with the air of birds who were masters of the situation, but who had no time to lose. No other magpies came near these two.

"I thought," said Mr. Gray, "that magpies just roamed about at large?" "No," I replied, "each pair has its own reserve, and they work over it in this careful way." Presently, the male bird flew off to a neighbouring tree. With the field-glass we could see that the bill was full of insects. It had hardly returned when the female bird, with overflowing bill, flew up to the same place. "You see

MAGPIES (WHITE BACKED).

now," I said, "why they must work hard and systematically. They have to feed themselves and three or four hungry young birds."

As we turned to go home, we disturbed four blue-banded grass parrakeets. They behaved like ground birds, and did not fly far. As we quietly approached them, we saw that they were hanging to the strong grasses in search of seed. This is a parrot which has found it easier to make a living on the ground than in trees. Its tree-climbing foot, however, is still of use to it in holding on to corn stems and tall grasses while it takes the seed.

It was twilight when we recrossed the river, and a night heron flew overhead on his way to his favourite hunting-ground. As we passed through the stackyard, the boobook owl was coming on duty. Nature's eye never closes. As one bird's watch ends, that of another begins.

CHAPTER XI
How Birds Fly

"I notice," said Mr. Gray, next morning, "that bird students can tell a bird almost at any distance. How is it done?" "By the manner of flight," I replied, "or by recognition marks." (See page 2.)

One of our Spanish fowls, which had perched in a tree, flew back into the poultry-yard with a guilty air. "Do you notice," I said, "how difficult is the flight of birds of this class—the scratchers? Nearly all the scratchers have heavy bodies and short, rounded

STUBBLE QUAIL.

WHITE-FRONTED HERON OR BLUE CRANE.

wings, and fly in a laboured way. The wings have to be driven at a rapid rate to keep the bird in the air at all, and hence they never fly far. If at all near them, you can hear the whirr of the wings, and you can tell what kind of birds they are at any distance."

Near the foot of the home meadow, a pair of stubble quail rose, almost at our feet. The sudden flight and the strong whirr of the wings were startling. The birds flew low, and settled at a point within sight. "This bird," I said, "is a scratcher, just like the fowls of the poultry-yard. On many farms the quail, by eating insects, saves the farmer more money than his wife makes from the eggs laid by her hens."

At the lagoon we surprised a white-fronted heron. It rose into the air with easy power. There was a certain dignity about its flight that seemed to rebuke us for unwarranted intrusion. "There," I said, "is a bird built for easy flight, with light body and large wings."

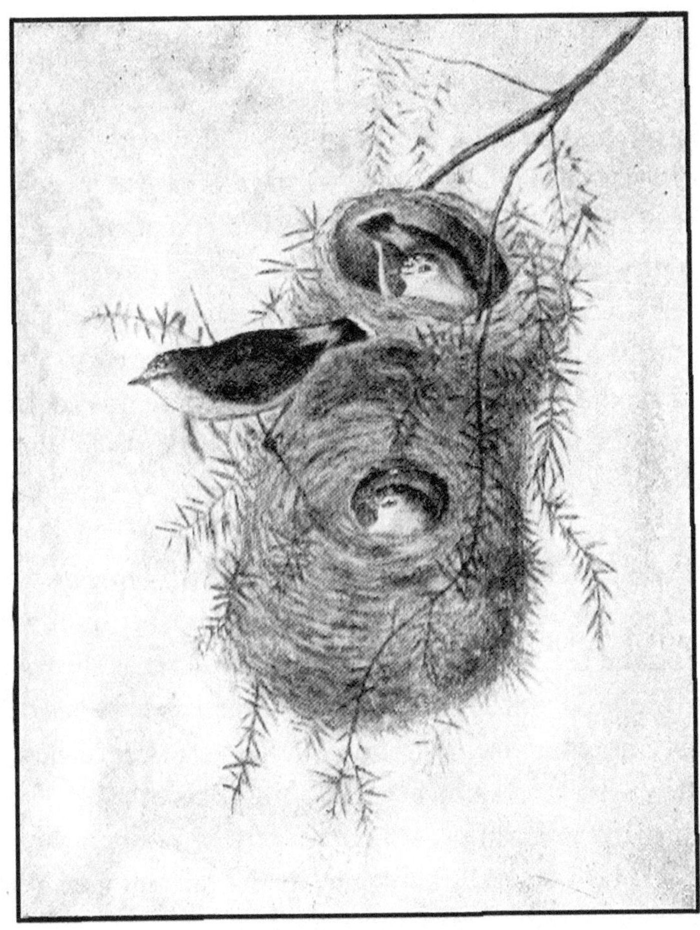

YELLOW-TAILED TITS.

"Caw!" came the cry of a crow from a great red gum tree. I levelled my stick at it, and it flew off at once. But with the crow, as with the heron, the retreat was a dignified one. With easy, leisurely flight, he made for a distant tree. "How different from the quail!" said Mr. Gray. "Yes," I said, "the crow has plenty of wing power. Indeed, he has, perhaps, relatively to his size, more sail-area than any other bird in Australia." "Ah!" cried Mr. Gray, "that goes well with his air of superiority. He seems to be thoroughly equipped at all points."

From the yard of a selector a sparrow flew out. "See," I said, "how it rises and falls in its course, as if it reached its goal by a series of efforts." Most of the finches, tits, and other small birds fly in that jerky way. Not always, however. When very much in earnest, they can fly for a short distance in a straight line. Just then a pair of sparrows flew out from behind the barn. Straight as a dart, they flew into a tree, where the chase was continued with movements so quick that the eye could hardly follow.

On the grass near some low scrub, we came upon a pair of blue wrens. "Here," I said, "is a little bird that flies straight, contrary to the usual rule." I clapped my hands, and the birds flew off to the scrub, not with jerky movements, but with continuous beat of wing and in a straight line. The long tail, which is always erect when the bird is on the ground, was on a level with the back. "This bird seems to be well born," said Mr. Gray. "Yes," I replied, "the blue wren is a king among the little birds of the bush."

Later in the day we saw a number of the red-browed finch. This little bird, so easily known by its fire tail and its red brow, is also recognized by its straight flight.

As we crossed the creek, we could see in a distant bend a little bird that flew in an undulating way across the water. "A fantail!" cried Mr. Gray. "I could tell it at any distance. It reminds me, in its beautiful movements, of the willie wagtail of England. One never tires looking at it." It was too far off for me to see the bird distinctly, but the manner of flight was unmistakably that of the white-shafted fantail.

A more accomplished fly-catcher than the fantail swept past—a house swallow. As we watched it making dive after dive, up and down, to right and left, Mr. Gray suggested that the fantail's erratic flight might be due to the same cause—the chase after flies.

High overhead a bird was moving in graceful flight. Then it stopped soaring, and began to hover as if watching one spot on the ground intently. Its wings beating rapidly, it continued thus poised all the time we remained to look. "That is our friend the insect-eating hawk—the nankeen kestrel." (See page 72.)

As we passed a cottage garden, we saw a little bird busy among the hanging blossoms of a gum tree. He was darting from flower to flower; falling sometimes from one branch to another with the agility of an acrobat. An occasional somersault was taken with graceful ease. Mr. Gray was amazed at the number of blossoms visited in the few minutes we stopped to watch.

"You need not tell me," he said, "that that is a honey-eater." "There are several honey-eaters," I replied, "but perhaps you can see the little crescent-shaped white band on the neck. That is the *recognition mark*. We know it as the honey-eater with the moon-mark on its neck. I hope to show to you the spine-billed honey-eater, which hovers like a humming-bird about the blossoms, the wings moving so fast that you see only an indistinct blur." (See pages 43 and 44.)

Passing from a clump of trees into a meadow, we saw a bird rise from the ground into the air, singing as it rose. One could tell at once from the song that the bird was a lark. Was it the bush-lark or the brown song-lark? The bird rose high—higher than the brown song-lark ever rises. "The bush-lark!" I said.

A magpie lark rose from the edge of a pond. With a heavy, laboured flap, it flew towards the river, making now and then a sudden turn or dip. "How different from the quick, easy flight of the magpie!" cried Mr. Gray. "Yes," I replied, "the magpie lark, so

MAGPIE LARKS.

graceful in its walk, is not at home in the air. Do you remember
Burroughs' impression of the peewit of Scotland—every move-

ment like visible music, but the moment it launches into the air its beauty is gone?"

We sat down under the scanty shade of a great white gum tree on the slope of a hill. Some small birds were feeding in the grass close by. Suddenly there was a terrified chatter among the birds. I looked up and saw, against the sky, a white-fronted falcon coming up. It was still 200 yards away, but it seemed only a moment till it made its swoop toward the birds. Too late! The birds had taken refuge among the branches of the gum-tree, and those that could not reach cover in time flew high into the air. "What speed!" exclaimed my friend. "Yes," I said, "the white-fronted falcon is one of the fastest birds in Australia. The stroke of the wings has remarkable force. One of these birds has been seen to chop off the head of a duck in mid-air."

As we talked over this, a laughing jackass, which had been on the watch on one of the branches above us, made a dive to the ground. "How softly it flies!" cried Mr. Gray. "Yes," I said, "the lizard is quick in action, and the jackass has to muffle his flight. It does this, though, at the cost of losing speed." I made a noise, and the jackass flew off with a somewhat slow, deliberate flight.

That evening we saw a bird still more accomplished in noise-less flight. Silent as ghosts, the boobook owls were flitting among the trees behind the stable. I took out a specimen of this owl from my cabinet, and we looked at the dense feathering of the head and the softness and fluffiness of the whole plumage. Even the feet were feathered down to the toes. (See page 62.)

CHAPTER XII

Birds' Nests

A rainy day came, and signs of damp in the ceiling showed that the roof needed attention. On going up, I found that the gutter was choked by a sparrow's nest. I tossed it down, and it fell at the feet of my guest.

"What a clumsy nest?" he cried, as I reached his side. "It reminds one of the slovenly house of a gossip!" It was a huge mass of feathers and straw, put together without any attempt at neatness, but a very cosy nest for the young.

"It is a good nest," I replied, "for a bird that builds in spouts and all sorts of odd holes. Birds show their high rank among the animals by their intelligent nest-building more than in anything else, and the sparrow is a clever bird." Some talk on nests followed, and we arranged to give the day to the study of nest-building.

As we walked towards the flats beside the river, we passed a swagman, a hardy nomad who could sleep in the open air all through the summer. "A reminder," said Mr. Gray, "of the primitive man, who slept under the sky! How far we have travelled."

"It is much the same with the birds," I replied. "They began by laying their eggs on the bare ground, and there is as much advance shown in the nest of a fantail as, in man's case, there is in a modern house."

We were now passing through a lightly timbered field near the river, the kind of place where the curlew likes to nest. We moved cautiously as we came near to the nest I was seeking; but the sitting bird had seen us before we saw her, and, as soon as she was sure that we were looking at her, she left the nest, ran fifty yards through the grass, and then flew away. On the bare ground—for there was no nest—were two eggs "of light stone colour." Here, then, was the primitive bird-dwelling.

As we skirted a stock water-hole, a dottrel—a bird about the size of a myna, with a black chest-band—rose suddenly and flew off in zigzag flight, as if with broken wing. At our feet, on the bare ground, were two eggs, brown in colour, and with dark lines and spots, to match with the clay on which they rested. A few particles of earth had been brought together to keep the eggs steady. Here was the beginning of a nest.

When we had gone twenty yards away, I turned and said to Mr. Gray—"Find the eggs!" For some time, so like were the eggs to their surroundings, he searched in vain, and in the end found them by chance. "The bird is not so careless as I thought!" he confessed.

Crows eat the eggs, and if these were easily seen, there would soon be no dottrels left. There is reason to think that the primitive egg was white, and the dottrel survives because its eggs have taken the colour of the earth and grass around.

Some birds, however, found it better policy, in order to escape ground-enemies, to leave the ground and lay their eggs in trees. "Here is one!" I said, as we came to an old gum-tree where a laughing jackass had his nest. In a hollow in the tree,

NESTING GROUND OF BLACK-FRONTED DOTTREL.

three white eggs lay on some decayed wood. There was no nest whatever. "Here we have the primitive white egg! There was no need for protective colour for an egg hidden in a hole." "Is it always so, then," asked Mr. Gray, "in the case of eggs laid in holes?" "Nearly always," I replied: "the eggs of cockatoos, parrots, kingfishers, and owls—birds that lay in the hollows of trees—are white; pigeons form an exception."

So far, we had seen no nest, but now it was time to see how the birds began to build a house. I led Mr. Gray to a field where I had seen a pipit's nest. Here it was, in a slight hollow under a tuft of grass. The nest was cup-shaped, and made of dry grass. There were three eggs, brownish-white, and with spots and blotches of darker brown. Nothing could be better than this scheme of colour for escaping notice. (See page 22.)

"I suppose," said Mr. Gray, "that some far-away ancestor thought it would be an advantage to have the eggs raised above the damp earth?" "Yes," I replied, "that was probably the beginning of house-building." A slight hollow also was chosen, so that the nest might sit more firmly. When man came into the land, bringing with him animals that leave tracks on the ground, the bird took advantage of these hollows. I led him to another pipit's nest, where the mother bird was sitting on the eggs. One of the three eggs was hatched out, and the bird sat boldly while we looked from a little distance. The nest was built in the track made by a horse's foot. So like to the grass around her was the little gray bird that a casual passer-by would never have noticed her.

Belonging to the same class was the nest of a wild duck, which we now visited. Here, however, there were two new features. The ten cream-coloured eggs, being easily seen, were covered with feathers plucked by the duck from her own breast. This the bird invariably does on leaving the nest. Again, this bird sometimes builds in a tree—an interesting feature, because it shows the transition from ground nests to tree nests.

And now we had to look for a nest which might show how

NEST AND EGGS OF BLACK DUCK.

those birds that left the ground began their attempts at house-building. We found a good type of this kind in the nest of a bronze-winged pigeon, which had built in the fork of a low branch of a she-oak. As the pigeon flew off with a strong whirr, we saw the sunlight glinting from the beautiful wings which give to the bird its name. The nest consisted entirely of twigs.

Standing below it and looking up, we could see the eggs. So loose, indeed, were the twigs that it seemed as if the eggs might fall through. "A well-drained house," said Mr. Gray. "No water can lie in that nest. Here, then, was the rudest attempt at house-building in the trees.

Later in the day we noted that the nests of the crow and of the magpie belong to the same class—that of the stick-nests—but are finished with more care. "We have a magpie in town," said Mr. Gray, "which used odd bits of wire for its nest. I see that it must have twigs or the nearest thing to twigs."

Having now seen a nest that rested on branches, I wished to find a nest that hung suspended from branches. This kind of nest we found in a bush of leptospermum beside an orchard—the nest of a yellow-faced honey-eater. "It is a great fruit-eater," I explained, "and when the young are being reared this orchard will suffer." The dainty nest was open and cup-shaped, formed of grasses covered with moss and spider's web, and it hung suspended from a branch. Two eggs were in it, light buff, with red and purple spots. The shrub was beautiful in its pure white flower, and, with the neat nest, made a picture which lingers in the memory.

The nest we had just seen was open, and I now wished to show a nest suspended from a branch and provided with a roof. The place was favourable. Fencing in the orchard was a thorny acacia hedge, still gay in its pale yellow blossom—an ideal place for the nest of the yellow-tail tit. As we reached the hedge, a tit flew out with a graceful little flutter, and then another and another—all merry, busy birds.

Mr. Gray was now thoroughly interested in the story of nest development, and he ran along the hedge like a boy, pricking his face and hands in his eagerness. The nest which we sought for is a bulky one, and we were soon successful. It had a side entrance, but on the top of the roof was what looked like a second nest. (See illustration on page 83.)

"Why!" exclaimed Mr. Gray, "we have two nests here!" "We are not sure," I replied, "about the purpose of the upper nest. Possibly, being open to view, it is meant to deceive the cuckoo or other enemy of the tit." "You mean," said Mr. Gray, "that the cuckoo may place its egg in the upper nest while the tits are being hatched in the lower nest?" "Yes," I replied, "I have found, though only on one occasion, the egg of the bronze cuckoo in the upper nest, while the young of the tit were in the lower nest. Had the cuckoo laid the egg in the lower nest before the tit began to lay, no doubt the tit would have reared her family in the upper nest. Many think that the spare nest is meant to be a resting-place for the male bird—a place where he may sit while the female is on the eggs. Others, again, suggest that the upper nest may be meant as a resting-place for the fledglings when they have overgrown the limits of the lower nest. All three guesses may have some truth in them."

"Is this nest with the spare room unique among nests?" asked Mr. Gray. "It is rare," I replied, "but not unique. The common wren of England builds in this way. The yellow-tail sometimes reverts to the ancestral practice of having only one chamber." In this case of a one-chambered nest, the tit has been known to cover a cuckoo's egg with feathers, and then to lay her own eggs on these. This, indeed, may be the first rude suggestion of the double nest of today. We noted that the eggs, being well shut out of sight, were white. "A most intelligent bird!" cried Mr. Gray. "Yes," I said, "and a bird of most engaging manners—a bird which would like to be on friendly terms with men, if boys and cats would allow it."

CHAPTER XIII
Birds' Nests

PART II

NEST OF BLACK AND WHITE FANTAIL.

"I wish now," I said to Mr. Gray, "to show you a nest which is protected, not like this one by a roof, but by overhanging leaves." I led him to the creek-side, and there, in the fork of a dead branch which stretched over the water, we found the nest which we sought—the nest of a black and white fantail. Three yellowish-white eggs lay in a neat, open, cup-shaped nest, artistically woven of grass and fine shreds of bark. The outside was covered by a thick felt of spiders' webs.

"What a beauty!" cried Mr. Gray. "Yes," I said, "it is one of the neatest of nests, and, though quite open, you notice how it is protected by the overhanging branch. The nest is not always screened in this way, but it is evident that the bird seeks a place hidden from the eyes of the hawk."

"I shall take you now," I went on, "to a ground-nest which is protected by a roof—the nest of the ground-tit." I led my friend to a field where trees were plentiful and grass high. "I came on this nest," I continued, "by chance, and, though the bird rose almost at my feet, I had to search for the nest. Here it is!" Under a thick-leaved native shrub was a nest of dry grass, lined with feathers. It was roofed over with grass and moss, in exact keeping with the surroundings. The nest rested in a slight hollow, and so was level with the surface of the ground. In this snug home lay an egg of brown-red, a beautiful egg of unusual colour, and one which, in the shallow chamber, could not be seen from the outside. The parent birds were hopping about uneasily at some distance.

"You call it a tit," said Mr. Gray, "but it seems to me like a pipit." "In some ways," I replied, "it is a tit, in others a pipit. Possibly it is a tit which has, through some stress of affairs, become a ground bird. That may explain its dome-shaped nest—so different from the nests of other ground birds. When a bird has to change its way of living, its form and habits change to match the new conditions; but some ancestral trait gives us a hint of the family history."

As we passed a farmhouse, Mr. Gray pointed to a swallow's nest in the eaves, and said, "How does this house come into your story of the nest? It seems strange that so fine a bird should be content to make a nest of mud." Making no reply, I pointed to a pair of swallows which were seated on a fence, and handed to Mr. Gray my field-glass. "Look," I whispered, "at the short, feeble feet, and at the wide, soft bill. In these two features of the bird you have the key." (See page 16.)

"You mean," said Mr. Gray, "that the swallow has not the feet and beak for weaving a good nest?" "Exactly. Strong feet and beaks are needed for good weaving. The birds that have feet for perching, and those that have strong bills for eating hard-shelled insects, are the birds that build the best nests. The swallow rarely needs his feet, and, for catching flies, a soft, wide beak is the best."

I led my friend to a steep bank of the river, and pointed out the holes of the black and white swallow drilled into the sand. "There," I said, "is one way of solving the difficulty. The bottle-neck nest of the fairy martin, which we saw below the bridge, is another way. A bird which cannot weave grasses or twigs can readily plaster together pellets of mud. In the house swallow—an advanced bird—we have some grass and feathers mixed with the mud." "And how does the swift manage?" asked Mr. Gray. "The swift," I replied, "is forced to get its materials from the air, since it does not set foot on the ground. It picks up feathers and winged seeds as it flies, and mixes these with a secretion from the mouth. When the air is too pure to furnish such material, as in the case of the sea-swift of China, it makes the nest entirely of this secretion." (See page 29.)

The advent of man has been of advantage to the swallow tribe. Road and railway cuttings have been of use to the swallow that lives in tunnels. The fairy martin, which used to build under hanging rocks, or under the huge warts on great trees,

NEST AND EGGS OF DIAMOND-BIRD

now uses also bridges, woolshed eaves, and verandahs. The home swallow, the highest of the family, has virtually made a partnership with man, to the great advantage of both.

We called at the hut of our friend, the Russian, on our way back. "Yes," he said, "the birds trust me. One spring I went to town for a few days. On my return I found that a pair of swallows had entered my room through a broken pane, and were building their nest under a shelf. I allowed them to go on, and in a few days the sitting bird was so tame that it would let me stroke its back."

When we left the hut of this lonely man—softened and refined by his care for these beautiful birds—I led Mr. Gray to a gum-tree where a colony of the babbler had nested. "I wish to show you another bird, which, like the fairy martin, builds in groups." As we neared the tree, some of the babblers were feeding in the grass. They were hopping about very actively over the ground, with tail raised and wing spread. On our approach they flew into a young wattle, and jumped restlessly from branch to branch. It was chitter-chatter, flitter-flutter all the time.

"A social bird!" cried Mr. Gray. "Yes," I replied, "the people about here call them the happy family. Its love of company brings it many advantages. In winter time, when food is scarce, and the lonely bird might starve, ten birds hunting together, and calling out at every discovery, may do well. Then, at nesting time, they join in building a number of nests together. With all the birds working, a nest is finished in a day or two."

On the overhanging branches of the gum-tree were three large dome-shaped nests, and a fourth nest which seemed to be used as a sleeping place. Most birds use their nests only for the breeding season, but these birds seem often to use their nests for sleeping.

We made a slight detour on our way home, and skirted the lagoon. A few feet out from the edge was a floating round mass of plucked water-weeds, which had stranded on a clump of reeds. The mass was almost level with the water, and was suggestive of the nest of some huge water-spider. "You would not have taken that for a bird's nest?" I said. "No," said Mr. Gray, "I should never have suspected it."

Wading in, we lifted off the weeds on the top, and found a rude bowl-shaped nest, with four eggs of dull white. "Thrust your finger into the grass below the eggs," I said. Mr. Gray did so and cried, "Why, it's hot. Is this one of Nature's incubators?" "You have guessed rightly," I replied. The bird—the black-throated grebe—sits by night, but on warm days like this the heat of the

BLACK-THROATED GREBE OR DABCHICK.

sun and of the decomposing leaves carries on the work while the bird is absent. When sitting, the bird is half-covered by the outer parts of the nest, and before she leaves the nest she covers the eggs. She takes care not to rise into the air from the nest, but dives, and reappears at some distance.

"Wonderful," cried Mr. Gray, "are the ways of birds. I have never rated them high enough; they are as clever as they are beautiful."

During the evening Mr. Gray said, "I should like now to have the full life-history of a bird, so that I may gather together my scattered knowledge." This request delighted me, and I told him the following story of a Victorian magpie.

CHAPTER XIV

The Story of Bright-eye; Being the Life-history of a Victorian Magpie

For years a black-backed magpie and his mate—also a black-back—had nested in the fine old gum-tree at the foot of my garden. We called the male bird "Blackie," because most of the magpies in the neighbourhood were white-backed. (Compare figures on pages 79 and 107.)

I was reading one July afternoon under this tree, when some feathers came sailing through the air, and fell at my feet. I looked up, and saw that two magpies were fighting. One was Blackie, and the other a white-backed stranger. The hen bird looked on calmly, taking no part.

White-back, after the fashion of his kind, was a fierce, determined bird, and Blackie, getting the worst of the fight, flew off. White-back at one stroke had won a wife and an estate. Woe to the magpie that tried to share in the property—the old gum-tree, my garden, and the little clearing beyond.

In the first week in August they put in repair the old nest in the gum-tree, and by the middle of the month the first egg was laid. Next day another was laid, and on the following day a third egg completed the number. Each egg was laid between noon and one o'clock. The colour was light green. During the period of incubation in the nest, the mother bird was fed by White-back. Once in the morning and once in the evening she left the nest for a little.

In exactly the same order as the egg-laying, the three young birds broke shell, three weeks later, on three successive days. Strange to say, each bird left the shell about midday.

The old birds made no objection when I mounted a ladder and looked into the nest. The young were thinly covered with long down, and as yet there was no sign of quills. Pink at first, the skin gradually changed in a week's time to black, and the first quills made their appearance.

Why should the back of the young magpie, even when the bird turns out to be a white-back, so often be black? It seems to point to a black-backed ancestor, and a time when there were no white-backed magpies.

On the eleventh day from the egg, the oldest bird opened its eyes, and punctually on the two following days the two others followed suit. At a later stage this oldest bird—a male—became noticeable for his bright, knowing eyes, and we called him "Bright-eye," to distinguish him from his sister. He had his father's white back.

About this time I noticed that the youngest bird was not growing so fast as the others, and I was not surprised a few days after to find it dead at the foot of the tree. Probably it had been pushed out by the stronger birds.

The chief food for the birds at this time was the grub of a night-moth. The old birds would gather four or five grubs, mash them thoroughly in the bill, and then divide the mouthful between the two chicks. Each parent made four visits per hour to the nest, so that the young were fed once in about eight minutes.

Till the birds were three weeks old, I made a daily ascent to the nest. After that time I ceased to go up, lest I should scare them out of the nest before their time.

The birds were just a month old when I saw Bright-eye standing on the edge of the nest. He preened his feathers, and then went back into the nest again. The other chick was also restless. Five days later both birds ventured from the nest to the branches above.

For some time after this they spent part of the day in the nest, and the old birds continued to feed them for fully a week.

On the ninth day after their first effort to leave the nest, they followed the old birds in their search for food. Each parent took charge of a chick, and kept as far from the other two as the limits of their ground would allow. One day the young got too close, and there was a violent quarrel. Then I understood why the young were kept apart at feeding time.

Tuition went on entirely by example. White-back would turn over a piece of bark or of dried cow-dung with his bill, pick up a grub, and then, running to another piece of bark, repeat the process. Bright-eye, in the rear, turned over smaller pieces in the same fashion. In this way all the light litter on that ground was turned over every few days.

Now and then, when White-back made a good "find," he would allow the chick a share; for the young birds were not yet able to get all the food they needed. After about three weeks' education, the chicks could leave the old birds and search for food for themselves, and, from this time on, the young birds were less quarrelsome.

When Bright-eye was about four months old, I heard him try to sing. He had not yet got all the notes, and he piped in a low key. In a month's time he could give the full song, but his baby cries were kept up till he left his parents.

One day, in mid-April, I noticed an unusual stir among the birds. They moved about restlessly, and finally all flew off to a clump of trees in a neighbour's field. Here they were joined by other parents and their families, all meeting in a friendly way as if a rendezvous had been arranged. It was the great annual meeting for mating.

The proceedings began noisily. Everyone seemed to be talking at the same time, and there was much warbling and piping. This carnival went on for some days, and then the parent birds withdrew, and left the young birds to go on with their wooing.

In due time the old birds returned to the scene and drove the young couples away to seek new homes. Bright-eye and his bride came back to the old tree the first night, but the old birds would have none of them, and beat them off.

Bright-eye's sister, having failed to find a mate, came back, dejected, to the old home, to the disgust of her parents, who bit and chased her without mercy. But she would not be beaten off, and it was not till April in the following year that she disappeared.

A clearing had just been made around a new bush-school, and here Bright-eye and his mate made their new home. They had hardly settled down when another newly-mated couple came up; but Bright-eye, who had all the white-backed magpie's courage, drove them off with fierce charges.

Bright-eye was proud of his mate and home, and the next few months of his life were a happy time. His white became whiter, his black deeper, and the brown eyes were brighter than ever. Alive to his feather-tips, the day seemed too short for the joy of life.

September came round again, and a new brood was being reared in the old gum-tree at my garden foot. The young were still in the nest when the father, who had been thrashing a neighbour's fowls, was shot. Next day I noticed the widow at the nest, and a new bird with a black back was with her. Blackie had returned!

BLACK-BACKED MAGPIE NESTING.

Had he been faithful to his mate all this time? Had he been watching for this chance for a whole year?

A few days after, I found, at the foot of the tree, a young white-backed bird. It did not seem to be hurt, and I put it back in the nest. On the following day it had been thrown out again. Blackie would have nothing to do with white-backs.

Blackie, like most black-backed magpies, was a good singer. It was like old times when his mate sang the morning song and Blackie joined in with his rich warble, prolonging the last note after the hen-bird had ceased.

One fine day, late in spring, as I passed by the school paddock, I saw Bright-eye and his mate busy teaching their young. They had five chicks—an unusually large family, and strict discipline was necessary to keep order. Feeding was going on.

One of the young birds seized a tit-bit out of his turn. Immediately the stern Bright-eye knocked him over on his back, and there he had to stay till his turn came.

As I watched, I found that the discipline in the school-house was not more severe than in this bird's family. Father and mother spared no pains in seeing that their large family was well fed, and they took equal pains to drill the young birds in good behaviour.

When the feeding was over, one of the young birds got into the company of some other young magpies. This was promptly checked; no intercourse with strangers was allowed. Just as I left, the parents rose to fly into the roosting tree, and the young followed at once. I understood by this time how this prompt obedience had been got.

Bright-eye's selection was rich in grubs, and there were

always scraps to be had from the dinners of the school children. But the bird was losing his good temper.

He had been brought up in a quiet neighbourhood, and had had the good temper of birds that are treated well. But a new enemy called "boy" had entered into his life, and was fast making him savage. He was a brave, high-spirited bird, and would stand no nonsense.

Next time I passed that way, he was making a fierce swoop down on some boys, who were guarding their eyes with their books, and beating him off with their slates. The boys told me that Bright-eye would attack any living thing that came near, even a horseman a quarter of a mile from the roosting tree.

Later in the season, when Bright-eye's family had grown strong, I saw the whole seven birds chasing a hawk. The hawk took refuge in a thick teatree, and was still under siege when I left.

One fine evening, during the New Year holidays, I met two boys near the school-house. They were town boys out for a day's shooting. Something led me to look again at one of the birds which they had killed. Could it be Bright-eye? Yes, it was my brave bird. There was the scar on the bill where his sister had pecked him.

The beautiful gloss was already fading from the feathers, and the bright eyes were closed for ever. My own eyes were dim as I turned away.

CHAPTER XV

The Partnership Between Birds and Plants

Next morning we sat on the verandah listening to the carol of a magpie, which was hidden in the great gum-tree. "I am struck," said Mr. Gray, "by the close partnership between the birds and the trees. A magpie in a treeless land! I can't imagine it." And then I laughingly proposed to examine him on the points of this partnership between trees and birds. "In a partnership there is mutual service. Now, what do the trees give to the birds?"

Just then came the distant call of the pallid cuckoo. "There," said Mr. Gray, "you have my first point. That cuckoo is calling from a tree-top; the tree helps him to get a sweetheart."

"Then the very movement of a tree must be pleasant to a bird. Do you remember Wordsworth's delight in watching a green linnet fluttering among the topmost leaves of a hazel tree, perched in ecstasy as the tree rocked in the breeze? Don't you think that that brother of the dancing leaves was glad to be there?"

"Then," continued Mr. Gray, "when the day is hot, the trees give shade to the birds, and when it is cold they give shelter." "Yes," I said, "it is a pretty sight to see a bird and his wife marshalling the young family on a snug branch for the night—all close together for warmth."

"Then," I went on, "we have to remember how the tree protects the bird from his enemies. Yonder silver-eye flees into the pepper-tree if a hawk comes sailing up. The bird also builds his

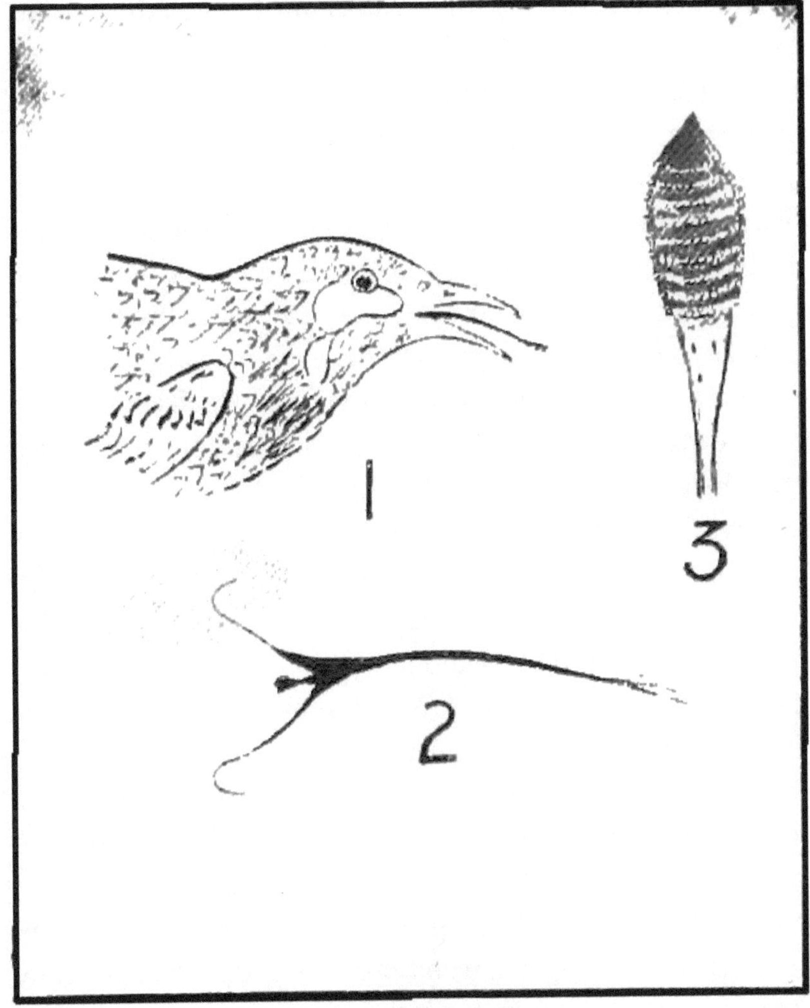

1. HONEY-EATER. 2. TONGUE OF RED-WATTLE BIRD.
3. SPIKE OF TUBULAR FLOWER.

nest in its branches to escape the many ground enemies that prey on him or his young."

Some pink berries fell to the ground, as the silver-eyes picked at the ripe fruit of the pepper-tree. "Here we have another point," continued Mr. Gray; "the tree is not only bed for the bird, but board." "Yes," I said, pointing to the gum-trees on the hillside, "every one of those gum-trees is getting ready nectar for the honey-eating birds; and the honey-eaters, in their turn, are counting the days till the honey-pots open."

Later in the day, we saw a hawk perched high on the branch of a dead gum-tree. We sat down on a log and watched him for a quarter of an hour. The grey bird sat as still as the grey branch beneath him, save that his head moved slowly as his eyes travelled all round. His flexible neck enabled him, without turning the body, to see even behind him—a power which belongs also to the owls and nightjars. Here, then, was another way in which trees help birds to their food. But, indeed, birds use trees as observation towers for a score of purposes.

While we were watching the hawk, a tree-creeper began to run up a tree close by. It had been there all the time, but so like was it to the bark that we did not notice it till it moved. "This bird," said Mr. Gray, "gives to us still another point—the insect food that trees furnish for birds like this."

"And now," he went on, "let me change roles, and ask you what the birds do for the trees. It seems to me that the birds get more than they give." "I doubt it," I replied. "Let us see. We have point number one in the help which yonder tree-creeper gives to the tree in freeing it of wood-boring insects. The amount of damage done to trees by the larvæ of moths and flies is great; but for the birds it would be much greater."

Then we saw the other day how the honey-eating birds help in freeing leaves of the scale-insects and of the honey-dew, which harbours the sooty mould fungus.

How much the birds help the trees by eating moths, flies, and beetles on the wing passes all reckoning. If we could suddenly destroy all the insect-eating birds in the world, the trees could not long survive them. No grass would clothe the fields, no woods the hills. "Surely," cried Mr. Gray, aghast at the picture, "you exaggerate?"

"No," I said; "with locusts and grasshoppers eating the grass above, and wire-worms, cockchafer grubs, and crickets at work on the roots, we should soon have bare fields." I stopped at a dead wattle tree, and, having torn off a strip of bark, showed how bark and wood were grooved and drilled in every direction by larvæ of various kinds. These insects ring the tree as effectively as the woodman's axe. "Here," I said, "you have the fate of every tree, if insect life multiplied unchecked by birds."

A flock of the green 'keet[4] flew out of a gum-tree. One or two lingered behind the others, unable to tear themselves away at once from the nectar-laden blossom.

"I suppose," said Mr. Gray, "that the tree gets something in return for these sweets." "Yes," I said, "the nectar is offered because the tree needs the services of the birds. The pollen-bearers have to be paid. The honey-eating parrots are great travellers. Just as a shearer will work his way from the early-shearing districts in the north to the late-shearing stations in the south, so the honey-eating parrots follow the flow of honey from Queensland to Tasmania."

In the same way, the spine-billed honey-eater and the tawny-

4   *Glossopsittacus concinnus*

crowned honey-eater and other small birds help to distribute the pollen of flowers, serving in Australia the same purpose that the humming-birds serve in South America. Of the native birds of Australia, honey-eaters of many kinds form the largest family. This is no chance arrangement, but is due to the fact that honey-bearing eucalypts fill a corresponding place among the trees of Australia. "Ah!" said Mr. Gray, "that is the most striking evidence we have had of the partnership between birds and plants."

"I haven't finished yet," I replied. "We have still to see how the birds serve the trees in carrying seed. For, just as a bird drives away its young lest the old home should be crowded, so the tree seeks means of sending its seed to a distance."

I led my friend to a gum-tree, on which, at several points, the parasitical plant we call the mistletoe was growing. "It lives by tapping the sap of the gum-tree, does it not?" asked Mr. Gray. "Yes, the mistletoe is an unasked guest, and lives on the hospitality of the tree. But how do you think the seed of the mistletoe gets there?" "If the seed of the mistletoe falls to the ground," replied Mr. Gray, "I suppose that would be of no use?" "None," I said; "the seed must be taken to another branch or to another tree, and placed where it can germinate and strike root into the wood."

"The seed-carrier," I continued, "is the mistletoe-bird. This bird, which is like a little robin, with a deep blue back, eats the sweet, glutinous seed within the hard berry. This seed, on passing through the bird, adheres to the branch on which he is seated, and the smallest crack in the bark is sufficient to enable it to germinate. The missel or mistletoe thrush performs the same service for the mistletoe of England."

A sparrow rose from the grass near us, and a red object drew us to the place where he had been busy. The red object was the berry of a Cape-thorn hedge, which bordered a neighbouring road. We walked up to the hedge, and found that many of the berries had been eaten by birds. "Here," I said, "is another illustration of the way in which birds carry seeds. Just as the gum-trees offer to the parrots a fee of nectar for visiting their blossoms and distributing pollen, so the Cape-thorn offers food to the bird carriers who can scatter its seed. Birds have wonderfully keen eyes for the colours which advertise their favourite fruits."

While walking near the river, we disturbed a white-fronted heron, a bird which preys on small fish. "There!" I said, "is another seed-carrier." "What!" cried Mr. Gray, "does the heron eat fruit?" "No," I said, "but it eats fish that eat seeds. Now, the heron is not fond of seeds, and will often eject the seeds from its stomach in the form of pellets. In this way, or by passing the seeds through its body, the heron distributes the seeds of water plants."

We had stopped to look at a pond which was half-covered with water weeds. I thrust my stick into the pond-mud, and, holding it up, said, "There are probably seeds enough in the mud at the end of this stick to stock a dozen ponds with weeds." "How do you know?" asked Mr. Gray. "From Darwin's researches," I replied. "He took from the edge of a pond a cupful of mud. This he dried and spread out, and placed in his study. In six months 537 plants grew from this earth." "You astonish me!" cried Mr. Gray, "but how does this bear on the partnership between plants and birds?" "Birds," I replied, "in flying to a distance with muddy feet carry seeds with them. Darwin took from the foot of a partridge, killed three years before, a ball of earth. From this earth there grew 82 plants of various kinds. By this means birds that migrate, and birds that are blown out of their way by high winds, must carry seeds to great distances."

"Well," said Mr. Gray, as we reached home, "you have proved your point. The birds give full return to the plants for all they get."

CHAPTER XVI.
The Birds of the Town.

PART I.

Mr. Gray wished to spend part of his holiday at the coast, and I agreed to go with him. *En route* we gave two days to the birds of the town.

Mr. Gray lives in a suburb where there is good cover for birds, and where thrush, blackbird, and starling will soon be as plentiful as in the outskirts of an English town. These birds, with the Indian myna and the sparrow, will, year by year, become a more important feature of town life.

I found that Mr. Gray's children looked on all these birds as Australian birds, and were not at all inclined to think of them as "introduced birds." This is as it should be. These birds, equally with the children, are Australian natives. The children hear occasionally the songs of the blue wren and the magpie; but these songs are not part of their daily life, as are the songs of thrush and blackbird, and the chatter of sparrow and myna.

The sparrow and the myna are so common that few people take notice of them. And so it comes to pass that few town dwellers know much about them. Just as they overlook their fowls, except when they fly into the flower-plots, so they pay no heed to the two birds which come closest to them in their daily life.

This seems to us a mistake. These clever birds that have been living about the feet of man for centuries are worth watching. There is really more to notice in these birds than in the birds of the bush, just as the dingo, which has never gone to school under man, is much less interesting than the dog, which, in looking up to man's face for ages, has caught something of his intelligence.

Apart, too, from the interest of the study, every fact, even the smallest, that is ascertained about these creatures that share our lives so closely is important. We ought to know whether the sparrow is, on the whole, a friend or an enemy; whether the starling should be protected by law or left to fight his own battle; and whether the blackbird kills snails enough to pay for the strawberries he eats. "Do you think," said Mr. Gray, "that that would settle the question? A pair of blackbirds that nested with us last spring forced us to put netting over the strawberry bed; but we are very sorry that they did not come back this spring." "You mean," I said, "that the birds, besides killing insects, make our homes more interesting, more home-like?" "Yes," said Mr. Gray, "that must be reckoned in balancing the account."

I found that town dwellers are on better terms with the sparrow than country folk. The birds are looked on as harm-less, happy chatterers, who help to make life lively; and most townspeople agree with the bird-lover who said that a town without sparrows is as dull as a house without children.

No doubt, the sparrow helps himself to some grain in the fowl-yard, destroys a few tree buds, and pulls up young peas; but, then, is he not busy all the winter in picking up the seeds of weeds or the larvæ of insects, and does he not, when nothing better offers, feed on the green fly which infests your roses? If the sparrows never left town, we might let the matter rest there; but many have settled in the country, and, when the time of harvest comes, some of the town sparrows pay a visit to their brethren in the country. On his way to the wheat fields, the sparrow visits the orchards. Guns, bogies, and hideous noises cannot keep him off the cherries. Accustomed for ages to feed on red berries—on hips and haws—the sparrow cannot resist the call of the cherry tree, as the fruit hangs red in the November sunshine. The fruit-grower must shoot and poison, if he is to live at all. As to the wheat fields, who can say how much of the harvest goes to the flocks of sparrows? Only those who have watched have any idea of the amount of grain they take.

"Then you condemn the sparrow?" said Mr. Gray. "He is good," I replied, "in the town, bad in the country; and he must be kept down. We can never exterminate him, but we can keep him within bounds."

"What of the starling?" asked Mr. Gray, as we walked in the fields. A flock of starlings was feeding near us, and we stood to watch them. Black and with yellow bill, they are sometimes mistaken for blackbirds. The starling is a smaller bird than the blackbird, and the bill is of a paler yellow.

"I never see starlings and blackbirds together," said Mr. Gray. "No," I replied; "the blackbird is a solitary bird. He associates with no other, save his mate, and even with her only for a time. Whoever saw a flock of blackbirds?" More starlings joined the flock, and we noticed that one of the new-comers hustled and pushed aside a thrush. The thrush, though quite as large, is no match for the starling, which is a bird of great energy and push. It is to be feared that the starling has helped the sparrow to frighten away small useful native birds.

THE STARLING (*ENGLISH ILLUSTRATED MAGAZINE*)

"Then you think," said Mr. Gray, "that the starling will make good his footing in Australia?" "I have no doubt of it," I replied. "He may, indeed, become too plentiful. Few birds are more adaptive. In the north of Australia there is already a starling, which does not come south of Queensland. The bird we are looking at will probably fill the whole field from Cape Otway to the border of Queensland."

"Then you think that there is no need for protection?" "None; the bird can take good care of itself; it is as clever as the sparrow. That flock seems to be feeding at random, and without sentries, but watch how the birds behave as this boy gets near them." Along a footpath came a boy whistling, but before he came near enough to be dangerous, the whole flock rose in a body. We could not hear the signal, but signal there must have been to secure such unity of action.

As the birds rose into the air, the sunlight glinted beautifully from the under-wings. Rising with admirable precision against the wind, the flock closed and wheeled as one bird, and then, opening out, flew towards the next field. Upon this they descended with graceful sweep, and settled at once to pick up grubs. "They seem to be doing useful work," said Mr. Gray. "Yes," I replied, "they must eat larvæ innumerable, but what I fear is that here, as in England, they may develop a liking for cherries, pears, and apples. The starling is a sprightly bird, of engaging manners, but it must be watched."

When we got back to the house, the gardener showed us a starling's nest in the hollow of an old gum-tree. Five pale blue eggs lay in it. The nest was roughly put together of straw and grass, with a little wool for a lining. Breeding, like the sparrow, in holes in houses and trees, it has the same loosely-built nest.

As we sat on the verandah, two thrushes flew from the shrubbery onto the lawn, and began to search for worms. One a few feet behind the other, but not in the same line, they moved over the grass. But now the male stops, and with head to one side, listens intently. Can it be that the fine ear of the thrush hears the worm moving up his tunnel towards the light? Presently, with a little leap and a quick dive, he pounces on the worm. A miss! Now it is the wife's chance. The tiny leap, the quick pounce, and the worm is caught.

Mr. Gray's little girl took us to the wall, and showed us the nest among the ivy. It was a large nest, made of grass and moss and small twigs, coated inside with clay. Three young birds gaped a welcome as we peered into the nest, and there were two beautiful blue eggs still unhatched.

Then Jenny took us to the end of a garden path; and there, under a weeping willow, was the "snail-stone." "A snail-stone?" cried Mr. Gray. "What is that?" "It's the stone the thrushes use to break the 'shell-backs' on!" Round the stone were little bits of snail-shell. The smaller shell-backs can be crushed in the beak, and the large ones are dashed on this stone. A thrush flew up towards the willow, and, on seeing us, swerved and continued his flight. The bird flies rapidly, and rises and falls in his flight in gentle curves. It flies just high enough to clear the trees, and never flies far.

CHAPTER XVII.
The Birds of the Town.

<u>PART II.</u>

We had been hearing blackbirds singing from the pine trees, and now one of them flew into sight. Descending with a gentle, sweeping flight, the bird alighted on the edge of the lawn. As the feet touched earth, the tail was gracefully tilted, and then the bird set about looking for worms, insects, and snails. The food of the blackbird is similar to that of the thrush; and, indeed, the bird is simply a 'thrush in ebony.'

The blackbird kept a sharp look-out, and for a time remained close to the shrubbery. "It seems," said Mr. Gray, "to be a more difficult bird to watch than the thrush." "Yes," I said, "the blackbird will never feed in the open when it can get all it needs in cover. People call it a bird of furtive, skulking habit; but such words are misleading. The bird is still, to a greater extent than its cousin the thrush, a bird of the woods; and hence there is greater timidity."

"You mean," said Mr. Gray, "that the birds that come about the homes of men have to acquire confidence by degrees?" "Yes. Who can say for how many centuries the sparrow has hopped in the streets; and who can tell for how many ages the Indian myna has been man's companion? As far back as the books take us in

THRUSH AND BLACKBIRD (AFTER SHARPE).

the history of India, we read of the myna sharing in the life of
the peasant and his cattle. In many of the old representations
of their god Ram, you may see the bird perched upon his hand."

In old countries like England, where little of the primitive
forest is left, the birds have had to come out into the open
country. First, they came into the fields, and then some of the

bolder birds into the gardens; and a few, greatly daring, ventured into the streets.

"Do you think, then, that a similar process is at work in Australia?" "Undoubtedly!" I said. "In public gardens where birds are protected we already have the silver-eye, honey-eaters, blue wrens, reed-warblers, and some of the tits; and, as time goes on, some of the other country birds may come in. It is to be hoped that the yellow-tail tit may be among these. This little busy bird, with the pretty ways, probably needs only to be kindly treated for a few generations to become a dweller in all suburban hedges. Living entirely on insects, it is a bird that can do us good service. The scrub-wren is another insect-eater which might be tempted to come into our gardens; and the fairy martin, if encouraged, might build among our homes."

"I was much struck," said Mr. Gray, "while travelling in Norway and Sweden, to find that the magpie bore so good a character. The people are kind to it, and it comes to their doors, and even enters their houses. It has little of the sly cunning which one sees in the same bird in England." "You mean," I said, "that the difference of character may be due to the difference of treatment. In England every man's hand is against a bird that is reckoned a rogue, and so the bird lives up to his reputation. Treat a bird as a rogue, and he becomes one!"

Meantime, our blackbird, in the absorbing pursuit of worms, got further away from his beloved cover. We stole closer to watch him, but he saw the movement, and flew off, with a flurried *giss, giss, giss*. This cry of alarm, which is often continued till the bird finds cover, is one of the commonest cries in English woods, and is now familiar to residents in Melbourne suburbs. The bird flew low, with wavering, fitful flight, and darted into a clump of bushes. We moved up to the thicket, and, in the shadowy light, saw the blackbird turning over the leaves with his golden bill.

Late in the afternoon we stood to watch a blackbird which was singing on a high branch of a pine tree. Presently, the bird noticed that it was being watched, and flew off, as if making for a distant point. When it had gone about a hundred yards, it dropped as if to earth, and then, keeping a hedge between itself and us, came back to the same tree with low, skimming flight. The ruse was a pretty one; and we respected the bird's wishes, and turned away.

In a neighbour's garden we were shown a blackbird's nest. Though placed deep in a thick laurel bush, it had been easily discovered through the loose straws and twigs that hung from the nest. It was made of grass, leaves, and fine twigs, and the cavity was lined, as in the case of the thrush, with clay. Over the clay, however, was a lining of fine grass, and on this lay six eggs of greenish-blue, thickly spotted with reddish-brown.

We leant over the fence to look at a fine Jersey cow. It was grazing with quiet content in a little field besprinkled with the yellow Cape-weed. An Indian myna was feeding near the cow's head. As the cow moved on, the bird advanced, keeping always a few feet from the animal's nose. "Is it by chance or by design that it keeps there?" asked Mr. Gray. "Design, I think. The cow's warm breath disturbs the little flies that live in the grass, and the bird takes advantage of this. The myna, no doubt, learned this device in India."

Presently the myna flew up and alighted on the Jersey's back. The cow paid no heed. "One can guess," said Mr. Gray, "that that is also a habit learned in India." "Yes," I replied, "the myna and the little cow of India are close friends. Perhaps the cow appreciates the service the bird renders to her in freeing the grass of flies."

Other mynas settled in the field, and then a flock of starlings. "The mynas and starlings seem to get on well together," said Mr. Gray. "Yes," I said, "they are cousins, and they have a good many habits in common. Both have a wide range in food, which, unfortunately, includes fruit, and both are gregarious and garrulous. The myna builds a nest not unlike that of the starling, and both birds lay the blue egg which is so rare among our native birds."

"They differ, however, in flight. Look!" I clapped hands, and all the starlings flew off. The mynas remained. When birds have a common foe, the signal of alarm of one kind will often be obeyed by the others. But the myna is a bird of character, and judges for himself. I clapped hands more loudly, and, this time, the mynas flew up, moving more slowly and less gracefully than the starling.

"Listen to the locust, father!" cried Jenny, "it's the first I've heard this year." "It does not seem to be the full sound," said Mr. Gray; "perhaps it is tuning up its instrument for the summer concert." I knew that the cicada was not due for two months, but I said nothing. Presently a bird moved in a tree overhead—a bird with yellow-green back and yellowish belly. "There is the locust!" I cried; "the greenfinch of England!" A year or two before, I had been deceived in the same way. An English naturalist, writing of this bird's monotone, says that it is unique among the sounds of the animal world. He had not heard our cicada.

This bird, which is one of the singing birds of England that have been introduced into Australia, has not made so much progress in popular favour as the others. There is nothing striking in the bird's appearance or character; and, indeed, few people know that we have such a bird. The best that can be said of the song is that it is a good song for a finch.

An English bird which is more popular is the goldfinch. About the same size as its cousin, the sparrow, it is easily distinguished by the crimson forehead and by the yellow band which makes of the wings "a fairy fan of golden spokes." It flies in flocks, and may often be seen in the Brighton gardens feeding on the seeds of weeds—the thistle and groundsel being its favourites.

It is a pretty sight to see it perched on a thistle-head picking at the seeds; and, indeed, so much is it associated in the popular mind with this weed that, in Germany, it is called the thistle-bird. We looked along the hedges, but failed to find the nest of the goldfinch[5]. It is a cup-shaped nest, beautifully built of moss. It is lined with horsehair and feathers, and the outside is covered with lichens. The egg is blue-white, spotted with grey and reddish-brown.

During our evening talk, I said to Mr. Gray—"Have you ever noticed that the only birds familiar to town-dwellers—and these make up half of our people—are birds that have been introduced from England and India?" "Never," replied Mr. Gray, "until we talked today of the native birds which have not yet learned to live beside man."

"Yes," I said, "that partly accounts for the retiral of the native birds; but there is another reason. The forms of life existing in Europe belong to a later and more advanced stage of development than the forms of life in Australia; and hence the European animals and plants are hardier and more adaptive than

5   For descriptions of nests and eggs of the Australian Finches consult 'Nests and Eggs of Australian Birds," A. J. Campbell.

those of our country. This is why the English weeds, snails, and other pests take possession of our gardens; why the imported hive-bee is displacing the native bees; and why the sparrow and starling take the place formerly occupied by half a dozen useful native birds."

"Don't you think," said Mr. Gray, "that the introduced birds are equal to the task of keeping down insect pests?" "Well," I replied, "they do excellent work in the larger gardens which have lawns and shrubberies; but, in the smaller gardens, which are little visited by thrush or blackbird, starling or myna, the little birds that have been displaced would be of great service. In England even the smallest garden is watched over by tits, wrens, robins, and finches. Most of the birds that have been introduced from England were brought partly for the sake of their singing: it may become necessary to bring in some birds and insects for the sake of their usefulness in keeping down pests. Such introduction would involve risks; but the problem will need to be faced. As knowledge of Nature increases with the growth of Nature-study, we shall be able to restore Nature's balance with less danger of error."

"You mean," said Mr. Gray, "that we must seek in the country which bred the pests for the natural check to their increase?" "Exactly," I replied; "I think that pests grow so fast in our climate that artificial remedies are not sufficient. Sooner or later we shall be forced to fall back on Nature's methods."

"But," said Mr. Gray, "the eggs of pests must come to us in food-boxes and fruit-cases from all parts of the world." "Yes, and we must go to the breeding-place of the pest, wherever it may be—to England or America, to Sicily or Turkey. If the merchant, seeking a market, brings the ends of the earth together, the gardener, the orchardist, and the farmer must do likewise."

"I see," said Mr. Gray, as we went off to bed, "that Nature has some very subtle ways of teaching us that the World is One!"

CHAPTER XVIII.
The Songs of the Town-birds.

Next morning the dawn-chorus of the birds awoke me—a fitting beginning to a day which we had set apart for hearing the songs of the town-birds. Thrushes and blackbirds were singing from the neighbouring pine-trees. At this season, when family cares fill up the day, the thrush is best heard in the morning and evening; and so I called Mr. Gray to hear the thrush's song.

"What does he say?" asked Mr. Gray, as we listened to the bird with the speckled breast. "Who knows?" I replied; "each bird-lover has his own rendering of the song. Tennyson hears it say, 'New, new, new, new! here again, here, here, here!' and Burroughs, listening in the evening, when lovers walk, hears it cry 'Kiss her, kiss her; do it, do it; be quick, be quick; that was neat, that was neat; that will do!'"

These are good renderings; but, perhaps, Macgillivray succeeds as well as anyone in imitating the inimitable:

> *"Cheer up, cheer up, cheer up!*
> *Qui, qui, qui, kween, quip.*
> *Tiurru, tiurru, chipiwi,*
> *Tootee, tootee, chiuchoo,*
> *Chirri, chirri, chooee,*
> *Quiu, qui, qui!"*

But, indeed, as the bird never repeats his song in exactly the same way, the best transcription cannot be more than a help to the memory.

It is a sprightly song, for the bird sings only when he is glad; at mating time, or when sunshine follows dark days in winter, or when a shower gives promise of plenty of worms. Occasionally there is a tender note, but, as a rule, the song is the song of the blithe heart.

"Can you hear the melody that the poets write of?" asked Mr. Gray. "No," I replied, "the bird seems to have much to say, and no time for a measured strain. Out it tumbles, in shrill sharps."

Mingling with the thrush's song was the song of a blackbird on a tree close by. Here there was less of eagerness—a mellow, unhurried strain. If the thrush was a child pouring out his gladness in stammering haste, the blackbird was a man of happy experience, speaking out of a deep content with life. In accord with this is the fact that, while the eager thrush can spare little time during the day from family cares, the blackbird steals a few minutes at intervals all through the day to tell us that the spring world is a good world, and that it is a joy to be alive.

I arranged that we should go, early in the forenoon, to a part of the coast where the skylark may be heard. My wish was that Mr. Gray, who had no idea that the skylark of England could be heard in Australia, should get a surprise.

On our way we heard again the monotonous note of the greenfinch; and, soon after, the light but sweet notes of the goldfinch. The goldfinch flew with quick, undulating flight to another tree, hovered for a moment, and then perched on the highest branch.

We had stopped for a few minutes under an old gum-tree, when a number of starlings flew up. They settled on the upper branches and began to talk. One bird called plaintively as if in trouble. The call of another suggested the not unpleasant sound of a good violinist tuning his instrument. In a third call we heard the slight crack of a child's whip, and, in still another, the harsher sound of a boy's rattle. Then we were startled to hear a spirited imitation of the blue wren's notes. But the leading note, the note most characteristic of the starling, was one which suggested the breath drawn in with a musical sound. After this lively and varied performance, it was not difficult to believe that the bird has been taught to say the Lord's Prayer without missing a word!

It was still early in the day when we reached a sandy plain near the mouth of the Yarra. Little knolls of sand, held together by the sand-grass, were frequent. Seated on one of these, we looked round upon a wide stretch of open land of the kind that larks love. Patches of the richer land between the knolls were gay with the yellow flower of the hibbertia and the pink stars of the noon-flower. Overhead was the light blue of the spring sky and this was reflected in the beautiful blue of the sea, which shimmered in the morning light.

While we were looking at this view, we did not at first notice that larks were singing at some distance; but presently some birds closer to us added their songs to the chorus, and all at once Mr. Gray cried out sharply—The skylark!—is it possible? I thought there was no skylark within 10,000 miles!

And then I explained to him that, in 1865, the Acclimatisation Society had set free some English skylarks on the shore of Port Phillip, and that the birds were now firmly established on the low, open plains near the sea from Sandringham to Williamstown.

Several larks were now singing near us, and the air was vibrating with the music. So commanding was the strain that, for a time, all other sounds were forgotten. So pervasive, too, was the sound that Mr. Gray imagined a lark to be singing just behind him when the bird was high in air.

"Ah! now I see one!" he cried; and, following his finger, I saw the bird that floats flutteringly in the blue—the skylark of England. Down came the stream of sound, jubilant, penetrating, unceasing—a song of pure ecstasy! Would the bird never tire?

"It is the very sunshine singing," said Mr. Gray, who had lost the bird again, and was looking up with dazzled eyes. "It must be many a day since that bird left the woods and became a creature of the light and of the open fields!"

When the first gladness of discovery was over, Mr. Gray said—"It is a blithe song, an exhilarating song! Who could be in dull spirits with a song like that in his ears? But I can't lay hold of it. There seems to be no fixed succession of notes." "No," I said, "the bird's vocal resources are endless, and he never exactly repeats himself. He just says—always in the same way, and yet always in a different way—that he is glad to be alive on this beautiful morning, and to be looking down on the little brown bird that shares his home."

"How is it," asked Mr. Gray, "that the air is so full of the song? Half a dozen thrushes singing together would not take possession of the ear in this way." "Well," I replied, "the sound comes from above us; and, also, there is the burr, which makes a kind of undertone to the higher notes. One may easily miss this humming undertone, just as one may not notice the monotonous deep notes that accompany a lively air. But it is a marked feature in the lark's song, and has much to do, I think, with its power to pervade the air."

The bird was now hovering for a moment before coming down. The little quivering creature, now at its highest, was distinctly visible. Mr. Gray, who knew the bird much better from the poets than from actual observation, was disappointed that it did not lose itself in the blue.

It came down quickly, descending in a straight line and by stages. All this time the song continued, nor did it cease until the bird, a few yards from the ground, stopped abruptly and dropped among the grass. From our knoll we could see that, on alighting, it ran along the ground. Later in the day we saw a lark which made the descent differently. It descended as usual, but, before reaching the ground, flew for some distance close to the earth. The lark rarely descends straight upon the nest.

As we walked on quietly, we were startled by the bold opening notes of a lark that rose from the other side of a knoll. I noted the time, and we sat down to watch and listen.

No sooner was the bird clear of the ground than it began to sing; and it seemed to pour out its notes as vehemently as when it is high in air. This may be an error of the ear, but it is clear that the song is heard best from a height.

And now we followed the bird as it rose rapidly, its tremulous wings beating the air tirelessly. Wonderful is the vigour of the bird as it climbs up, singing with all its might! "What a delightful little spendthrift of its powers!" cried Mr. Gray.

After the first upward rush, it continues the ascent, not in a straight line, but in a spiral movement; and the radius widens as the bird rises higher. Now the wings quiver against a great white cloud, and now the bird has wheeled off again into the blue. So wide at last becomes the circle that the bird seems to be about to wander at large through the fields of heaven. But, no! It is but a wider spiral, and ever the centre of the circle is the home in the grass where the wife sits listening.

When the bird reached earth again, I found that the whole performance had taken place in seven minutes. Later on we watched a lark which took only three minutes. The time varies according to the season, the weather, the time of the day, and the mood of the bird. It would be of interest to know how often the same bird rises to sing from daylight to dusk. It cannot be so often as is commonly thought, because the minstrel is also the father, and the family has to be fed. The strain, too, of singing and mounting must be great.

Long after we had ceased to give it close attention, the singing of the larks formed a pleasant background to our thoughts and talk. It is perhaps in this way that we most enjoy the lark-music. Certainly it is in this way that most people know it, and it is this that stirs the memory most subtly.

Evening was coming on as we moved home. On a wall overgrown with ivy, a flock of mynas was settling for the night. We could hear them long before we arrived at the spot, and, when we came close, the noise was deafening. They seemed to be chattering at the top of their voices, and all speaking at the same time. There was a flutter of brown and white along the wall as the birds sought easier perches.

"What a babel of tongues!" cried Mr. Gray. "They talk with the vigour of birds beginning the day's work." "Yes," I replied, "they seem to be going to roost because the light is failing, and not because they are tired. It is a strong bird, the Indian myna." "Are they talking of the grubs they have caught?" said

Mr. Gray, "or are they quarrelling about the best roosts, or are they screaming out of the pure joy of living?"

The myna is a true starling in this habit of evening chatter, and, as the starling increases in numbers, we shall often hear the bird settling for the night in the same way.

The mellow note of a blackbird came to us from the woods near home, and the same thrush that we heard in the morning was singing from the same tree. It appeared to me that the strain was less hurried than in its morning performance. It seemed, as a vesper-hymn should, to fit in with the peaceful close of day.

CHAPTER XIX.
Sea Birds.

"We must have a look at the sea birds," said Mr. Gray, "before we finish our bird-studies." The beauty of sea birds had long been a cause of pleasure to him, and in arranging a cruise down the Bay the pupil was as eager as the master.

It was a fine October morning when we stepped on board at St. Kilda; a morning to provoke that zest in a pursuit which gives inspiration and insight—qualities as necessary to the seeker after Nature's secrets as painstaking work.

The sky, pale blue after a night of rain, was flecked with white clouds. Silver gulls, beautiful in their pure white as the clouds themselves, were sailing between blue sky and blue sea. A breeze from the south rippled the water and filled the sails.

It was fitting that we should begin with the silver gull, a bird which is a kind of link between the land birds and the sea birds. One may see this bird all round the long coast line of the Australian continent, mingling its white with the white of the breakers; and one may see it on the Murray a thousand miles, by river, from the sea. Numbers of silver gulls were seen in the Lake Eyre district by Professor Gregory's recent exploring party.

In stormy weather scores are to be seen picking up refuse at the Yarra wharves, in the heart of the city. At all times, a few of the birds patrol the river from Footscray to Heidelberg, doing useful work as scavengers.

"Do you mean to say," said Mr. Gray, "that these beautiful birds live on the refuse of that dirty river?" "Yes," I replied; "if man could combine the useful and the beautiful as Nature does, how much better a place the world would be to live in!" "The gull that patrols the Yarra, it is true, is not so clean as these gulls on the Bay; but that is not the bird's fault. Some day the city air will be smokeless, and the river will run clear, and then the river gull will be a thing of beauty."

"I know," said Mr. Gray, "that this gull takes readily to land-life. I had one to help the gardener to keep down the snails." "In Europe," I replied, "one often sees the gull following the plough to pick up worms."

Strikingly different was another bird which was fishing near us; a large, black, and somewhat ungainly bird—the white-breasted cormorant. This bird has the reputation of being one of the greediest of birds; and certainly the quantity of fish it can consume is astounding. It is, however, doubtful whether, in proportion to size, it eats more than some of our favourite small birds. A blue wren kept in captivity ate 100 grasshoppers, March flies, or cockroaches per day! Equally careful observations of other birds might show that the cormorant, whose rapacity has passed into a proverb, is not so greedy as we think. When a fishing-ground fails, the blame is often placed on the cormorant. The reasoning is not sound, for the bird had been fishing for centuries before man came on the scene.

It cannot be denied, however, that the bird sometimes suffers from his eagerness in feeding. We have found a young shark 18 inches long in the stomach and gullet of a cormorant. It is worthy of note that several worms one inch long were found in the stomach of this bird. A young cormorant, still unfeathered, found at Kerguelen Island, was infested by worms. These had probably been received with food from the parent bird. Can it be that the cormorant is troubled more than other birds with worms? Can this have anything to do with its great appetite?

The cormorant near us suddenly dived; and one forgot his ungainly appearance in admiring his splendid fishing powers. There is no better fisher in the world than this clumsy-looking bird, unless it be the penguin. As becomes a good fisher, the cormorant knows that a river-mouth is a good place for fishing, and so the bird is generally to be seen at the Yarra mouth, picking up fish as they come or go out with the tide. Occasionally, too, a few cormorants are to be found far up the river.

Another bird was fishing for whitebait near the shore. It looked like a silver gull, but, on closer view, one noticed that the flight and the manner of diving were different. The flight was quicker, and the jerky movement contrasted with the graceful ease of the silver gull. But nothing could exceed the grace of the tern in diving; the poise, the lightning descent, and then the return to air with the silver fish in the black bill.

Later in the cruise we saw a tern which was engaged in the tedious process of swallowing a garfish twelve inches long. The head and half of the body had been already digested.

But what means this commotion among the terns? Ah! it is the skua, the pirate of the sea! A brown and white bird has come up rapidly, has singled out a tern which is rising with a fish, and has given chase. The tern tries to escape. In vain! The fierce bird with the hawk-like beak presses his attack, and the

AUSTRALIAN GANNET ROOKERY. (PHOTO BY H.P.C. ASHWORTH.)

gull coolly drops the fish. Down darts the skua, and seizes the fish before it touches the water.

"Does the skua never fish for himself?" asked Mr. Gray. "Never!" I replied; "if he had to dive for fish, he would probably starve. But you can't call him a lazy bird; he works actively for a living, and the birds that he makes use of don't distress themselves much about the blackmail which he levies. It is the natural tribute to his superior courage. Through long habit, they can fish for him as well as themselves without undue strain."

"It seems strange that so small a bird should be so much feared," said Mr. Gray. "It is his courage," I replied, rather than his size that is feared. The skua is little larger than a silver gull, but he is very strong of wing. He is sometimes found hundreds of miles from land."

Wandering Albatross (from Buller's Birds of New Zealand").

Near Mornington, a flock of gannets was fishing. It is a bold bird, the gannet, and came so close to the boat that we could see the long, strong tapering bill—a perfect instrument for piercing. Presently the quick, easy flight was checked; the bird poised, and then, almost in a straight line, dashed into the sea. So strong was the plunge that the spray was thrown up for several feet.

"I understand now," said Mr. Gray, "how the gannet can be caught by fixing fish on boards placed below the surface. I can see that the bill would pierce fish and board, and how the catcher would be caught." "We are lucky in seeing these gannets," I said. "During this month, the gannet, the terns, and, indeed, all the birds we have seen today, go to one of the islands in Bass Strait for the mating season."

Opposite to Dromana we had the good fortune to see an albatross. This fine bird is only an occasional visitor to the Bay. The breeze had freshened, and the great bird was soaring majestically without a flap of the wing. Using the field-glass, we guessed the distance from wing-tip to wing-tip to be about eight feet. No wonder the bird can keep up with ships for weeks together. No wonder it has been found as far from home as the coast of Norway.

The bird is made for the open ocean; and it seemed out of place in the Bay. And the fresh breeze that made the yacht heel over was but as a zephyr to the bird which is never so much at ease as in the fiercest gales of the Southern Ocean.

"I like," said Mr. Gray, "to think of the bird in those desolate wastes of ocean where keel of ship has never been, riding with joy on the wings of the wind." "The words," I replied, "which you have used, 'the wings of the wind,' are literally true; for the bird seems to have solved the problem of flying by using the force of the wind. The stronger the wind, the less the bird needs to flap the wing; and, as the wind is almost unceasing in these southern seas, the bird has learned to move with motionless wing.

The albatross swept near us again, and we watched its maj-

NESTING GROUND OF WHITE-CAPPED ALBATROSS.
(PHOTO BY H.P.C. ASHWORTH.)

esty and grace of movement. The silence, too, of the bird adds to its dignity, in striking contrast to the noisy garrulousness of gulls and terns.

We landed at a little wharf beyond Dromana, and pushed across the sand hills to the outer ocean, in order to visit the mutton-bird rookery. Striking the sea some distance from the rookery, we made our way along the beach.

In a little bay among the cliffs we saw a pied oyster-catcher—a handsome black and white bird with red bill and red legs. The bird was running in a fashion that suggested that it was seeking to lead us away from its nest. Taking this hint, we followed the print of its feet backwards, and came to the nest, which was simply a depression on a small sand-mound a little above high-

MUTTON-BIRD ROOKERY.

water mark. The two eggs, stony-grey with brown spots, were so like in colour to sand and shingle that we might have stepped on the eggs before noticing them. Later in the day we saw one of these birds using his long, strong bill to prize limpets off the rocks, and another at work digging for sea-worms.

Mutton-bird is the popular name for the short-tailed petrel, which nests in the islands of Bass Strait. These birds, in great numbers, come to us yearly in the spring months. They remain through the summer, and disappear during the five coldest months of the year.

The numbers observed by the early colonists are almost incredible. When Flinders and Bass, in 1798, were exploring Bass Strait, they saw a flock of the sooty petrel passing. The stream of birds continued for ninety minutes, and Flinders reckoned that the birds must have numbered over a hundred million.

The bird prefers to nest in lonely islands near the land, but here and there we find a small rookery in unfrequented parts of the coast. The mutton-bird rookery which we had now reached was one of these.

On a raised beach, twenty feet above sea-level, partly covered with tussocky grass, was the rookery which we sought. The birds lay only one egg, and this is placed at the end of a tunnel about three feet long. No nest is made, and the egg, true to the rule which we had already noticed, is pure white.

The birds arrive in September for their spring cleaning, and, having put the holes in order, go to sea for some weeks, and then return for the breeding season in the third week in November. Where the rookery is large, this return of the birds is described by the fishers as the "mutton-bird gale." As our visit was in October, the rookery was deserted.

"Then we shall not see the petrels?" said Mr. Gray. "No," I replied, "and even in the season you might find the place, to all appearances, deserted. The sitting bird is hidden in its hole and its partner is out at sea fishing. Just when night falls, however, about 8 o'clock, the petrels appear suddenly in the half-light and whizz past your head on their way to the burrows. From that time, till 4 o'clock next morning, the rookery is alive with the cries of the birds. By day-break the bird that is off duty has gone to sea."

As we turned away, no sound broke the stillness of the primeval scene but the roar of the sea and the faint rustle of the evening breeze among the stiff grass.

On the cliff top we turned to take a last look at the sea. Clouds, fiery with the flush of sunset, were working up from the horizon. The weird *weeloo* of the sea curlew came from a distant bay. A few weeks ago the eerie call of this very bird may have sounded in the ears of the Russian fur-hunter as he skirted a lonely marsh in North Siberia!

CHAPTER XX.
The Earth-worm.

<u>THE ANIMAL THAT PREPARES THE
EARTH TO BE MAN'S HOME.</u>

We had heavy rain for two days after our return from the coast. On the morning of the third day we found so many earth-worms on the garden walks that we could not help trampling on some of them. The earth-worm must have moisture, but it may get too much, and these worms, flooded out of their holes, were sick or dead.

"It has a perilous life, the earth-worm," I said; "few creatures have more enemies, and yet so well has it played its part in life that it has managed to spread over the whole world. Where is the land in which the fisher can find no worm for his bait?" Mr. Gray was not interested. "I can go on as long as you like with bird study," he said; "bird life is delightful; but I can't feel much interest in this creature, except when I go a-fishing."

"Mr. Gray," I said, laughingly, "you will change your mind within fifteen minutes." In less than that time I gave to him the gist of Darwin's wonderful book on earth-worms—a book which shows that no other animal has played such a part in history as these lowly creatures!

Having thus gained his ear, I made an experiment to find

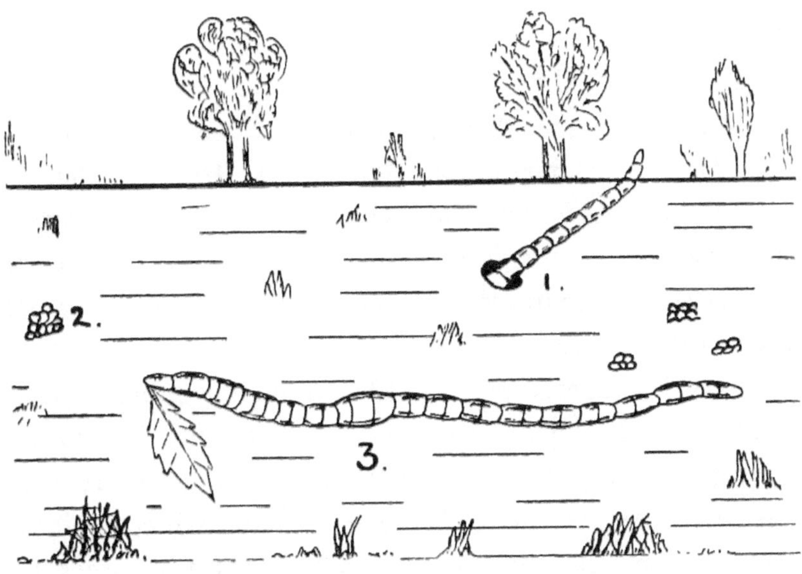

1. Earth-worm entering a burrow. 2. Castings.
3. Conveying a leaf to burrow.

how long a worm takes to burrow into the soil. "I loosened the earth of one of the garden-beds, and put a frightened worm on the surface. In three minutes the worm had disappeared. The worm, having pushed into the soil for half of his length, expanded so forcibly that the earth was thrust aside. Then came another advance and another expansion, and so forward. When soil less loose was used, the worm took from ten to twenty minutes to get out of sight. The power shown was astonishing, and the truth is that, helpless as the worm may appear, it has a highly developed muscular system.

"But how," asked Mr. Gray, "does it bore when it gets down into ground too hard to be pushed aside?" "Your question," I replied, "leads us to the most important feature in the worm life—it swallows the earth!" "Ah!" said Mr. Gray, now thoroughly interested, "that explains the worm-castings one sees on the lawn. They are formed, I suppose, of earth that has passed through the worm's body?" "Exactly!" I replied, "and you must remember that the worm, in swallowing earth, not only deepens his burrow, but gets his food. The earth that the worm frequents is composed largely of decayed leaves, and it is on these leaves that the creature chiefly lives. When the earth is not rich enough in vegetable matter, the worm carries small leaves into his burrow."

"Has this vegetarian," asked Mr. Gray, "any preferences in food?" "Yes," I replied; "an experiment made with the leaves of cabbage, parsnip, and celery showed that the worm preferred the celery. As becomes a creature of such distinction, it has its tastes. In calling it a vegetarian, however, you forget that decaying vegetable matter swarms with the minute creatures we call microbes and bacteria; also, that there is a good deal of decaying animal matter in the earth."

"I see now," said Mr. Gray, "why I have so much difficulty in getting worms for bait when the soil is sandy or poor. In such soil there can be but little decayed vegetable matter." "Yes," I said, "and you can see that the few worms that do live in such poor soil are making the soil richer."

"You mean," said Mr. Gray, "by the castings which they bring to the surface?" "Yes," I replied, "and by letting air and rain into their burrows. The truth is, that Nature had her ploughs at work long before Tubal-Cain forged a plough-share. Into the worms' tunnels the air passes to sweeten the soil, and the rain to give moisture and root-food."

"Then," said Mr. Gray, "the richer the earth, the more numerous the worms, and the more worms there are, the richer the earth becomes?" "Yes," I replied, "the more you enrich your garden soil, the more the worms will help you to keep it rich. In a very rich plot in New Zealand, worms were found at the rate of 300,000 per acre. Figures like these help one to understand Darwin's calculation that, in many parts of England, a weight of more than ten tons of earth annually passes through the bodies of worms in every acre of ground, and is brought to the surface. In this way the entire surface-bed of vegetable mould actually passes through their bodies in the course of every few years!" "Wonderful!" cried Mr. Gray. "I can never tread carelessly on a worm again."

And not only do worms create the soil which gardeners call good growing soil, but they smooth the surface of the earth. Long before man levelled his fields with patent graders, Nature was at work filling up the hollows."

Here Mr. Gray led me to a croquet-green, and said: "This was originally a poor, rocky bit of ground with few worms in it; but I had some rich earth spread on it, and now you see from the castings that worms are plentiful." "Yes," I said, "and the birds know it." I pointed to a thrush that was pecking at a worm at the far end of the lawn. "I fear that we must set this habit of the thrush to the debit side of his account."

"Part of his fee for singing!" laughed Mr. Gray. "Does the worm charge no fee for his services?" "None," I replied, "we have nothing to set against the worm except that the castings sometimes make the lawn look untidy. On account of this, some gardeners lose no chance of killing worms! You may see them chopping them with the spade as they dig!" "You remind me," said Mr. Gray, laughingly, "of the gardener who cried out indignantly to a frog, as he struck at it with his hoe, 'I'll larn you to be a frog!'"

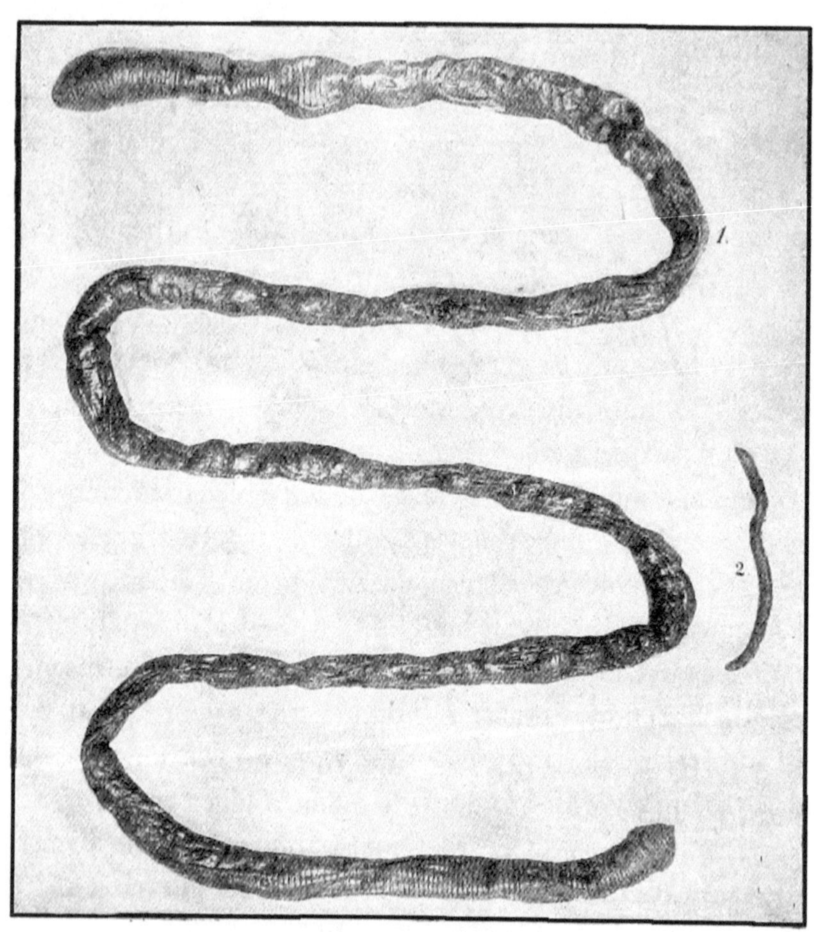

1. THE GIANT EARTH-WORM, 5 FT. 6 IN. LONG.
2. COMMON EARTH-WORM, 4 IN. LONG.

"If the thrush," I continued, "lived entirely on worms it would long since have become a night-bird like the owl." "You mean," said Mr. Gray, "that the worm comes out only at night?" "Yes, the nighttime, cool and dewy, suits the worm better than the warm, dry daytime, and it is then safer from its enemies. By day, it spends much of its time with its head close to the mouth of the hole."

"Ah! now I understand the thrush's way of worm-hunting," said Mr. Gray. "The bird knows this habit, and dives into the hole before the worm can retreat." "Yes," I said, "and you notice how lightly the bird hops when he is near a hole. The worm has no ears, but it is very sensitive to vibration. Even the hop of a robin is often enough to give it warning."

Mr. Gray, who had been examining a worm with his pocket lens, said: "It seems to have no eyes." "No," I replied, "but Darwin found by experiment that it was sensitive to light. It feels the difference between day and night." "It seems," continued Mr. Gray, "to have some hooked bristles along the body." "Yes," I replied, "it is by means of these and the muscular rings that it can move so quickly."

Turning over a large, flat stone, we found some worms that had made for themselves lairs in the security of this cover. Beside them lay a few worm-cocoons. These round, jelly-like balls contain the eggs. The cocoon is secreted by the *saddle*, the thickened zone to be seen in the middle of the worm. This jelly-like cover serves as food when the egg becomes a worm.

We noticed a burrow plugged with small bits of leaf, apparently meant as a protection to the entrance. Stones are sometimes used for this purpose. These plugs may serve to keep out centipedes and other enemies of the worm.

Then we carefully laid bare some of the burrows, and found that, as a rule, the direction was oblique. This oblique direction makes them less liable to be flooded, and also keeps the worm in the richer earth near the surface. In one of our excavations we disturbed a colony of ants, and I was reminded of the great service that these little creatures do to man in a country like ours, where the soil is often too dry, or too hard, or too poor, for the operations of the earth-worm.

Darwin says: "When we behold a wide, turf-covered expanse, we should remember that its smoothness, on which so much of its beauty depends, is mainly due to all the inequalities having been slowly levelled by worms. The earth-worm ploughs, drains, airs, pulverizes, fertilizes, and levels." Had Darwin been a native of Australia, he would have associated the ant with the worm in this beneficent work. He would have added also the burying-beetle, which covers with earth the droppings of horse and cow.

As we walked towards the house, Mr. Gray said: "I retract all I said about the worm. I see that this gentle, tireless creature has changed the face of the earth and made it fit for man's home."

"Yes," I replied, "the earth-worm slowly covers the seats of dead empires, but the empires were built upon his lowly labours."

CHAPTER XXI.
A Word for the Snail.

Next morning was showery. When the clouds cleared off, I went into the garden. The sunlight was broken into fresh beauty by the raindrops that hung from every bush, and the faint smell of honeysuckle blossom was in the still air.

I found Mr. Gray bending over a bed of carnations, and picking off snails. He was tossing them, with a movement of disgust, into the road. "Don't do that, Mr. Gray!" I exclaimed. "It is cruel to the shellbacks. Kill them outright!" Mr. Gray, gentlest of men, who taught that everything that breathes should have our sympathy, was startled, and I added, "I'm sure you would agree with me if you knew the snail."

Mr. Gray, whose whole thought had been of his beloved carnations, said, "I'm sure you're right; I've learned, by this time, that among living creatures there is 'nothing common or unclean.'"

"It's a rare chance to get rid of some of them, though," he added, as he looked ruefully at his flowers. "One rarely sees them except in showery weather." "In rainy England," I replied, "they are to be seen often enough by daylight, but in Australia they are becoming creatures of the night. Our heavy dews give them a chance of getting through the spells of dry weather."

A large snail was moving over the bed towards the fence.

THE SNAIL.

Every muscle of its body was straining, as the frightened creature sought cover. The two feelers were diligently exploring, and the eye-stalks were at full stretch to get a commanding view of the path ahead. Every part of the under surface of the snail touched the earth, and a trail of glistening slime marked the track. "You can see why the snail is not much abroad in the daytime," I said. "When the earth and the leaves are dry, the expenditure of the slime must be great. No wonder it is a lover of damp earth and moist leaves."

I took up the shell, and the creature at once withdrew within its house. "It would shut the door, I suppose, if it had one," said Mr. Gray. "Its house is not so complete as that of some of the sea-snails." Presently the snail began to come out of the shell and to move along my finger. The shell was held fast between finger and thumb, and I felt the drag as the strong muscles of the belly-foot contracted, and the creature sought to pull the shell forward. The force of the pull was remarkable.

This led to a twisting of the fore-body to the left, and the breathing-hole on the right became clearly visible—just within the shell. Holding the shell up to the light, we could see into the breathing-cavity. The tortoise-shell pattern of the outer surface shone through the shell, and, in the thin layer of flesh, we could see distinctly the network of veins which bring the blood to be freshened.

"I feel ashamed," said Mr. Gray, as he looked at all this through his pocket lens, "when I remember how contemptuously I have kicked this creature out of my way. It is out of ignorance that we maim it or put it to death by slow means."

I wished to show to Mr. Gray the famous tooth-ribbon of the snail; and I placed the creature in a box containing a fresh cabbage-leaf. In the evening, the snail fed eagerly; and, on listening attentively, we could hear the rasping movement of the teeth as they rubbed the leaf into green mash. On closer examination, we found that the tooth-ribbon was a kind of strap, covered, in symmetrical fashion, with minute teeth. When this toothed-ribbon is moved backwards and forwards, it acts on the tender leaf like a file. The pretty pattern formed by the regular rows of teeth varies in each kind of snail according to the nature of the food. So marked, indeed, is this adaptation of tongue to food, that the varying pattern of the teeth has been used as a basis for classifying snails, shell-fish, and other molluses.

"In the sea-snails," said Mr. Gray, "I suppose that the file is fitted for rougher work?" "Yes," I said, "in most cases. Some of the vegetarians among the whelks live on sea-plants, which are almost as tender as any land plant; but the dog-whelk and other molluscs that prey on shell-fish need a very strong file." "You mean," said Mr. Gray, "that they have to file through the shell of the fish which they eat?" "Yes," I replied, "you must have noticed how many cockle-shells on the beach are drilled with holes." "Yes," said Mr. Gray, "I've often seen the children stringing cockle-shells together by these holes."

Mr. Gray, who had been looking at the eye-spots on the points of the long horns, asked if they were not exposed to danger in a position so prominent. I touched one gently, and, quick as thought, the eye-spot was drawn into the tube very much in the same way as the point of a tight glove-finger is sometimes drawn in when we seek to withdraw the hand. It was a pleasure to watch the smooth working of this mechanism and to see how well the eye was protected.

We found the snails in great plenty hidden among the inner leaves of the honeysuckle which covered the fence. "How happens it," asked Mr. Gray, "that the leaves of the honeysuckle are not riddled?" "The snail," I replied, "is a dainty feeder, and refuses to touch certain leaves. He will not touch, for example, leaves which have a bitter taste; and to this distaste, no doubt, we owe it that many of our medical plants have survived. Nor does the snail care to walk on hairy or on prickly leaves."

In a damp, shady corner of the garden, beneath an old board, we found the eggs of a snail. They are like small peas, of a pretty pearly white. Sometimes the eggs are buried in the soil; and one often turns them up in digging. A large number of eggs is laid; and, if the summer is not too dry, there may be a second brood about the beginning of autumn.

In time of drought, the snail secretes a kind of temporary door to his shell, and then goes to sleep until the rain awakens him. This faculty of summer-sleep, so useful in a country subject to drought, is possessed by many of our animals.

In another part of the garden, we found that the houseless snail, which we call the slug, had been busy among the pansies. The slugs had not attacked the green leaves, but had eaten away parts of the pretty flower faces—here a brow and there a chin! The maimed faces looked up with a patient, injured air!

"What dainty feeders these slugs are!" cried Mr. Gray. "I suppose that the slug is just a snail without a shell?" "Yes," I replied, "and there is reason to believe that the slug at one time had the shell. In the early stages of the slug's life, the shell still appears."

In the evening, Mr. Gray read aloud an account of the snail-sties in which the Romans fattened snails of various kinds for table; and how the competition of the snail-farmers resulted in snails of fabulous size being produced. When the Romans spread over Europe, they took their tastes in food with them, and the snail which is eaten in France to this day is known in the south of England as the Roman snail. This snail, which is common in the chalk counties, has not been brought to Australia. One may still see, in one of the oldest streets of Paris, a huge snail of gilded wood hanging as a sign over the door of an eating-house. There is evidence, too, in English literature, that the Roman snail was once an article of food on English tables. Ben Jonson, in Every Man in His Humour, speaks of dressed snails as a delicacy.

As usual, Mr. Gray wanted the poets to have the last word. "In England," he said, "I once met an old woman who told me that in her youth it was the custom of girls to consult snails on May Day morn as to the names of their destined sweethearts. The snail, when placed on a dusty slate, traced out the initial letter of the name! I have since found these lines in the works of the poet Gray:

> *'Last May Day fair I search'd to find a snail*
> *That might my secret lover's name reveal!'"*

CHAPTER XXII.
What We Saw at the Beach.

PART I.
ANEMONES, CORALS, SEA-JELLIES.

The next day was set aside for a visit to the seashore at Black Rock. The day was warm, and our hearts leapt as we caught sight of the sea-blue, under a cloudless sky. When Mr. Gray drank the large air, and took off his hat to let the cool south breeze play upon his brow, he looked like a sea-worshipper doing homage to his god.

"All the rivers run into the sea, yet is not the sea full!" he chanted. "I can follow, in imagination," he said, as we descended by the cliff path, "the wonderful circle of water—from sea to air, from air to river, from river to sea—but what of the solid matter, the mineral substances that are being washed from land to sea perpetually? They do not leave the sea again to join the eternal cycle!"

For answer, I pointed to the shells that lay on the beach, the dead sea-tangle on the sand, and the living green and brown weeds that were swaying in the flow of the beautiful green water. "You mean," said Mr. Gray, "that the solids go to build up shell and seaweed? What wonderful chemists and builders the shells and seaweeds are."

"I suppose," he continued, "that the whelk secretes a shell just as the snail does?" "Yes," I replied, "just as a man throws out upon the skin the moisture that he does not need, so the shellfish throws out the lime that forms its shell."

"What is this?" said Mr. Gray, as he poked at a dark red knob of what seemed to be opaque jelly. "A sea-flower," I replied—"an anemone. It is not worthy of its name as you see it now; but, watch!" I threw on it some spray, and, presently, the mouth began to open and to show the lighter red of the arms. Another douche of the sea-water and the arms were opened wide. This was not enough, so I turned over the stone into a rock-pool so that the creature was fully submerged. Immediately the arms were stretched out, and the beautiful circles of ray-florets were complete. We had anticipated the tide by half an hour.

"How does it live?" asked Mr. Gray. "It fishes," I replied, "for twelve hours daily for small fish and for crabs, mussels, and limpets." Just then, at the bottom of the pool, a small stone moved, and, when I lifted it, a little crab ran out. I caught it and held it to the arms of the anemone. They closed on it at once, and, when we left the spot, nothing was visible but the prominent eye-stalks. "Poor crabby!" said Mr. Gray, "his last look at the world!" Later in the day, we gave a shrimp to an anemone, which grasped it eagerly. This was evidently a choice morsel.

"Can the anemone move at all?" asked Mr. Gray. "Yes," I replied, "it can move along on its base in snail-like fashion, but much more slowly than a snail. That the anemone knows the advantage of being able to move is clear from the habit of one anemone which is often found fixed on the shell the hermit-crab lives in. Wherever the crab goes, the anemone goes. As a rule, however, it moors itself for life on some rock where the currents will bring to it all the food it needs. In places where the current is rich in life, as at the entrance to harbours, the anemones are often in great numbers."

"How is it," asked Mr. Gray, "that it can lengthen the arms so quickly?" "Each arm," I replied, "is really a tube into which the animal can drive water from the interior of the body. This enables the anemone to thrust forward the feelers to a great length. Each feeler has a minute hole at the tip through which water can be expelled when the anemone shrinks."

"Are all the anemones solitary in habit like these ones?" asked Mr. Gray. "Nearly all," I replied; "but in one or two kinds the separate anemones are joined by a common fleshy trunk, such as is frequent among the corals." "Are the corals, then, related to the anemones?" asked Mr. Gray. "The corals," I replied, "are just social anemones which have learned the secret of joining their forces. If you look at a live coral colony, such as you may see off the Queensland coast, you will find that the individual coral creatures are just anemones, waving their arms and getting their food like the animals we have been watching. Some of the corals, indeed, live solitary lives, and the only important difference between the solitary coral and this Black Rock anemone is that the coral secretes a skeleton of lime to support the soft body. In the colony-building corals, the lime also cements together the separate animals that make up the colony, and hence we have the formation of coral reefs."

Soon after, we picked up a piece of coralline. Looking through a lens, we could see how the delicate, branching, shrub-like stems were built up. "This," I said, "is the work of another family of anemone-like creatures. This gelatine-like structure is the dead framework or skeleton of their common life. When new individuals are born in a colony like this, they are not set free, but are added by an extension of the branches to the parent colony." "I see," said Mr. Gray, "it is the old patriarchal system. The son adds a new farm to the paternal acres, and continues to live as part of the family."

Nearly all the animals that are low down in the scale of life have more than one way of multiplying. The anemone increases occasionally by means of buds or fragments detached from the broad foot, but chiefly by means of germs which grow into young anemones within its body. These, when ready for independent life, are launched into the sea through the mouth. Sometimes, too, one sees an anemone in the aquarium dividing itself into two. In a week or two each half becomes a perfect anemone, exactly like the parent.

"It would seem, then," said Mr. Gray, "that among the lowest animals the methods of increase are very like to those which we have in plants?" "Yes," I replied, "the three processes I have given are very similar to the three methods of multiplying plants— the method of slips, the method of seeds, and the method of root-division."

Just then we saw a sea-blubber in the clear water of a rock-locked cove. The beautiful, transparent disc was slowly flapping its way through the water. "If I could show to you the first form of this creature," I said, "you would hardly believe that this mass could spring from it. The egg hatches out into a minute creature, which swims about by means of the hairs that cover it. This free-swimming creature settles down after a time upon a rock, and becomes fixed like an anemone. At this stage it is about half an inch long. Like an anemone, too, it has waving arms by which it feeds. By-and-by it throws off bud after bud, each of which becomes a free-swimming disc-shaped jelly. In time this creature, sprung from a half-inch parent, reaches the size of this jelly-fish before us. Specimens have been found 7 feet across, and with feelers 50 feet long! The eggs produced by this huge creature grow, not into a jelly-fish, but into the little anemone-like creature which is fixed to a rock."

A mail steamer, outward bound, was passing down the South Channel. "The shuttle," said Mr. Gray, "that weaves the nations together! The wisest men of old thought that the sea was meant by heaven to keep the nations apart: today the sea unites the races of the earth even more than the land itself!"

CHAPTER XXIII.
What We Saw at the Beach.

SPONGES, WORMS, AND SHRIMPS.

"Surely this is a sponge?" said Mr. Gray, as he handed to me a small dead sponge that had been washed ashore. "Yes," I said, "this is the skeleton of the sponge-animal that covers some of the rocks out yonder, as moss covers a stone. Just as the chalky

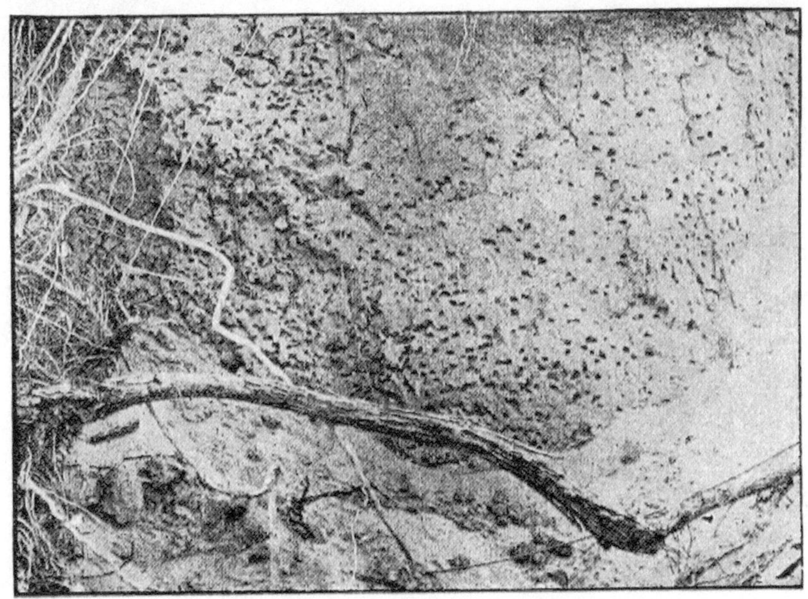

DISUSED HOLES OF SAND-HOPPERS.

GREEN SHRIMP MIMICKING GREEN SEAWEED.

structure which we call coral is the skeleton of the coral-anemone, so this sponge is the framework of the sponge-animal."

"In its live state the sponge has as much beauty as moss, and more variety of colour. Some are crimson, others green, and one common kind is pale yellow. This sponge is probably from a rock near the low-tide mark, where it is protected from the light by masses of growing seaweed."

On looking at the sponge through a lens, we saw that the surface was pitted with very small holes (a, b, fig. 2), and that, here and there, there was a large hole (d, fig. 2).

The sponge, in its first stage, is a free-swimming creature

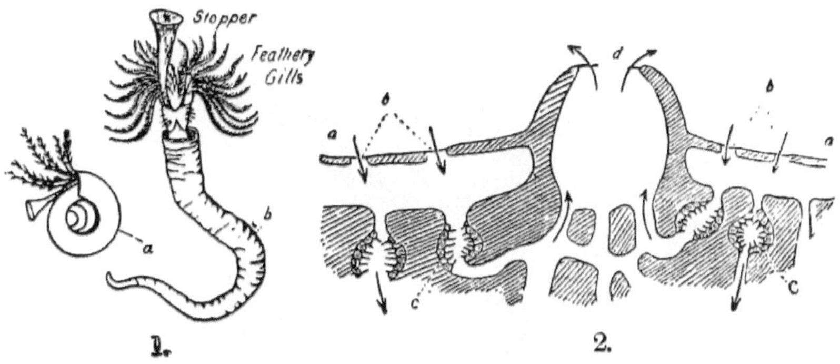

FIG. 1. A, SPIRORBIS TUBE-WORMS. B, SERPULA

FIG. 2. SECTION OF SPONGE. A, B, INHALENT PORES. C, CILIATED CHAMBERS. D, EXHALENT PORE.

of very simple form. Then it fixes itself, mouth downwards, on a shaded rock, and grows into a colony of cells, which form a kind of living filter. The water enters by the small holes and passes through the sponge, leaving behind minute forms of life on which the cells feed. The water, having finished its journey through the sponge, is passed out through one of the large holes which we see so plainly on the bath-sponge (d, fig. 2, above).

This beautiful arrangement for airing and feeding the colony is finely described by Huxley as "a kind of submarine city where the people are stationed about the streets in such a way that each can easily take his food from the water as it passes along!"

"But how," asked Mr. Gray, "is the water drawn into the sponge?" "Here and there, along the passages," I replied, "are special cells with long hairs, always moving in the same direction (c, fig. 2). These suck in the water, much as a ventilating-fan in a mine draws in the air."

"What an admirable scheme!" cried Mr. Gray. "If only the

Nature Studies in Australia

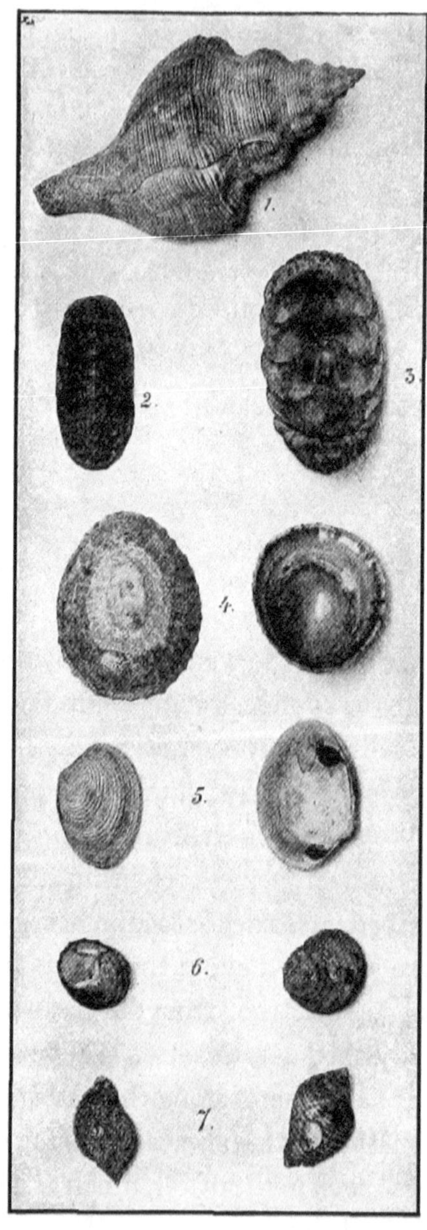

1. WHELK 2, 3. MAIL-SHELLS (TWO SPECIES) 4. LIMPETS (UPPER AND LOWER VIEWS)
5. COCKLES (VIEWS WITHIN AND WITHOUT) 6. PERIWINKLES
7. A WHELK THAT FEEDS ON MUSSELS

human family had a system as perfect for attending to the needs of the body, we might be set free for the life of mind and soul!"

Presently we picked up a mussel-shell which was riddled with small round holes. "Here," I said, "is the work of a small sponge which often kills mussels and oysters. The little cells of the sponge-animal secrete an acid which enables them to bore into the lime of the shell." We afterwards picked up numbers of these riddled shells.

Mr. Gray, who was still looking at the mussel-shell, said: "This shell seems to be as rich in life as an old fence-rail. What is this?" He was pointing to a white, chalky, winding tube, fixed on the surface of the shell. "That," I said, "is the *serpula* (figs. 5 and 6, page 164, and fig. 1, page 153), a worm which lives in a tube of lime." And then I told him of this worm, which is as common on the beach as the earth-worm is in the garden. The rocks are often white with them—living and dead.

When the tide is out, the worm retires within the tube, which is provided with a plug that acts as a door to keep in water and shut out enemies. When the tide comes back, the plug is thrust out of the tube by a long stalk, and the glistening hair-like gills begin to play. This action of the gills brings food as well as air into the mouth. The gills have a beautiful feathery look, and can be studied in rock pools or in a home aquarium. The living worms (a, fig. 1) build frequently on the tubes of dead worms, and often form a crust of some thickness, just as the coral-animal rises by building on the skeletons of the innumerable dead.

"Here," I continued, as I picked up a piece of seaweed, "is another of the tube-worms" (a, fig. 1). The fronds and floats of the weed were covered with a small white tube, coiled into a flat spiral. This tube*6 has a smooth, glistening, shell-like surface—a pretty object when closely examined. This little creature also has a stopper and feathery gills. It is one of the commonest objects of the beach, being found on nearly all the weeds of tough texture.

"Is this another tube-worm?" asked Mr. Gray, as he picked up a little tube of sand. "Yes," I said, "the worm which was the tenant of this tube lived under a sandy bottom, with this tube thrust up so that the gills might play in the water. There is another kind," I continued, "which strengthens the sand-tube with bits of shell." We noticed that the tube had a firmness due to some gluey fluid which the worm had added to the sand.

"I suppose," said Mr. Gray, "that there are also sea worms without tubes?" "Yes," I replied, "the common sand-worm used as bait is an example. Most of the worms of this kind lie quietly in their holes by day, and come out in the dusk to seek food. They swim most gracefully."

A boy with bare feet was walking cautiously over some rocks which were white with the acorn-shell. "You would never guess," I said, "that this creature belongs to the same family as the shrimps, lobsters, and crabs!" "Well," said Mr. Gray, "I've seen a hermit-crab that had taken up house in an empty whelk-shell, and I suppose that this is just a creature of the same family that makes its own shell!" "Yes," I replied, "but, while the hermit-crab can poke its head out of the shell, this acorn-barnacle spends its life upside down, and can thrust out only its feet."

"The acorn-shell," I continued, "is in several pieces. Two of these open when the tide comes up, and the legs are pushed out in search of food. The barnacle that fixes itself to ships is

6   *Spirorbis.*

similar to this one. As, however, the movement of the ship gives it a greater variety of food, it grows to a larger size."

On turning over a mass of seaweed, we disturbed some sand-hoppers. "Here," I said, "is another member of the shrimp family—a member which can't live in the water. When sand-hoppers venture below high-water mark, and are caught by the returning tide, they leap quickly out of reach of the wave."

We found, on the dry sand above high-water mark, the burrows of the sand-hoppers. Sometimes the holes are dug in the hard dune-sand, a good way back from the beach. In cases where the land is sinking, this firm dune-sand becomes, in time, submerged, and may be hardened into rock. The burrows would remain in this rock as holes, and this may be the explanation of the small holes which often honeycomb the rocks on the Sorrento Ocean-beach[7].

"I have seen," said Mr. Gray, "the sand-hoppers, in thousands, on the Ocean-beach, dancing in the twilight." "Yes," I replied, "they do not appear much in the daytime; but, as they feed on decaying seaweed, you can find them under nearly every mass of tangle on the beach. The hooded dottrel knows this, and may be often seen turning over seaweed in search of them."

"They seem, then," said Mr. Gray, "to be beach-scavengers." "Yes," I replied, "they do the same good work on the beach that their cousins the shrimps do in the sea." "Do you mean to say," said Mr. Gray, "that the shrimps are scavengers? Why, they look as if they lived on air, these dim, ghostly creatures of the pools and shallows!" "Yes," I said, "the shrimps have as keen a scent for decaying matter as their grand relations the lobsters."

7　　　　Explanation suggested by Mr. D. Le Souef, C.M.Z.S., in the *Victorian Naturalist*, November, 1901.

"Now," cried Mr. Gray, "I understand better the exquisite purity of the sea. Thousands of sea-creatures must die daily, and yet that fringe of foam is as pure as the snow that has just fallen.""Yes," I replied, "Nature's plans for keeping the world-house sweet and fresh were perfect long before Man rose to the idea of a scavenger." "And yet Man is the crown of Nature," said Mr. Gray musingly. "What a world this will be when he has come to his kingdom!"

As we sat among the rocks, and listened to the soothing plash of the advancing tide, Mr. Gray looked out dreamily to sea, and said: "The face of the land changes from age to age, but the face of the sea is the same today as when Homer stood on the shore of the Ægean. This *lap, lap* of the tide fell on his ears three thousand years ago, as it falls on ours today. You can hear the whisper of summer seas in his verse. And his song is the story of Man's fight with the sea—a story that came out of a dim past, and from sources that no man knows. What a link with the Past is this whispering sea!"

CHAPTER XXIV.

What We Saw at the Beach.

"See what a lovely shell;
Small and pure as a pearl,
Lying close to my foot;
Frail, but a work divine,
Made so fairily well
With delicate spire and whorl,
How exquisitely minute,
A miracle of design!"—Tennyson's Maud

PART III.

SHELL-FISH AND STAR-FISH.

We had been picking up "counters" on the beach. The "counter" is a white, disc-like body, marked on one side by a spiral line. This disc is the lid of the periwinkle called the warrener. On turning over some stones near low-water mark, we found a live specimen. The shell is dark brown on the outside, but the white inner surface is beautifully marked with green.

Between this low-tide mark and the high-water line, we noticed whelks and periwinkles of various kinds. Shape and colour are closely adapted to their habits and homes. The thickness of the shell, too, is determined by the extent to which they are exposed to the force of the waves. The more sheltered have thinner shells than those which, like the dog-whelk, bear the full force of the waves. The shells of those which live in the great depths beyond the line of "breakers" are often quite thin.

On the rocks which were almost out of reach of the waves, we found the little greenish periwinkle which forms a link between the sea-snails and the land-snails. Many of these shell-fish are submerged only on rare occasions.

"I suppose," said Mr. Gray, "that the garden-snail is just a periwinkle that lives on land, with lungs instead of gills?" "Yes," I said, "snails and periwinkles and limpets all walk on the broad *belly-foot*: that is the family mark. Snails and whelks are alike, too, in having a tooth-ribbon—a kind of strap covered with many minute teeth. When this is moved backwards and forwards it acts like a file. The snail files its leaf into a green mash before swallowing it." "What do the periwinkles eat?" asked Mr. Gray. "Some," I replied, "live on seaweed; others prey on cockles and other bivalves, into which they bore with the tooth-file."

On the beach we found a cockle-shell (fig. 5, page 168) with a neat hole bored in it. "Ah," said Mr. Gray, "is that how it happens? I've often seen children stringing cockle-shells together by these holes!"

"Can you tell," asked Mr. Gray, "from the look of a whelk whether it is a vegetarian or a flesh-eater?" "As a rule," I replied, "in the vegetarians the mouth of the shell is unbrokenly round, an example being the edible periwinkle. In the whelks (fig. 1, page 168) which prey on bivalves, the mouth of the shell is notched or produced into a canal, as in the dog-whelk. The dog-whelk can burrow into the sand in search of cockles, and on oyster-beds it destroys large numbers of the bivalve."

"Was not the *murex*, from which the Tyrians got their purple dye, a shell-fish of this kind?" asked Mr. Gray. "Yes," I said, "and

I've no doubt but that some of these whelks would yield a dye if it were worth trying." "I like," said Mr. Gray, "to think of those who lived 'in the purple' in these old days, and how this lowly creature contributed to their pomp and power."

We now returned to the edge of the rocks in order to watch the tide waking up the cockles, mussels, and limpets from their inter-tidal sleep. Mr. Gray tried to take a limpet (fig. 4, page 168) from the rock, but it was too quick for him. The sucker-like foot closed on the rock with such force that he could not dislodge it. "Here is one travelling!" cried Mr. Gray. The tide had just covered it, and the limpet was slowly moving over the rock. On returning, after a time, we found that it had travelled six inches, and was feeding on some green seaweed.

On this limpet there was fixed a peculiar tuft of weed, and by this mark we were able to identify the creature when we visited the beach two days later. It had returned to its old home—the spot on the rock to which it had fitted its shell. As the limpet cannot alter the rock to fit the shell, it moulds the shell to fit the rock. In this way, it is able to conserve water enough to tide it over the time when it is high and dry; also, it is able to guard itself the better against its enemies—the oyster-catcher and the wharf-rat.

Attached to the rock were mussels of all sizes. On watching a large one which had just been submerged, we saw the valves opening to receive the water. "How does it feed?" asked Mr. Gray. "It seems to be as stationary as an anemone, but it has no arms." "The gills are at work," I replied, "though you can't see them. These gills are covered with vibrating hairs, which draw in food." "Can it move at all?" asked Mr. Gray. "A very little," I replied. I tore the mussel from the rock, and we looked at the threads by which it had been moored. These, when first secreted, are soft and silky. When the creature wishes to move, it casts off the old cable, extends its foot, and attaches a new thread to a new point in the direction towards which it desires to travel. Repeating this operation, it can go forward very slowly.

The mussel has many enemies, the most deadly in our seas being a whelk, which children often gather from the piles of the Port Melbourne wharves. The mussels killed by this shell-fish may often be seen on the piles, the open, empty shell still hanging by its cable to the wood.

We looked for the mutton shell-fish, which hides among the rocks, but failed to find one. On the beach, however, we found several shells of this creature. The shell is ear-shaped, and is like a huge periwinkle that has been flattened. It is pierced with a series of regular holes which admit water to the gills. The outer surface is generally covered with a rough limy deposit, but the interior is lined with brilliant pearl. This shell-fish, which is closely related to the limpet, clings to the rock by its large foot.

The last mollusc that we found was the curious mail-shell (figs. 2 and 3, page 168). This shell-fish we found adhering to a rock between the tide-marks. Eight separate plates of mail were arranged over the back. When we took it from the rock, it curled up into a ball. This creature seems to be an eccentric member of the limpet family.

On rolling over a large stone near low-water mark, we found a number of the cushion star-fish. The star-fish (figs. 3 and 4, opposite) are sociable creatures, and are generally to be found congregating together. The colour varied from brown to black and yellow. The leathery skin was strengthened by a kind of scaffolding of lime, and among the numerous little swellings

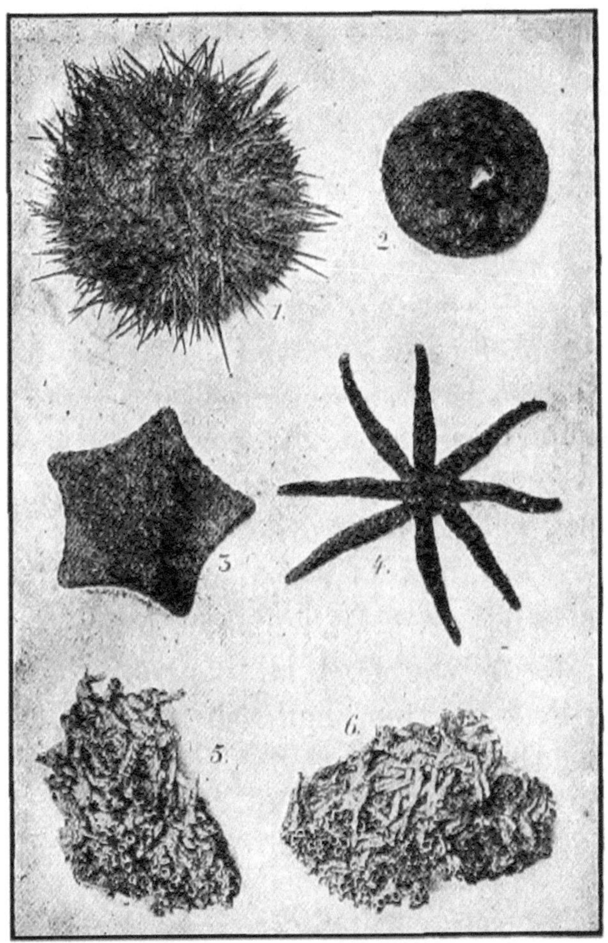

1. SEA-URCHIN 2. SEA-URCHIN (WITHOUT SPINES)
3, 4. STAR-FISHES 5, 6. SERPULA

there was a greenish, spongy disc at a little distance from the centre. This is perforated with very small holes, and serves as entrance to the system of canals which radiate through the body and the five arms. The water is thus filtered before entering the body, for the object of these water-channels is not to feed the star-fish but to provide a means of walking and grasping.

On turning over the animal, we saw, in the grooved under-surface of each ray, rows of white sucker-like tube feet, some of which were drawn in, and others at full stretch. These tube feet are connected with the canals, and the star-fish has the power to squeeze water into them when it wishes to thrust them out. By help of these feet and the suckers at the end of them, the animal can walk. We turned one over, and were surprised to see how cleverly it managed to recover its usual position.

These tube feet are also used to grasp the shell-fish and shrimps on which the star-fish lives. The outer feet pass the shrimp on to those nearer to the centre, and so on till the mouth—which is in the centre of the under-surface—is reached. The star-fish which frequents oyster beds is, perhaps, a greater consumer of this bivalve than even man himself.

On the beach we found the shell of a relative of the star-fish— the sea-urchin (figs. 1 and 2, page 177). This shelly-ball is the limy skeleton of an animal which lives on the rocks below low-water mark. It is sometimes called the sea-hedgehog, because, when alive, it is covered with spines. These spines are generally rubbed off by the waves before the shell is thrown on the beach.

The shell is pierced by numerous little holes in regular double rows, which radiate at intervals from the centre to the circum-ference. Through these the urchin pushes white sucker feet, exactly like those which we saw in the star-fish. By means of these feet, the urchin can pull itself along, or hold itself so firmly to rock or weed that the waves cannot dash it off. These feet, as in the star-fish, are worked by the water which radiates in canals through the body. The spongy disc which serves as entrance to these canals is placed near the centre of the upper surface. Both urchin and star-fish lie mouth downwards.

While walking along a sandy part of the shore we found

the shell of the sand-urchin. This creature lives on a sandy bottom, and is in continual danger of sinking into the sand. To guard against this, the shell is lighter and flatter than that of the rock-urchin.

"I am struck," said Mr. Gray, "with the number of sea animals that are built on the beautiful radial plan—the anemones, the jelly-fish, the star-fish, the urchin, and, no doubt, many others." "Yes," I replied, "and it is also one of the main plans of form among trees and flowers. The truth is, that the infinite variety of form in Nature is based on a few simple plans of structure. When we have mastered these we are no longer bewildered by the endless differences."

As we left the beach, Mr. Gray's eye caught the glint of the sun on the pearl of a fine ear-shell. "I wonder," he said, "if the little living will that used to move this house of pearl had any pleasure in its beauty?

> *Did he stand at the diamond door*
> *Of his house in a rainbow-frill?*
> *Did he push, when he was uncurl'd,*
> *A golden foot or a fairy horn*
> *Thro' his dim water-world?"*

CHAPTER XXV
The Rose Green-fly

I found Mr. Gray in the garden next morning getting for himself a nosegay. He had just picked a fine bud of *The Bride* rose, and was impatiently flicking off the green flies. "A most interesting creature, this rose aphis!" I exclaimed, mischievously. "Interesting!" cried Mr. Gray; "it would interest me very much to hear that they were all banished from the earth!" "In that case," I replied, "a wonderful life-history would be lost to Science."

I handed to him my pocket-lens, and he said, "Well, I never before noticed how beautifully the light is broken on their wings. And here's a green one moving!" I took the lens, and looked at the little creature with the black, staring eyes, and the long waving antennæ which explored the way as it sprawled slowly over the leaf. Something unusual must have happened to make it move; for its fellows were sucking the leaf-sap as if nothing else mattered at all in the world. Even when touched they kept their suckers buried in the leaf, and continued to feed.

"Most of them seem to be reddish-brown rather than green," said Mr. Gray. "Yes," I said, "the aphis has several colours; but the green-fly is the best known, and so has given its name to the family. The colour protects the insect; and, while green is the best colour on some plants, the aphis which settles on the young shoots of the rose is often better concealed by a reddish tint."

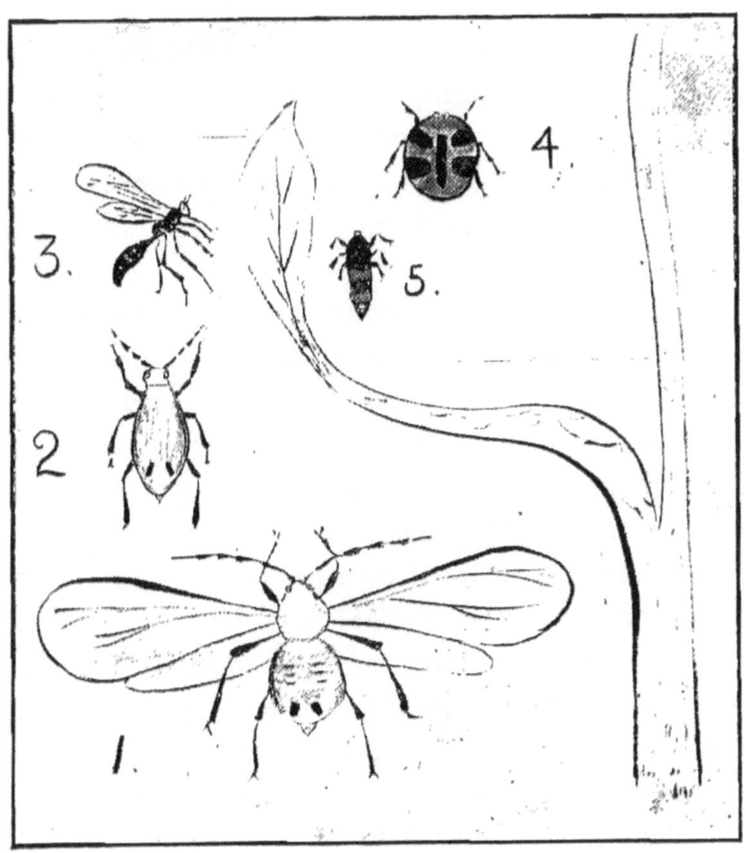

THE GREEN-FLY (APHIS)-1, WINGED GENERATION; 2, WINGLESS
GENERATION; 3, AN ENEMY OF THE APHIS; 4, LADY-BIRD BEETLE; 5,
THE LARVA OF 4, WHICH DESTROYS LARGE NUMBERS OF THE APHIS.

"I notice," said Mr. Gray, "that they crowd most just where
one does not want them—on the buds and growing shoots."
"Yes," I replied, "just as you prefer the heads of asparagus to
the stems. The mother who laid the eggs last autumn on that
bud chose the place well."

"Most of them," continued Mr. Gray, "seem to be wingless.
Are the winged flies the males?" "No," I replied, "there are no
males to be seen till autumn; and it is here that the life-history of

the aphis is most wonderful. During the whole growing season, the aphis goes on producing young, very much in the same way as the plant which it feeds on produces new shoots during the whole of the growing season. The creature multiplies at such a rate that the descendants of one aphis in a single season must be reckoned by millions."

We looked about until we found an aphis which was engaged in this process of multiplication. The parent aphis took no further trouble with the young aphis than to move forward a step to allow to the newcomer a free space of leaf to feed on. A summer aphis, kept in a warm chamber and supplied with food, continued to produce young in this way for years.

"It must be a creature of low type," said Mr. Gray, "since it multiplies at such a rate." "You are right," I replied, "in thinking that rapid increase is usually a sign that an animal is low in the scale of life; but the strange thing is that the aphis stands comparatively high. It ranks with the cicadas, which we call musical locusts. Possibly it is an insect that has fallen in the world."

"Is there any evidence that it has fallen?" asked Mr. Gray. "Yes," I said, "when food gets scarce, towards autumn, it multiplies in the usual way. Winged male and female aphides are produced, and from these we have a generation which passes through the same stages of growth as the higher insects. Again, as you notice, some of these summer aphides are winged. On the whole, we may suppose that the aphis, from being an active winged insect, has degenerated into this sluggish creature."

"Your idea, then," said Mr. Gray, "is that the aphis has sunk in the scale as the result of too easy a life?" "Yes," I replied, "that is generally the result with insects as with men. Possibly the change began with the advent upon the earth of man and the introduction of numberless sappy plants."

And here it is of interest to note that the great flow of sap in a good growing year seems to hurt rather than to help the aphis. The creature seems to thrive best in bad seasons when the flow of sap is slow.

"These honey-tubes, too," I went on, "may indicate that the insect suffers from excess of food." I pointed to the two little tubes on the back of the body which serve to get rid of the excess of sugary fluid which the insect absorbs in times of plenty. We looked about until we found on one of the aphides the little blobs of honey-dew which had been expelled. The leaves of the rose bush, below the cluster of aphides, were spotted with shiny patches caused by the honey-dew which the insect had allowed to drop.

"Here comes a honey-eater!" I cried, as a little black ant came running up the stem. The ant approached the aphis confidently, and proceeded to suck the tiny drops of honey-dew. Another ant was licking the smear of honey on a leaf below. Looking at it through the pocket-lens, we could see that it ate with relish.

"Is this another partnership?" asked Mr. Gray. "Yes," I replied, "and so close a partnership that the aphis has been called the ant's cow." The second ant, seeming now to be dissatisfied with the honey smears, approached a large green aphis, and touched it. The insect seemed to find the caress agreeable and, presently, there appeared small drops of liquid from the honey-tubes. The ant ate eagerly.

"The arrangement seems to give mutual satisfaction," said Mr. Gray. "So much so," I replied, "that certain ants have been seen to take charge of the eggs of the aphides during the winter.

SCALE-INSECTS ON LIGHTWOOD TREE.

The eggs are carried into the nests of the ants to save them from the perils of frost and rain. In the spring, the eggs are placed out on the leaves of the plants that suit them. Still more wonderful, there are underground ants which, according to Sir John Lubbock, keep 'herds and flocks of the root-feeding aphides.' In the mallee there is an aphis which feeds on the stems of young gum-trees; and ants have been observed to guard this aphis under a domed roof of bark and grass. The object, of course, is to secure a constant supply of the honey-dew. Scale-insects are also protected with this purpose."

As we turned away, Mr. Gray said, "The rose bush, then, has to grow and bear flowers, and support besides all these aphides and ants; it is a great drain on its strength." "Yes," I replied, "it hurts the bush just as *this* aphis hurts the apple tree."

I was pointing to a Ribston pippin apple tree, which was curiously marked with white fluff on the underside of the branches. When we looked closer, we found that in almost every crack in the bark there was more or less of this woolly fluff. "The gardener calls it the American blight," said Mr. Gray. "Do you mean that it is caused by an aphis?" For answer, I took some of the fluff, and showed the reddish-brown aphis that lay concealed under the white, silky threads.

Every one of these creatures was busy tapping the juices of the tree, and diverting the sap from shoot and fruit. Nor was this all the damage done. The irritated bark was swollen into lumps wherever the insects were feeding, and unsightly excrescences showed the damage done in previous years.

The roots, too, of the tree had swollen so much that near the stem they had risen close to the surface. The winter eggs of the apple aphis are placed not on the buds of the tree, but on the roots. Also, in the hottest part of summer, the insect retires from the hot branches to the cool roots. Hence that swelling of the roots which gradually kills the tree.

"From this tree," I said, "you can judge of the trouble which is caused by the vine aphis—the phylloxera." "Then the phylloxera is an aphis?" cried Mr. Gray. "Yes," I replied, "a root-eating aphis, which spoils the roots of the vine with galls or lumps, just as the apple aphis has spoiled the roots of this pippin."

"Here," I said, pointing to a cabbage-plant, "is another aphis which often protects itself like the apple aphis." The green fly on the cabbage was covered with a mealy coat, which matched the bloom on the leaves. This fly, if possible, is still more sluggish than the rose aphis. Its whole life consists in piercing the leaf which it was born upon, in sucking up the juices, and in producing young.

At the end of the garden were three peach trees. One of these looked as if blasted by fire. "Can you tell me what is wrong with this tree?" asked Mr. Gray. "Yes," I replied, "the peach aphis!" A few green leaves, curled up and wilted, remained and, inside of these, we found the green aphis, dreaded by the peach-grower. Much of the bark was covered with the sugary, sticky fluid, and this "honey-dew," in closing the breathing-holes of the bark, must help in the work of destruction. Among the green flies on the peach leaves were some black aphides. The latter come first, just when the sap begins to move freely in spring. Then, with the full leaf, comes the green fly to complete the work.

"Has Nature no remedy for this pest?" cried Mr. Gray, impatiently. "Creatures," I replied, "that multiply quickly, die easily. A heavy shower or a hot wind may destroy many. The little red, black-spotted lady-bird beetle kills thousands; but we have far too few of these lady-birds. Other flies of the lace-wing order help also, in their larval stage, to keep them down."

Artificial remedies, too, must be used vigorously, for we must remember that, while Nature checks the over-increase of an insect, she makes no effort to exterminate it.

"I can see now," said Mr. Gray, "that the aphis is a creature of commercial importance." "Yes," I replied, "taking only the aphides which attack the vine, the peach, the apple, the cabbage, and the turnip, the annual cost to the grower must be hundreds of thousands of pounds. But the cost is not too great!"

"Not too great!" cried Mr. Gray. "I mean," I continued, "that these pests have compelled man to study thoroughly the relations between insects and plants. The best science of the day is even now working at the problem; and the result will be not only a mastery of the situation, but a raising of the status of the grower. Farming and fruit-growing will become scientific pursuits, as interesting as any learned profession, and demanding as much skill. For the people at large, too, the impetus given by these pests to Nature-study will be of high value in adding to the interest of open-air life."

What We Saw in the Pond: the Beginning of Life

In the evening I found Mr. Gray on the verandah. He was dividing his attention between a book and the mosquitoes. "These pests," he cried, "demand one's attention; and they certainly get it." "If," I replied, "they got a little more attention we might get rid of them." "You mean," he laughed, "that a mosquito-bite is a stimulus to Nature-study?" "I do," I replied. Some talk followed that led us, next day, to seek the beginnings of mosquito-life in a pond.

As we walked towards the pond, I said: "You can't touch pond-life without being fascinated by the wonderful variety of life it contains. It is a little world in itself. There is hardly a creature in the sea which has not its counterpart in the pond—the shark, the octopus, the anemone, the lobster, the whelk, and a dozen others."

"How," asked Mr. Gray, "do all these kinds of life get into a pond which is cut off from the waters of the earth?" "Ah!" I replied, "in that question you raise a most interesting point. Most of the life of a pond consists of minute creatures which are capable of sleeping through long periods of drought. When the pond dries up, they are borne by the wind in the form of dust to regions often remote from the starting point. If we had sharper eyes we could often see clouds of germs being thus conveyed from point to point through the air. Of these, some must drop, at times, into the pond."

"Then," I went on, "we have seen how birds carry seeds on feet and bill. We know that they carry in the same way minute eggs, plants, and animals. Again, if the pond be in the neighbourhood of a river, then, through floods, it is occasionally connected with the river. Every flood, therefore, may add new forms of life. Wandering cattle may also help to people a pond."

"What causes the bubbles to rise so often?" asked Mr. Gray, as we came to the pond. It was a clear-water pond, and we could see them rising before they burst on the surface. "It is caused," I replied, "partly by the used-up air which escapes from all the pond-dwellers that have no gills. These have all to come to the surface now and again to take in air. See! Look at these whirligig beetles!"

Some of these active little creatures, which we had frightened to the bottom, were now rising, and began to dart about on the surface. The grace of their quick movements, and the ease with which they avoided collision, made us forget all else for some minutes.

"Then," said Mr. Gray, reverting to his question, "the beetle exists below the surface very much in the same way as the man who takes a long breath before diving?" "Yes," I replied, "the beetle can take in a bubble of air through a hole near its mouth. This air it seems to be able to store under the wing-cases and on the under parts of the body."

"How they seem to enjoy their lives!" said Mr. Gray. Feeding among the beautifully divided leaves of the water milfoil were some beetles of smaller size. These rose to the surface at intervals, breathed for a moment, and then, with business-like promptitude, hurried back to their pastures.

Now and then we caught sight of the great water-beetle, which is the terror of the smaller pond-dwellers. He, too, shows a keen zest in life, as he darts here and there, and up and down, in his masterful way. A handsome fellow he is, as the sun glints from his shiny sides.

Presently a leech came swimming by, with easy, eel-like undulations. "A famous blood-sucker!" I said. "Enshrined in a proverb, he is also a reminder of the time when the best physicians thought it necessary to bleed the fever-stricken." "Yes," said Mr. Gray, "Wordsworth's 'Leech-gatherer' will not allow us to forget that."

On the surface of the pond was floating a snail—the pond snail. "Ah!" said Mr. Gray, "this is the snail that acts as host to the sheep fluke, is it not? How does the fluke

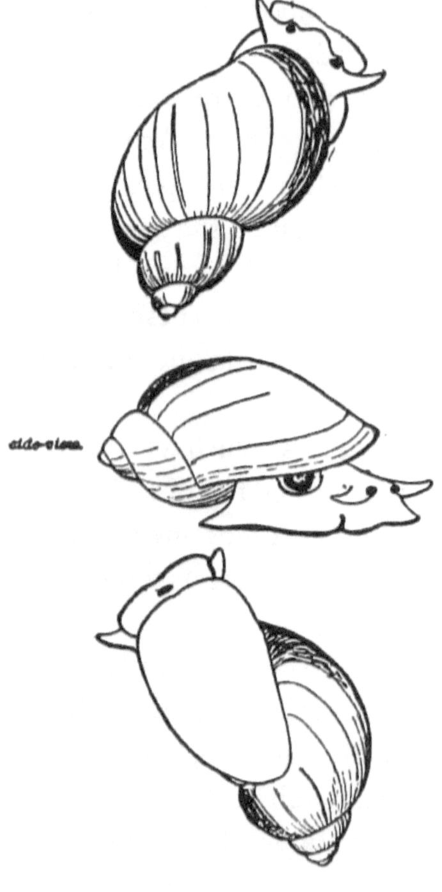

FRESH-WATER SNAILS,
MAGNIFIED THREE DIAMETERS.

get into the snail?" "In the liver of the sheep," I replied, "the fluke produces eggs, which find their way into the water. In order to mature, the egg must now pass into a pond snail, where it grows into another form, that leaves the snail and swims in the water. Then it attaches itself to a water plant, which the sheep eats. Finally, it bores its way to the sheep's liver, and becomes what we know as liver fluke. The magpie lark is fond of this snail, and in eating the snail helps to keep down the fluke."

"When I see how full of life these ponds are," said Mr. Gray, "I understand why the cattle that drink at them are often troubled with fluke and hydatids, and other parasites." "Yes," I replied, "it shows how careful one should be to filter water. Even in town, it is dangerous to drink unfiltered water, and in the country the risk is much greater."

A green dragon-fly flitted in rapid jerks over the pond, its beautiful wings glistening in the sun. "It has come, perhaps," I said, "to have a look at its native place." "What!" cried Mr. Gray, "is the dragon-fly a native of the pond?" "Yes," I said, "the larger part of its life is spent in the water, and in its pond life it hunts the larva of the mosquito as fiercely as it is now chasing the winged mosquito."

Fat, green-backed tadpoles were turning their silver bellies to the light; red mites swam along as if on urgent business; pond-flies skated on the surface; and, near the bank, there was a shoal of little brown darting creatures. "What are these?" asked Mr. Gray. "Some mosquito-wrigglers, just out of the egg," I replied. We caught a few of these, and took them home in a glass bottle, in order to watch them growing.

The water at one end of the pond was coloured green by vast numbers of a minute creature which can be seen only under the microscope. "Are these creatures plants or animals?" asked Mr. Gray. "They behave," I replied, "in some ways like plants, and in other ways like animals. Nature laughs sometimes at our hard and fast names. We are here on the dim borderland between plant and animal. These tiny one-celled creatures can increase their number by the simple process of splitting in two."

We took up some of the sediment at the bottom of the pond, and that evening, by the help of the microscope, we found in it a speck of living jelly, glassy-looking and irregularly shaped. This animated dot can move very slowly, and can receive food at any point of its body. The jelly opens in order to close round the food, absorbs what it can of it, and then opens to reject the rest. It has neither head nor mouth nor stomach, nor any special organs. When we looked at this simple, one-celled creature, we knew that we were looking at the beginnings of life! Some of these dots of living jelly can be seen with the naked eye.

I filled a long glass vessel with the water of the pond. When we held the glass up in a good light, we could see one of the wheel-plants, a minute green globule, gently moving about. In the evening we looked at this wheel-plant with the microscope, and found that the beautiful little green ball had many long hairs. Using these as oars, it rolls forward; turning over as it goes like an animated cricket ball.

If this little green globe be a plant, it is a plant without root, or stem, or leaf, and one which can move about actively. If it be an animal, it is an animal with the same colouring matter which gives to the plants their green colour. It contains a colony of smaller globes, and, when the containing ball bursts, these smaller globes set up in life for themselves.

Still more simple was the multiplication of a one-celled

plant-creature, which swam freely in the drop of water we were examining. At first it was oval, but gradually acquired the shape of an hourglass. The link between the two parts became narrower and narrower, till, with a final shake, the division was complete, and the tiny creature had become two distinct creatures. Mr. Gray, who had watched the process with breathless interest, said, "This is a case of multiplication by division!" "Yes," I replied, "this is Nature's simplest method of growth."

In order to provide food, and also to keep the water fresh, we had brought home in the bottles some branches of the myriad-threaded milfoil. When we placed on the object-slide of the microscope a tiny piece of this water-weed, in a drop of water, we saw the beautiful creature called the bell animalcule.

This minute creature is shaped like a wineglass, the stem of which is fixed to the plant. On the rim of the wineglass is

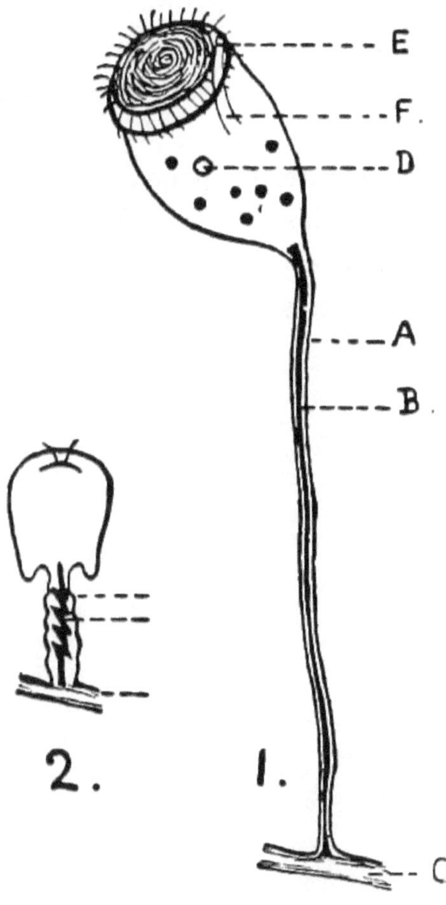

BELL ANIMALCULE— 1. EXTENDED:
A, STALK. B, AXIAL FIBRE. C, ATTACHMENT
D, CONTRACTILE VACUOLE. E, MOUTH.
F, GULLET. 2. RETRACTED

a fringe of hairs, which are kept in rapid play, so as to make a vortex that draws food into the mouth. The stem has within it a spiral spring, and, when danger threatens, the waving fringe of hairs disappears, the stem contracts, and the little creature is flattened against the plant. This we saw happening several times, and afterwards had the good fortune to find a colony of six, in tree-like shape, all attached to a common stem, and all, in the presence of danger, withdrawing like a flash by common action.

The bell animalcule is at no loss when the pond dries up. It secretes a tough case, within which it sleeps safe till rain fills the pool. Should the drought be severe, it may be blown into the air with the dust, and carried a long way before it is brought to earth again by a shower.

CHAPTER XXVII

The Story of the Mosquito[8]

On Returning from the Pond, We Placed the Larvæ of the Mosquito in a Glass Bowl, in order to watch their development. Meantime, mr. Gray begged to have at once the full story of a mosquito. And this is the story that I told him.

During the spring, the mother mosquito lays her eggs on the surface of a stagnant pool, or of a ditch, or even of a road puddle. Placed singly on the water they would sink, but many eggs are glued together, and these float like a raft. In two or three days, the egg hatches into a larva, with a head, thorax, and abdomen. This is the little brown darting creature which one sees so often in water-holes.

As the head is slightly heavier than water, the larva hangs head downwards, with the tip of the tail just appearing above the surface. Around the mouth are delicate hairs that move without ceasing. In this way an eddy is caused which draws the tiny creatures of the pool into the mouth. And so, while

8   The body of an insect is divided into three parts, *Head, Thorax, Abdomen.*
To the *Head* are attached the eyes, the antennæ (feelers), and the mouth. The mouth may be fitted for piercing, for sucking, or for chewing.
To the *Thorax* are attached the wings and legs.
The *Abdomen* has no legs, and has 10 segments, the last of these being furnished with an ovipositor or egg-placer. The ovipositor may be modified into a stinging instrument, as in the wasps and bees.

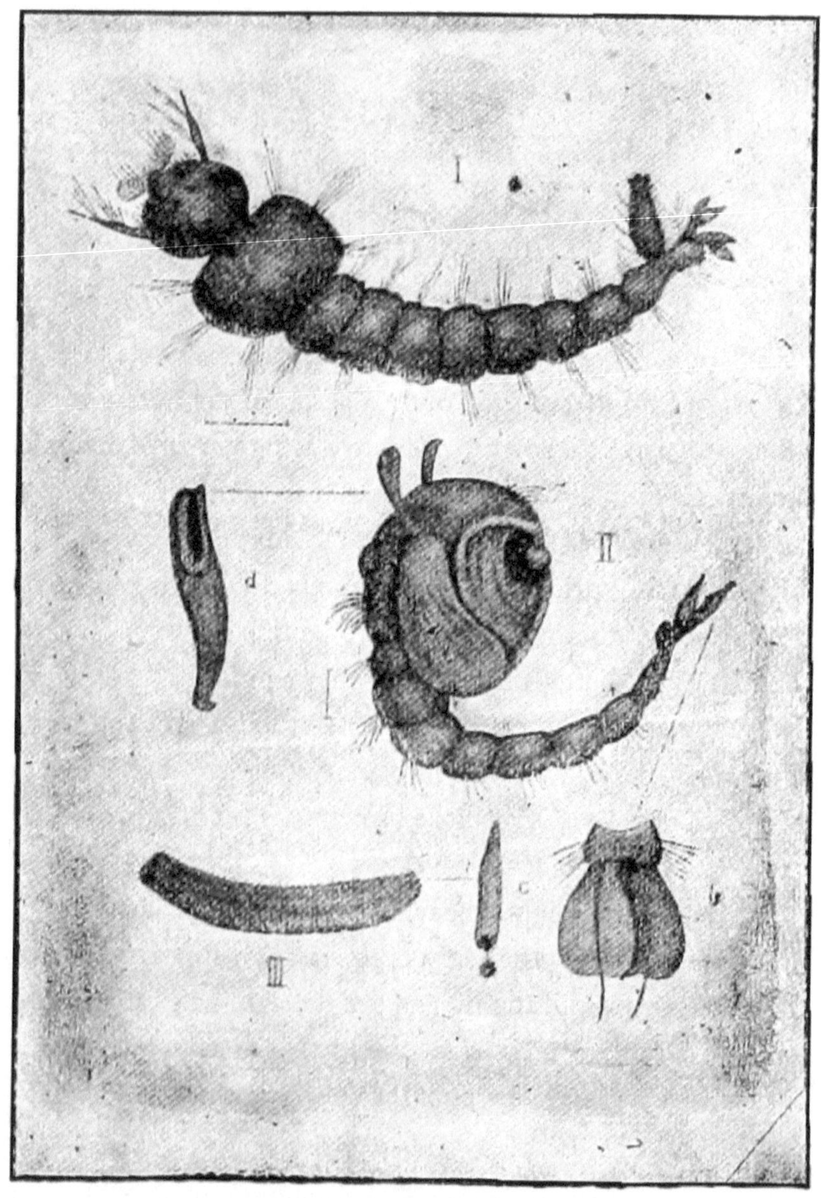

LIFE-HISTORY OF MOSQUITO.— I. LARVA.
II. PUPA: (A) ENLARGED RESPIRATORY SIPHON; (B) TAIL FINS.
III. (C) ONE EGG MAGNIFIED.

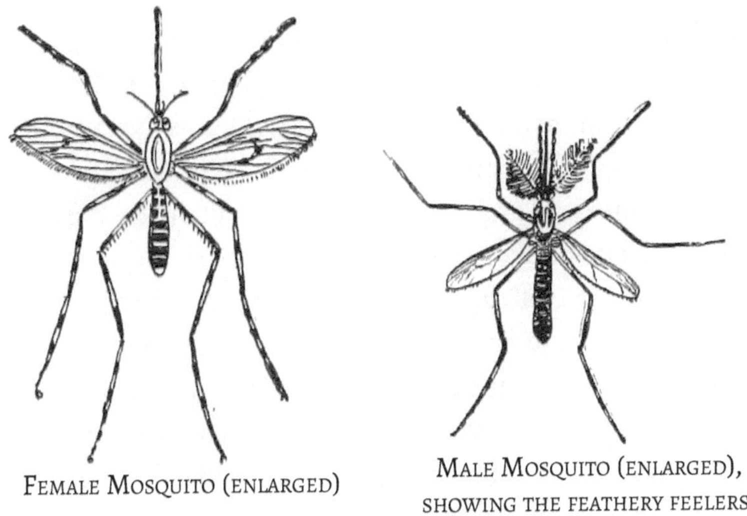

FEMALE MOSQUITO (ENLARGED)

MALE MOSQUITO (ENLARGED), SHOWING THE FEATHERY FEELERS.

POINTS TO BE NOTED.—(1) THE DIFFERENCE BETWEEN THE PIERCING AND SUCKING ORGANS OF THE MALE AND FEMALE MOSQUITO—THE FEMALE BEING A BLOOD-SUCKER AND THE MALE A VEGETARIAN; (2) THE DIFFERENCE IN THE ANTENNAE—THOSE OF THE FEMALE BEING PLAIN, THOSE OF THE MALE LARGE AND FEATHERY.

the larva hangs downwards and apparently at rest, it is really working hard for its living.

Behind the head is a large thorax, and behind the thorax a tail-like abdomen. This tail is jointed in such a fashion that the larva can jerk about with great activity. Try to catch the little creature and you will see how quickly it can dart from one side of the bowl to the other.

When we look at the end of the tail, we find out why the creature, when at rest, has the tip constantly above the water. It is a breathing tube. The mosquito larva cannot, like the tadpole, live in the water. Having no gills, it must rise now and then to the surface for air. If you frighten it, it may remain for some time below the surface, but rarely longer than fifteen minutes.

While under the surface, the entrance to the breathing tubes is closed by valves so well oiled that no water can enter.[9]

The mosquito continues in the larval stage for two or three weeks, and during this time changes its skin three times.

Then the larva changes into the pupa in order to get ready for the final change into a winged creature. In most insects this stage is one of apparent sleep; but not so in the mosquito. It does not eat, to be sure, during this stage, but it can move about freely while the mysterious transformation is being busily prepared within. When the pupa is at rest, the head is now uppermost instead of the tail, and, by a wonderful change in the breathing mechanism, the air tubes are now fixed in the thorax.

And now we come to a critical stage in the history of the mosquito—the emergence from the pupa-case. On the fateful day, the case cracks on the back behind the head; and the gnat slowly and cautiously extricates herself. Using the discarded case as a raft, she unfolds her wings and stretches her legs. Before the wings have dried and the legs hardened, the wind may blow her into the water, or her raft may suffer shipwreck. In either case she is drowned, for she is no longer a creature of the water. Should these dangers be safely passed, she is able to join her sisters who are trying their wings beside the pond before they fly off in search of blood.

"You speak of *her*; what of the male mosquito?" said Mr. Gray. "I have not spoken of the male," I replied, "because it is

---

9   The stages in the life-history of an insect which goes through a full course of change are (1)—the egg, (2) the larva, (3) the pupa, (4) the perfect insect—often winged.

The *Larva* (Lat. a mask) is so called because it generally differs in appearance from the parent. The caterpillar of a moth is a good example.
The *Pupa* is generally motionless. It is often wrapped in a covering of silky hairs called the cocoon. Hence the name pupa (Lat. a doll)

the female alone which bites, and it is with the biting mosquito alone that people concern themselves. The male is not a blood-sucker but a vegetarian. It is known, however, that the female can live on plant juices when no animals with blood are available. Mosquitoes in confinement have been fed for months on dried dates."

Late on the afternoon of the next day, we were seated under an oak tree on the lawn. A mosquito settled on my hand and began to suck. Mr. Gray was lifting his hand to brush it away when I seized his arm. "No!" I said, "let us watch the blood-sucking!" Holding it up to the light, we could see the blood coursing through the half-transparent body.

The evident enjoyment of the little creature, and the beauty of her delicate body, when seen under a lens, made one oblivious of the bite. "One is more tolerant, too," I said, laughingly, "of the sting, since we have found out that the poison serves to dilute the blood and make the act of suction easier. Even at the cost of a little pain, one likes to see work well done."

"I notice," said Mr. Gray, "that what we call a mosquito *sting* is not really a sting but a *bite*." "Yes," I replied, "the stinging organ in bees and wasps is the ovipositor at the end of the abdomen."

As we looked at the sucking-tube buried in the flesh, I said, "What if this mosquito carries on her lancet, the germ-laden blood of some sick man?"

"What!" cried Mr. Gray, "is *that* a possibility?" And then I told him of the part that mosquitoes play in spreading malaria and yellow fever, and of the self-sacrificing researches—sometimes at the cost of life—which give promise of mastery over these scourges.

To this Mr. Gray said, "I know nothing more depressing than

to be obliged to stand helpless before a disease of that kind; nor anything more exhilarating than to track a scourge to its causes and to feel the confidence and glow of mastery that comes with growing knowledge."

The subject is one of great interest to us. Several parts of Greater Britain are almost uninhabitable through malaria; and, in Victoria, we are said to have the particular mosquito which, in America, spreads the germ of yellow fever[10]. Some authorities, too, believe that plague, cholera, and typhoid may be carried by the mosquito.

Recent researches in Queensland have shown that one of our mosquitoes acts as host to a worm which infests dogs very much in the same way as the pond-snail acts as host to the fluke which preys on the liver of sheep. This mosquito, also, is suspected of having the power to convey the germ of malaria.[11]

"And the remedies?" asked Mr. Gray. "Nature," I replied, "has some checks. Fish, frogs, and water-beetles consume mosquitoes, at various stages, in millions. Dragon-flies, too, eat great numbers both in the pond stage and the winged stage."

"For man," I went on, "the main point is to abolish the breeding-places; to drain swamps and to fill up ponds. That there should be *no stagnant water* is now the first law in those parts of the world where malaria is being fought."

"Where ponds cannot be got rid of, the mosquito may be kept in check by spraying the surface with kerosene." "Ah! I understand," cried Mr. Gray, "the breathing-tube cannot act, and the larva is killed!" "Yes," I replied, "wonders have been

10   Address by Miss Georgina Sweet, M.Sc., read to the Field Naturalists' Club of Victoria, 8th September, 1902.
11   Observations by Dr. Bancroft of Brisbane. The mosquito is the house mosquito called Culex Skusei

accomplished in a mosquito-infested island by this means; and the time is fast coming when it will be reckoned a disgrace to a town council to have breeding-ponds within its area that have not been thus treated."

CHAPTER XXVIII.
What the Spade Turned Up.

"To watch the corn grow and the blossoms set; to draw hard breath over ploughshare or spade; to read, to think, to love, to hope, to pray—these are the things that *make men happy.*"

Mr. Gray read to me from Ruskin's *Modern Painters* the words that I have placed at the head of this chapter. "How we compass sea and land," he said, "to find happiness; and all the time it is at our door! I have never had from my large garden the pleasure that I used to get from the little patch of ground at the back of my first home. I dug and sowed with my own hands; and I reaped—I can't tell you all that I reaped. The peas and beans and lettuces, and even the flowers, were the least of the harvest. But a big garden with a gardener! That is different! Thoreau was right. It is not I who own the garden, but the garden that owns me!" "Why not take charge of a plot or two," I said, "the full charge?"

On the following afternoon I found Mr. Gray digging a plot which had not been turned up for some time. A stroke of the spade disturbed an ant's nest. "Poor things," said Mr. Gray, "I fear that I've wrecked that home completely."

A little later, an earwig's nest was laid bare, and two earwigs ran about defiantly with the tail forceps in the air. "How formidable they look!" said Mr. Gray. "Yes," I replied, "the forceps can be used as a weapon, but it is of still more account as a fearsome-looking thing which strikes terror into the earwig's enemies. How many men are there who dare to take up a threatening earwig?"

"But," I continued, "there is still another use for these pincers. After its flight in the dusk, the earwig folds away its wings under the wing-cases so carefully that few people know that the insect has wings at all. This is accomplished by a most ingenious process of folding, finished by a final tucking-in by the forceps."

"Is there any truth," asked Mr. Gray, "in the idea suggested by the name? Do they visit the human ear?" "Not at all," I replied. "The earwig annoys the gardener occasionally by eating flower-petals; but, otherwise, it is a harmless creature. As it is better known, it will be less disliked."

In examining the earwig's legs, Mr. Gray said that the creature seemed to be a poor digger; and I explained that the earwig takes advantage of the labours of worms and other excavators. When a thrush captures a worm, the earwig often occupies the tenantless burrow. In this hole it lays its eggs, and sits on them as faithfully as a bird does. When the eggs hatch out, the young earwigs keep close to the mother, and are often to be seen playing on her back.

From some surface rubbish there ran out a slater. "There goes," I cried, "a cousin of the shrimp, the crab, and the lobster! Nearly all its relations are creatures of the water. It must be long since the ancestor of the slater left the water; for it is now thoroughly at home on land."

"A centipede!" cried Mr. Gray, as the creature of many legs ran from under a clod. "How does this creature get a living?" "On worms," I replied, "and on the larvæ of beetles and moths!

It is a small insect to attack a worm; but its bite seems to be poisonous to small animals."

A little later a millipede was disturbed. At first it feigned death; but, as we continued to handle it, it rolled itself up into a tiny ball, which fell off the hand to the earth and was lost. The little creature had been too clever for us! The millipede lives on soft roots, but, in other respects, is harmless.

A nest of the black earth-spider was broken into, and the spider ran off with a ball of eggs below its body. It made a quick run, then stopped, listened, and watched; then another run and another pause; and, finally, it disappeared in a crack of the earth.

Then we turned up the familiar curly-white grub of the cockchafer-beetle, which does so much damage to the roots of plants. Later on, while digging a turfy patch, we came on another root-destroyer—the wire-worm. When grass without any apparent reason becomes sickly, the cause is often to be sought in this pale yellowish-brown worm. The wire-worm is the larva of the click-beetle, sometimes known as *skipjack*. When it has fallen on its back, this beetle can flip itself into the air and alight on its feet.

A stroke of the spade threw up the pure white silky cocoon of the mole-cricket. The pupa was fast becoming the perfect insect. Already all parts of the body could be seen; and the strong fore-legs—"the diggers," with the four claws spread out like a hand—were already outside the pupa case. Even the two long tails could be seen; these the cricket is said to use as feelers when moving backwards. It was plain that we should soon hear again the voice of the cricket in the land.

"It makes one think," said Mr. Gray, "of long hot evenings on the verandah chairs, just as the sound of the cicada calls up to memory, hot walks in the fields. Does the cricket do damage in the garden?" "Yes," I replied. "It is a clever, interesting creature, but it does a good deal of harm as a root-eater. It will also eat the lower leaf-buds in vines."

"It does good, though," I continued, "in airing the soil by its borings. It is a wonderful digger. If you hold a cricket between finger and thumb, you will be astonished at the strength of push and thrust that lies in its diggers. Put it on loose earth, and it will delight you by its skill in burrowing quickly out of sight."

As we rested for a few minutes, Mr. Gray asked: "Where do the larvæ of the cicada sleep during the winter?" "They spend the winter," I replied, "or, rather, many winters—for some are said to live underground for seventeen years—under trees. When the locust emerges, it crawls up the tree and begins the summer song." "Seventeen years!" exclaimed Mr. Gray. "Do you mean to say that the cicada lies in the dark for years preparing for three months' life in the air?" "I do," I replied. "We are not yet sure how long our Australian cicada takes to ripen; but a similar insect in America takes seventeen years. In country orchards, one sometimes finds the eggs of the cicada deposited in slits made by the insect on the bark of the peach tree. It is quite possible that the cicada which laid these eggs is sprung from an insect which, seventeen years before, laid its eggs on a gum tree occupying the ground in which the peach tree is now planted."

"You mean," said Mr. Gray, "that the young cicadas would fall to the ground and burrow under the root of the gum-tree? But, would their nest not be destroyed when the tree was rooted up and the ground ploughed for the orchard?" "Not necessarily," I

THE PLAGUE-LOCUST.

A.—1, EGG CAVITY FILLED WITH 18 EGGS; 2, EGGS BEING
PLACED IN CAVITY; 3, EGG CLUSTER; 4, SEPARATED EGGS.
B.—MALE. C.—FEMALE. D.—1, FEMALE DEPOSITING EGGS;
2, THE TWO ATTENDANTS (MALES); 3, RING OF ADMIRING MALES.
(FROM THE *AGRICULTURAL GAZETTE* OF NEW SOUTH WALES.)

replied. "The larvæ of the cicada are said to burrow very deeply
in the ground." "Quite a romance in insect life!" cried Mr. Gray.
Just then my eye fell on a small greenish insect resting upon

the leaf of a cabbage plant. "The first grasshopper of the season!" I cried; "the season of grasshopper and locust has begun."

"I suppose," said Mr. Gray, as we entered the house, "that the plague-locust of the interior will be getting ready for the summer campaign?" "Yes," I replied, "the breeding-grounds in the plains are almost alive now with the young locusts. These are from the eggs laid in the ground last autumn."

"In such breeding-grounds the surface is broken into tiny heaps of earth, about an inch in diameter. These heaps of earth indicate the places where the female locusts, in March last, made holes for their eggs. Each locust lays about 60 eggs. These heaps of earth often give to the land the appearance of having been scarified by a pronged hoe. The nests are sometimes so close together that there are about 170 to the square foot; and the locusts, when laying, often overlap one another."[12]

"The young," I continued, "are now coming out of these nests, but will need to change skin several times before they are ready to fly. Besides these inland locusts which fly to us from special breeding-grounds, there are, in every district, locusts which grow from eggs deposited by the swarms of the previous summer. These are already beginning to crawl about the fields and to eat the young grass. When these larvæ have become perfect insects, they will join the flying swarms from inland in attacking crops and orchards."

"Are means being taken to check the locust plague?" asked Mr. Gray. "Nothing at all adequate," I replied. "Naturalists, for many years, have been urging united action to destroy the locusts in the breeding grounds, or in the hopping stage, but the difficulties in a country like Australia are immense."

12   Richard Helms, of the New South Wales Agricultural Department.

The most promising remedy is one which was discovered in Cape Colony. It was noticed, a few years ago, that, in certain districts, great numbers of locusts were dying of a contagious fungoid disease. The germs of this disease, having been artificially grown, were used to spread the disease in other districts. It was found that a few disease-stricken locusts were sufficient to infect vast numbers of the others. This remedy is being tried in various parts of Australia.

"The great obstacle lies in the apathy of those who suffer from the locust plague. With the growth of Nature-study, however, the people will no longer behave as if the locust plague were a visitation of God."

"Is there not a sense in which it is really a visitation of God?" said Mr. Gray. "Is not ignorance often punished as severely as vice?"

We sat silent for a time, and then Mr. Gray took down a Bible and read aloud: "And the locusts went up over the land of Egypt: very grievous were they for they covered the face of the whole earth so that the land was darkened; and they did eat every herb of the land and all the fruit of the trees: and there remained not any green thing in the trees or in the herbs of the field through all the land of Egypt."

CHAPTER XXIX.
The Story of a Moth.

<u>A FAIRY TALE OF SCIENCE.</u>

We were watching some small moths in the garden, when Mr. Gray said: "What a pity we haven't more garden butterflies!" "Well," I replied, "some of our moths are as fine-looking as most butterflies. Here is one coming!" I pointed to a vine-moth which had just come over the fence and was flying past us in what looked like aimless flight.

It settled on the leaf of a Virginian creeper, and we could see that the rich black of the wing was crossed by a band of pale yellow, and that the wings were edged with white. The moth rose, showing the rusty-red bands on its body. "It does not seem to know what to do next," said Mr. Gray. "What is the purpose of a moth's life?"

"The great end of a moth," I replied, "is the marriage-flight. She has to find her mate and then to lay the eggs that continue the race. When that is done, she can die in peace, for her life-task has been accomplished. The life of some moths, indeed, is so short that they need no food. They pair, lay their eggs, and die. Others feed and enjoy themselves for a short period."

"Is life, then, all business for this gay-looking creature?" cried Mr. Gray. "No," I replied; "one sometimes sees it resting on a

VINE BRANCH, WITH CATERPILLARS OF VINE-MOTH.

sun-bathed leaf, or sucking honey from a flower; but, indeed, its whole life, if brief, must be a pleasant one. The joy of spring must be tingling in every nerve. But, see! it has settled on the grape-vine! You thought that it moved in a purposeless way. Now, the first thing it rested on was a Virginian creeper, and the next a grape-vine—the only two places out of the thousands in this garden where it can lay its eggs safely!"

"Then," said Mr. Gray, "you think that it is laying its eggs?" "I do. Watch!" I replied. We could see the movement from side to side of the ovipositor as it sought a rough place for the eggs. The moth seemed to lay only a few eggs at each point, flying then to another part of the vine, so that each caterpillar might have ample pasturage. A dozen parts of the vine were visited in this way, and then the moth flew off to seek another Virginian creeper. The moth takes care not to put all its eggs into one basket.

"How wonderful," said Mr. Gray, "that the creature should

fly confidently to the only leaves in the garden suitable for its young! It cannot be the result of instruction, for this moth has never seen its parents!" "We call it instinct," I replied; "but that is only a name to cover our ignorance. We are still in the guessing stage as to this and many similar wonders."

"Here is proof," I continued, "that vine-moths have been here before!" I pointed to a caterpillar on one of the vine-leaves. "Ah!" cried Mr. Gray, "I've often noticed that handsome fellow, but never connected it with the moth." The ground colour was white, banded and spotted with black, and with a bright red band round one of the rear rings. It was so handsome, and was eating the fresh green leaf with such evident enjoyment, that it seemed hard to kill the creature. "It must be done, though," said Mr. Gray. "One year, when we neglected the vine, we lost our crop of grapes."

"Here are the eggs!" I cried, as I examined some tiny dots lodged in a crevice of the rough wood. "Then the moth," said Mr. Gray, "does not always lay its eggs on the leaf?" "Sometimes," I replied, "it prefers the surface of the vine-wood or the vine-stalks. Indeed, the first eggs of the season are sometimes laid before the vine is in leaf; so that, when the leaf-buds break, the young caterpillars are ready to begin work." "The caterpillars must have a long season," said Mr. Gray; "we have to pick them off all through the spring and summer and far into the autumn." "But not the caterpillars of the same brood," I replied. "The moths have two or three broods in the season. This big fellow will soon have reached his full size, and whenever that happens he will stop eating, crawl down to the ground, work his way below the surface, and make for himself a cocoon."

"And then does he go to sleep?" asked Mr. Gray. "Well, he

eats nothing for a month," I replied, "but there must be great activity within the cocoon. The caterpillar is being changed into a winged creature, different in form, in limbs, and in manner of life. How the change is made we don't understand; but we may be certain that the work of pulling down one body and building up another must go on unceasingly. The cocoon, therefore, is by no means a mummy case."

"And then?" asked Mr. Gray. "And then there comes a great day in the history of the creature. The top of the case is pushed aside, and hey! presto! a winged insect emerges. What went in a caterpillar comes out a moth!" "No wonder it was thought a miracle by our fathers," cried Mr. Gray; "and it is still part of the daily miracle." "Yes," I replied. "Science but deepens the wonder and the mystery of life."

"You mean," said Mr. Gray, "that behind the processes which we understand there are always deeper processes which we do not understand? Well! I'm glad of it," he continued. "Man is by nature a seeker, and would not be happy if he knew everything." "Don't be afraid," I said, laughing. "Every discovery we make only suggests wider fields of research."

We had passed on to a seat beneath an old apple tree. "I like to sit here in the spring-time," said Mr. Gray. "The apple blossom seems to me the finest of the fruit-tree blossoms. Beautiful in its white and pink flowers, it also carries to us the very spirit of spring in its delicate scent. The beauty of the snowy blossoms of some of the plums and cherries is almost unearthly in its purity; but in the apple blossom we have just that touch of the earth that reaches the heart."

The gardener had bound round the stem of the tree a bandage of old sacking. "Ah!" I said, "you are troubled with the codlin

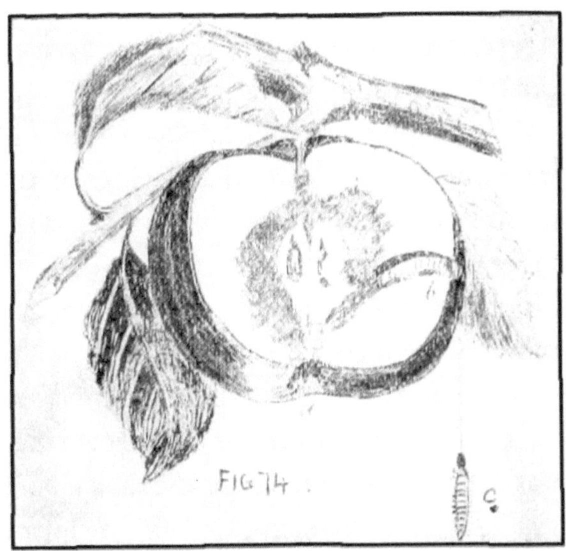

APPLE CUT TO SHOW THE CATERPILLAR OF CODLIN MOTH.
THE INSECT IS LAID IN (A), AND THE CATERPILLAR EMERGES AT (B),
AFTER EATING INTO THE PIPE; AT (C) WE HAVE THE CATERPILLAR
LOWERING ITSELF TO THE GROUND.—(AFTER *FRENCH*.)

moth." "I do not understand you," said Mr. Gray. For answer I unloosed the bandage and pointed to a grub which had been sleeping through the winter in this snug cover. It was one of a dozen others.

"This," I said, "is the grub of the famous codlin moth. The arrival of this moth in an apple or pear orchard is like the visit of a devastating army. Worse! for while the troop departs, the moth remains, and grows from year to year. To one grower alone last year this moth caused a loss of £200!"

"Can we see the moth itself?" asked Mr. Gray. "The earliest are now leaving the pupa-cases," I replied; "but they are night-flying moths, not readily to be seen in the daytime. In the twilight you may see them taking their marriage-flight wherever apple or pear trees are numerous. This moth is a poor flyer, and rarely goes far from the tree where it was born."

It is a small greyish-brown moth, faintly marked with bronze bands. By day, when resting with folded wings on the bark, it is almost invisible to the casual eye. "It lays its eggs in the blossom, I suppose," said Mr. Gray. "As a rule, it does," I replied, "but it may lay the egg on the fruit at any point, or even on the leaves. In most cases, however, when the grub emerges from the egg, it crawls to the calyx-eye of the apple and bores its way into the pips. Long before the apple is fully grown the grub has eaten the pips and reached its full size; and then it bores its way through the side of the fruit, spins a silken thread, and lowers itself to the ground."

"Ah!" said Mr. Gray, "I've seen this escape from the apple. Last autumn, while seated here, a little white caterpillar, with a delicate pink flush, lowered itself onto my book. I suppose I ought to have killed it!" "If," I continued, "you had watched it, you would have seen it crawl to the stem of the tree to look for a winter retreat. Probably it found just what it wanted in this bandage; and, indeed, it may be one of these very grubs before us!"

Here the gardener came up, and, on seeing the loosened bandage, explained that he had forgotten to kill the grubs during the winter. "The moth breeds two or three times during the season," he added, "and I have to look at the bandage and kill the grubs all through the summer and autumn." "And where," asked Mr. Gray, "did the grubs hide before you began to bandage the trees?" "In crevices of the stem and under broken bark," was the reply.

"I suppose," said Mr. Gray, as the gardener left us, "that

the codlin moth has also its natural enemies?" "Yes," I replied, "but it is better guarded than most insects. Inside the apple, and while hidden away under bark, it is not much exposed to attack. In the brief moth stage it is eaten by spiders, bats, and night-flying birds."

CHAPTER XXX.
Ants, Wasps, and Bees.

THE INSECTS THAT FORM SOCIETIES.

One morning I found Mr. Gray looking at an ants' nest in the garden path. "What are they doing?" he asked, as I joined him; "they seem to be moving about with a busy aimlessness." "There is purpose in every movement," I replied, "just as there is purpose in the movement of men in a busy street. Now, let me prove what I say!"

I killed three house-flies and placed them close to three separate doors of the ant-nest. We strolled down the path, and, on our return, within five minutes, were just in time to see one of the flies disappearing down door number one.

Door number two had to be reached by climbing over a heap of small loose stones, and a strong detachment of ants was trying to drag the fly up this hill. But the footing was treacherous, and they seemed to make no headway. Now came a gallant rush, and the heights were almost scaled; but a speck of gravel bigger than usual—a boulder to the little garden ant—got in the way, and the fly and the clinging ants slipped down again to the hill-foot. Three times the gallant creatures rushed up the hill; but at the end they were farther from the door than when we arrived.

Then we passed to door number three, and here the fly—a

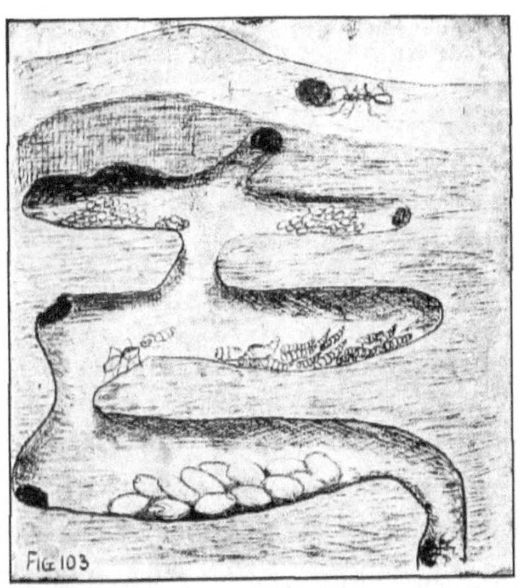

CROSS SECTION OF
ANTS' NEST.—

TOP FLAT, SHOWING EGGS.

MIDDLE FLOOR, FOR GRUBS.

BASEMENT, SHOWING PUPÆ.

large blue fly—lay untouched. "And yet," said Mr. Gray, "there are plenty of ants near!" I handed him my pocket-lens, and, on looking at these ants, he reported that they were coming out of the hole, bearing in their jaws little specks of earth and quartz. These they carried for some distance and then put down. "Is it," he asked, "a new nest that is being excavated?" "No," I replied, "it is an old nest that has its pathways blocked by sand washed in by last night's heavy rain. The road-making officials of the ant-village have a busy time after a heavy shower, just as the street and channel cleaners have among ourselves. Also, the tunnels and drives have often to be lengthened in order to provide for an increase of numbers."

"Some of them," continued Mr. Gray, "seem to be lazy. They put down their burden so close to the hole that it will soon tumble in again. Others carry their stones to the edge of the heap of rubbish and throw them down like a navvy emptying his wheelbarrow over a ridge, while a few conscientious carriers go quite beyond the hill before dropping their burdens.

All, however, are no sooner free than they race back to the nest for another load."

"And now," I said, "you can see why the fly beside this nest is untouched. If these road-menders have seen or smelt it, which is doubtful, they pay no heed: it is none of their business! In the case of the other two flies, some foraging ants, no doubt, espied the treasure."

"Do you mean," cried Mr. Gray, "that the ants have arrived at division of labour?" "I do," I replied. "We have, perhaps, to go to a human community to find a society so well organized as an ant-village. Besides road-makers and food-seekers, there are workers set apart to nurse the young, and others to defend the nest from attack. Among these little garden ants the general workers seem to be able to turn their jaws to anything; but in the case of many kinds of ants there are regular castes."

"But here," I continued, "comes a forager at last." An ant bearing a grass-seed in its jaws was approaching the hole. Although the fly lay in her way, she hardly paused in passing. The task on hand had to be finished before she was free even for treasure-trove of this kind. She had hardly passed when a forager, outward-bound, came along the track, and almost ran up against the huge carcass. The tiny creature promptly seized a leg, and began to pull. It was as if a bull-dog had tried to pull the body of an elephant. The great body shook, but would not move. The plucky creature continued to pull desperately.

"Why doesn't she run to the nest for help?" cried Mr. Gray. "They rarely do that," I replied, "if they can stir the object at all. The garden ant is an independent little creature." "But that," said Mr. Gray, "is not a sign of intelligence." "Perhaps not," I said; "their efforts are often clumsy and slow, for want of an overseer to make them work together. But they rarely fail in anything they undertake, if you give them time. Besides, as this ant is on the beaten track, it can depend on getting help."

Sure enough, other foragers outward-bound came up, and soon there was an ant pulling at every leg. As the prize came near to the nest-door, numerous ants, summoned perhaps by the first discoverer, came out to help, and the fly was moved forward at a run and drawn head first into the hole. Then came a block, for the body was much too large for the door.

Presently, we noticed that a larger ant than the foragers had come to their help—an ant with very large head and powerful jaws. This giant made herculean efforts to enlarge the hole. With jaws in the ground and legs kicking vigorously, he was soon smothered in dust. But the ground was hard and dry, and progress slow. The smaller ants, in trying to help, would sometimes get into the way of the vigorous legs and be kicked back among the stones. One, more sensible than the rest, took up the stones as they were kicked aside by the giant, and carried them further out.

Meantime, a forager arrived bearing a grass seed. The seed was almost as large as herself, and we watched admiringly the spirited way in which the hill of *débris* was surmounted—the seed being held high in order to avoid the obstacles. Almost spent by the final effort, she arrived to find the door blocked. With admirable sense, and perhaps a little temper, she threw down the seed and rested. Other foragers arrived, and soon a dozen seeds and two small beetles were lying near the door.

At last, one of the road-making ants set to work to make a new entrance close to the old one. Others joined her with evident zest. As their jaws broke into the earth, their legs kicked the dust back, and in twenty minutes the seeds and beetles were being carried in through a new door. The work of enlarging the old door was still going on when we left.

That evening, after dark, we looked at the hole by lantern-light, and found that the ants were still at work. The new door had been joined to the old one to make one large entrance, and the task was almost accomplished. "Why don't they leave the fly till tomorrow?" said Mr. Gray.

"Because," I replied, "night-wandering beetles would be almost certain to take it."

As we returned to the house, Mr. Gray said, "I noticed that the ants seemed to be able to communicate news." "Not a doubt of it!" I replied. "They have a way of touching with the antennæ which conveys information."

"I was struck also," continued Mr. Gray, "with the variety of food which the ants were bringing to the nest." "Yes," I replied, "they can eat almost anything that man can eat, and a good deal more. That is one reason why they have been able to hold their own so well all over the world. The ant is, among the insects, what the sparrow is among the birds."

"I have noticed the good work they do as scavengers," said Mr. Gray. "Yes," I said, "we owe much to the ant. The rat that dies under the floor soon disappears, and of the thousands of insects that must die daily, we never see a dead body left to pollute the air." "It is rather a humiliating thought," said Mr. Gray, "that we are only now beginning as a people to assist Nature in her wonderful scheme for keeping the air pure!"

"Did you notice," said Mr. Gray, "that the homeward-bound foragers often collided with the outward-bound ants?" "Yes," I said, "they have eyes, but they do not see well. This was to be expected in creatures which spend much of their time in dark tunnels. Like most hunting creatures, they depend on smell. That is why they cannot go straight to an object, but must keep to the beaten track."

As we passed the ants' nest next morning, Mr. Gray said, "Why do they drive their tunnels where the earth is so hard?" "Because," I replied, "in soft ground the tunnels would readily collapse. Galleries are driven in all directions from the main shaft, some being used for store rooms, others for the eggs, others for the larvæ, and others again for the pupæ. In the case of the garden ant one often finds the larvæ and pupæ—so-called *eggs*—under a stone close to the door of the nest."

I led Mr. Gray to the end of the path, where I had noticed an ants' run. On lifting a large flat stone near to the nest entrance, we found a large heap of young ants in the pupa stage. As soon as this nursery was uncovered, a scene of amazing activity began. The village became alive as if an alarm-bell had sounded; but for the human ear all was silence. Every able-bodied ant seized a baby in its mouth and bore it off to the inner chambers. Many mouths make quick work, and, in a wonderfully short time, every baby had disappeared.

Looking with a lens at one of the pupæ, we could see the two black specks where the eyes would be. "I am struck with the helplessness of the young of the ant," said Mr. Gray. "How different from the young aphis, which drives its beak into the leaf, and begins to suck almost as soon as it is born! But I suppose that this is an illustration of the rule that, as one goes up the ladder of life, the period of helplessness in infancy increases?"

"Yes," I replied, "from this fact alone we could have guessed that the ant is high in the scale. The parental care continues, too, for some time after the young ant has been helped to draw itself out of its pupa-clothes. It is taught to clean itself, to use its antennæ in talking, and to nurse the larvæ." "This long-continued care for the young must develop intelligence and sympathy," said Mr. Gray. "Yes," I replied, "it is Nature's chief plan for drawing out the traits that mark the higher animals. From the self-dividing jelly-creature upwards, Nature seems to be striving to produce the perfect mother. Self-sacrifice, intelligence, and courage have been learned in this school more than in any other."

"Do the ants, then, show the trait which we call sympathy?" asked Mr. Gray. "In a limited degree," I replied. "Besides their tender care for the young, they seem to help the sick. If, however, the illness be serious, they behave as uncivilized men do: they cast out the sick ant. No place has ever been found in an animal community for useless members. Among all these social insects—ants, wasps, bees—service to the community is the price of life." "Then," said Mr. Gray, "one could never see in some Troy of the ant-world the son bearing forth the aged parent from the doomed city?" "No," I replied, "that is a human, not an animal, trait!"

"How is the ant-village started?" asked Mr. Gray. "By a few perfect female ants which we name queens," I replied. "These females are born winged; so, also, are the few male ants. After the marriage-flight the males die, and the queens pull off their wings and settle to the laying of eggs."

"I suppose," said Mr. Gray, "that the life-histories of all the social insects—the ants, wasps, and bees—are similar?" "Yes," I replied, "they all begin with the egg and pass through the stages of larva and pupa; but there are many small variations.

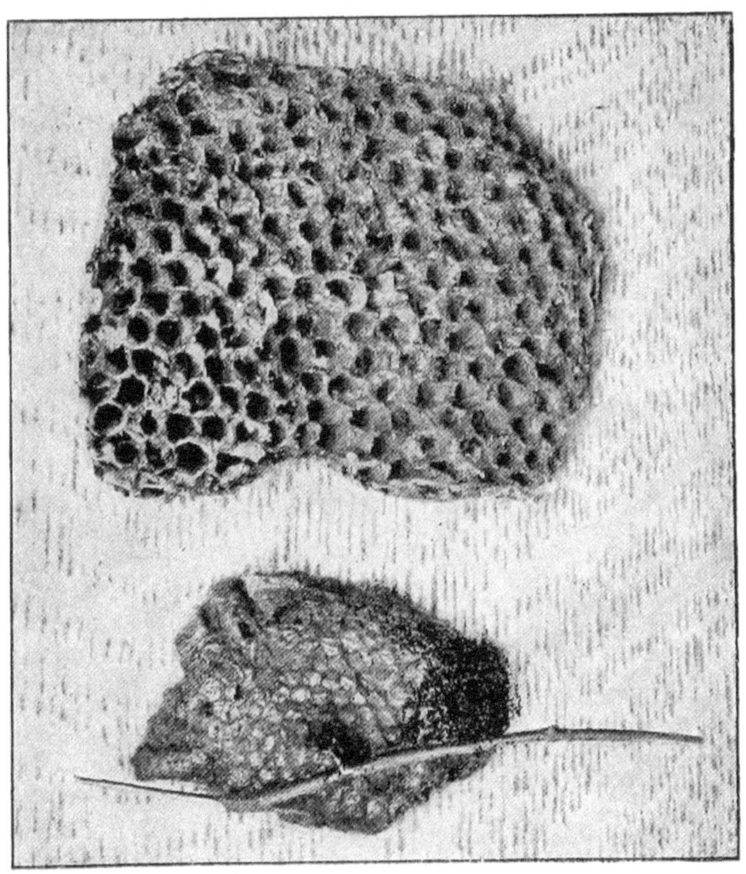

NESTS OF PAPER-WASPS—UPPER: FRONT VIEW, SHOWING OPEN
CELLS. LOWER: REAR VIEW, SHOWING ATTACHMENT.

In a bee-hive there is only one queen. When a fresh queen is born in the hive the old queen cannot live with the new one, and leaves the hive with a 'swarm' of workers to seek a new home. The caste system, also, under which the ants set apart special members for the work of fighting, is not found among the bees and wasps. All join in the work of defence."

"Would you place the wasp higher than the hive-bee?" asked Mr. Gray. "In almost everything," I replied, "except in the art of

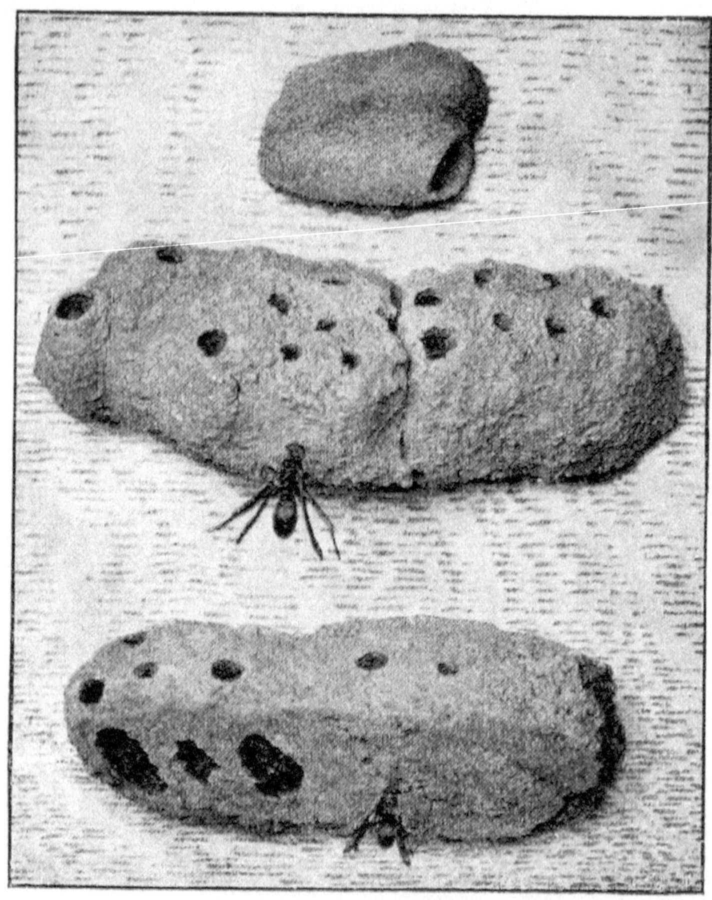

MUD NESTS OF HORNETS—UPPER: TWO-CELLED NEST, ONE STILL OPEN AND UNUSED. MIDDLE: MANY-CELLED NEST. LOWER: ENTRANCES TO SEVERAL AND THEIR CHAMBERS EXPOSED WHEN TAKEN FROM WALL TO WHICH THE NESTS WERE ATTACHED.

cell-building; in that respect the bee takes the lead of all insects. But, in general ability and in courage, the queen-wasp that founds a colony stands higher than the bee. No worker-wasp survives the winter; and, in the spring, the queen-wasp undertakes, without help, the task of building a new paper-house of many cells, and of peopling it with workers. It is a stupendous undertaking for a single pair of jaws."

"Do all the ants, wasps, and bees live in colonies?" asked Mr. Gray. "The ants always do so," I replied, "but there are many bees and wasps that lead solitary lives. There is, for example, a hornet found near Melbourne which builds a small nest of one or more cells in any kind of shelter—even in the keyhole of a door. The hornet lays an egg in the cell, places in it food for the larva, seals the cell up, and departs. Most wasps have a great range of food—nectar, fruit, meat, insects—but the solitary wasp has generally some favourite food for its larvæ. In the case of this hornet, a spider, alive but paralyzed, is sealed up with the egg in the cell. It is generally the same kind of spider."

Some of the solitary wasps are handsome insects. Some are blue-black, others are black, or black with yellow or white markings, and the sheen of their coats is like that of burnished metal. As a rule they are very quick in their movements. Nearly all show remarkable skill in paralyzing with their sting the beetle, or cricket, or spider which they choose for the food supply of their larvæ.

"All these social insects," said Mr. Gray, "appear to have the power to produce workers, or males, or queens at pleasure." "It seems," I replied, "to be mainly a question of food and of the size of the cell. The egg which would have produced a worker becomes a queen under the stimulus of better food and housing." "A hint," said Mr. Gray, "to us, if we wish to turn out a kingly race of men!"

CHAPTER XXXI.
The Partnership Between Insects and Plants

I found Mr. Gray next morning standing over a bed of pansies. The flowers were of many colours and patterns, and were mingled together without any planned order. They were from seed saved from the previous year. "I find three kinds entirely new in this bed," he said, "but I have lost the fine brown that I liked best last year." "The brown pansy still lives here," I said, pointing to some pansies dashed with brown; "and here; and here! The flies," I added, laughingly, "have been trying to make a new pansy. It is a wonderful thought that we owe so much of the beauty of the world to the insects."

"You don't mean," said Mr. Gray, "that the insects take a conscious part in making the flowers more beautiful?" "No," I replied, "but, in carrying out their own plans, they are made to help on the Divine plan, that the earth shall grow in beauty."

"Of course," I added, "if you give thought and work to this process of crossing flowers, you may do more for the beauty of the garden in a year than the insects could do in an age. Look at these fine roses! Out of the five kinds in that bed, only one was known to our fathers." "I wish," said Mr. Gray, "that we could improve men and women as quickly!" "Fear not! The day is com-

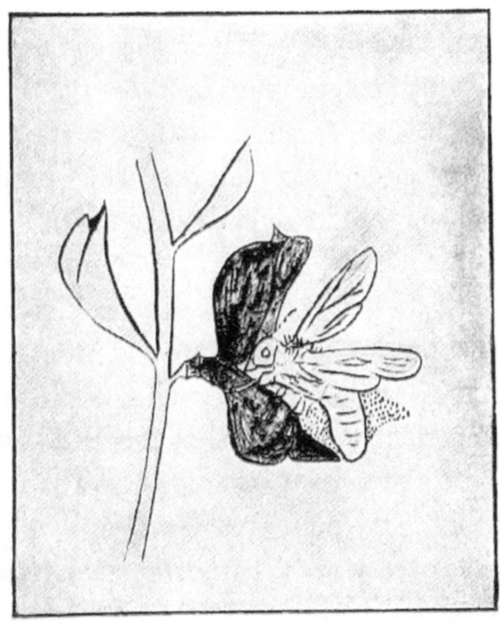

Bee bursting keel of furze, and liberating pollen grains.

ing when fine men and women will be reckoned the loveliest flowers of life; and in that day wonders will be wrought which we cannot even dream of today."

We were now standing before an Iceland poppy plant. An early bloom had pushed up its long, hairy stem, and was pushing off the green night-cap in which it had slept. We could almost see the movement of the petals as they pushed into the light. When we passed, five minutes afterwards, the night-cap had fallen, and the beautiful pale yellow cup was half open. A flower loses no time, and, already, the golden pollen was thick on the circle of stamens.

The flower was not yet fully opened when the first visitor arrived—a pretty, fly-like native bee. It seemed to know that it was the first comer, and it worked eagerly among the stamens. In a minute its legs and body were heavy with pollen. Then a hive-bee buzzed up, and thrust the smaller bee aside; then more bees. In the first fifteen minutes of its life the poppy-cup had entertained eight visitors; and all of these carried off pollen to other poppies, except, possibly, the first, which probably carried off its load of bee bread straight to its nest.

"Why this long, hairy stem?" asked Mr. Gray. "It is long," I replied, "because the flower must be easily seen. The rough hairs are probably meant to keep off ants and other honey-loving ground insects. Flowers do not like ants, because they do not keep to one kind of flower at a time, as bees and wasps generally do; and the plants have many ingenious ways of preventing the ants from reaching the honey."

As we passed over an uncut part of the lawn, I stooped to pick a head of white clover. The head was less than an inch broad, but was thrust up into the air above the other grasses on a stem twelve inches long. "Here," I said, "we have one reason why the white clover has spread over the world. It is easily seen, and it escapes the ants." Two bees came up, and were at once busy among the clover-blooms.

"We could spend an hour," I said, "in looking at the contrivances which make the clover-head attractive to the bees; but just look at this one!" I pointed to the outer, or lower, flowers in the head, which were all thrust down against the stem to be out of the way. These were the flowers that had been fertilized, and that required no longer the visits of the bees. The upper, or inner, flowers of the head are the last to open, and these, being in this case still unfertilized, were erect. By this device the bees can go at once to the flowers which are still charged with honey. The time of the bee is saved, and more visits can be paid to the flowers which still need its services.

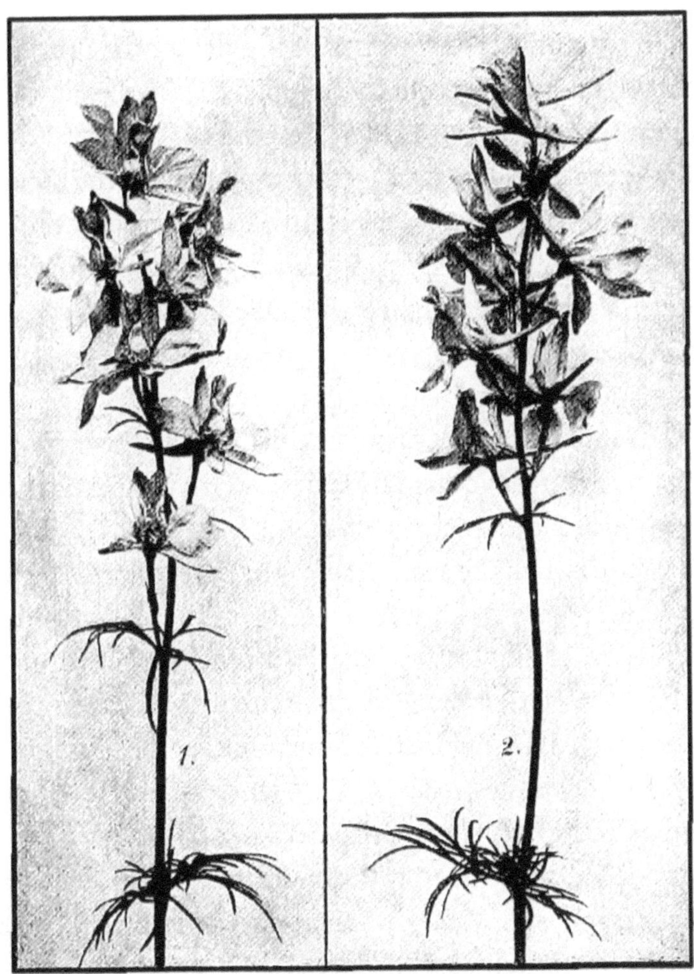

LARKSPUR—1, FRONT VIEW OF FLOWERS; 2, REAR VIEW.

"But here," I went on, as we came to a larkspur, "is a flower which is still more elaborately planned for the visits of insects." We picked a spike, the upper flowers on which were still opening, while the lower flowers were at all stages of ripeness. We noticed, first of all, how the honey was stored in a deep spur, so that the smaller flies might be unable to reach the nectar with their short sucking-tubes.

Then we noticed the devices of the flower for preventing self-fertilization. When the flower opens, the pollen is already breaking from the green anthers, but the stigma is still closed. The anthers are held firmly together in a bunch at the mouth of the nectary by the wings of the petal, these wings being provided with springs for this purpose. By this device the visiting insect is compelled to brush against the pollen. Later on, when the stigma is beginning to open, the clasp of the wings is relaxed, and the stamens fall down out of the way. The visiting insect now brushes against the stigma, which is ready to receive the pollen brought from other larkspurs; and so the purpose of all this beautiful mechanism is effected.

Still later, when the seed-case has been fertilized, the withering stamens are removed further from the track, while the ovary is thrust so far forward that, without a visit, flies can see that the nectary is empty. For, just as the stamens are pushed away whenever their work has been done, so the honey ceases to flow as soon as the seed-case has been fertilized. By this time the wings of the nectary-door have opened wide, for there is no longer need to make narrow the entrance to the honey-track.

"Each plant," said Mr. Gray, "seems to have its own scheme for attracting the right insect and for securing cross-fertilization." "Yes," I said, "flower-study is full of delightful surprises to one who is on the look-out. Colours, spots, lines, and shapes, seemingly meaningless, suddenly become invested with significance."

"It is a wonderful partnership," said Mr. Gray. "I can see now that the form of flowers, as well as their colour, depends a good deal on the visiting insects." "It would be quite as true," I replied, "to say that the form of the visiting insects depends a good deal on the flowers visited."

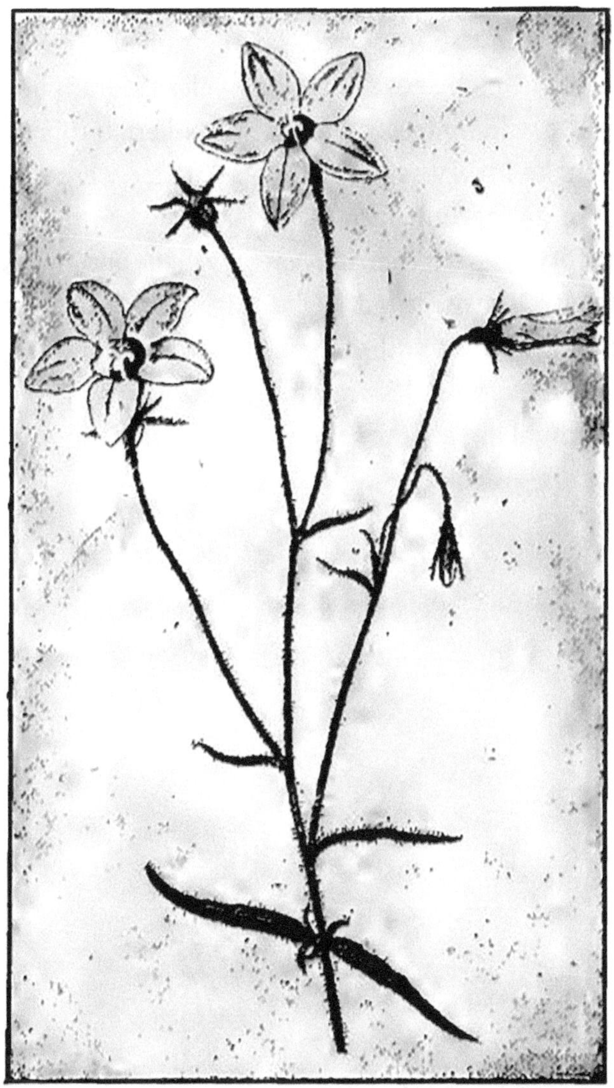

AUSTRALIAN BLUE-BELL

"We must have many cases," said Mr. Gray, "where a plant was imported without its insect partner." "Yes," I said, "many cases. A good example is the large clover introduced into New Zealand, which was not a success till its partner, the humble-bee of England, was also imported. In Australia we have a female flowering fig, which does not fruit so well as in Italy, because we have not the wild fig tree, which yields pollen. If this male tree, along with the small wasp, which is its partner, were introduced, the fruit might become larger and finer."

"What of the flowers which open only in the evening, when the bees and wasps have retired?" asked Mr. Gray. "They are visited," I replied, "by moths or other night insects; and here, again, the partnership is complete. Since white or yellow are the colours best seen at night, these are the colours of most of the night flowers."

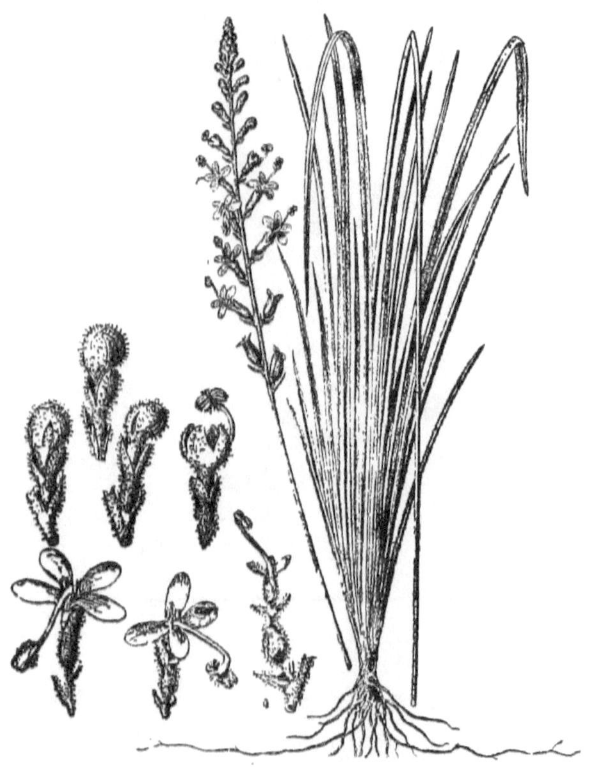

TRIGGER PLANT—FLOWERS IN BUD; EXPANDING AND EXPANDED FLOWERS (AFTER VON MUELLER).

The adaptation of colour to the needs of the visiting insect is possibly illustrated in the deeper tints of the mountain flowers. Many a man dates his first real interest in botany from his first acquaintance with highland flowers. "Is it the purer air of the mountains that gives the purer tints to these flowers?" asked Mr. Gray. "Many things contribute," I replied, "but one thing is clear. At these heights there are fewer insects, and hence the need of deeper colour, so that these few may not miss the flowers. On our Australian mountains, the blue-bell is deeper in colour and larger in form than in the lowlands; and this is true, also, of the trigger plant and of the heaths."

CHAPTER XXXII.
The Spider

As we sat in the shade of a great banksia rosebush, which overhung the fence, a tiny spider fell on my coat, from the branches above. Looking up, we saw that it had lowered itself by a thread. Following up the line, we found the nest. A curious nest it was, made of a mesh of many threads of silk, in the deepest folds of an old school exercise.

In this nest were numerous small spiders; and the many cast-off skins showed that the spiders had passed through one or two moults.

"Is there," asked Mr. Gray, "a full course of egg, larva, and pupa?" "No," I replied, "the young spider comes straight out of the egg, and is similar to the mother in all but size."

"There, no doubt, is the mother!" I pointed to a spider which was mending its web close to the young spiders' nest. "Last autumn, or early this spring, she wove a little saucer-shaped web, laid her eggs in it, added two layers of silk to make a cocoon, and placed the cocoon in this paper. She then left the young to shift for themselves, except that she wove a network of thread, to catch the young on leaving the eggs."

"When the young hatched out, the other day, they were soft and limp, and were huddled together in this mesh of web, which serves as a nursery. After several days, during which they shed

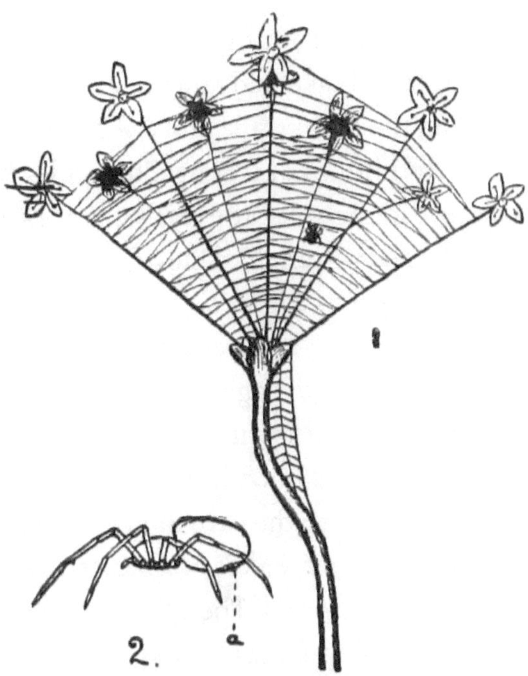

1. First Web of a Young Spider.
2. Adult Spider, showing spinnerets.

the skin twice, the venturesome spirits began to explore, letting themselves down by threads, or throwing out threads for the wind to blow about. When one of these threads touches a twig or a leaf, it sticks, and the spider, having run along the line, repeats the process from the new point. In this way she gets into position the cables which serve as framework for a web."

"Do you mean to say," cried Mr. Gray, "that the baby-spider is able to weave a web?"

"I do! Without a lesson from the mother, the tiny creature weaves a web; and a very pretty sight it is to see it throwing out the stout ray-cables from the centre, and filling in the delicate cross lines with the confidence of a veteran architect."

Intertwined with the rose-climber was another plant. On

one of the flower-heads, a young spider of a different kind had woven a web. It had taken advantage of the flower-stems which radiate from the main stalk; and the result was a dainty web made with a minimum of labour. The spider had merely put in the cross threads between the ready-made rays. The little architect, snugly settled within the delicate web, under the fresh pink flowers, made a pretty picture.

"You remember," said Mr. Gray, "that we saw an earth-spider carrying a white ball of eggs under her, as she ran away. Her habit must be different from that of this spider." "Yes," I replied, "the earth-spider is not a web-builder; and she seems to have more time to give to the care of her young. She either carries the cocoon under her, or keeps it stowed away in a kind of tubular retreat in the ground. The spider which we saw had been driven from her hiding-place by the spade, and was obliged, very much against her will, to expose her white egg-bag to the light. Where the egg-balls are not hidden away in this fashion, they are coloured, as in the case of birds' eggs, to match their surroundings."

The hole of the earth-spider is lined with silk, and the habits of this spider are supposed to be those of the primitive spider. Made at first merely to protect the eggs, the silk has been found useful in catching flies; and so has been extended beyond the hole for that purpose. We can follow the progress, step by step, in the habits of existing spiders.

Many still catch flies without the help of a web, by jumping, or by a quick rush, or by lying in ambush. We have in Australia a little green spider which can hardly be distinguished from the leaves on which it lives. We have also a spider which exactly resembles a bird's dropping. Spiders of these kinds make no web, but rely on a quick spring upon the fly. Another of our earth-spiders has added a trap-door to its silky tube. Another, which is better known, builds a very rough, irregular web in the corners of rooms and, among the more advanced weavers, there are many that do not build a full orb-web.

"You surprise me," said Mr. Gray. "I have always thought of the spider as the creature that builds the beautiful web. It seems to be the genius of the family. Is it true that it is greedy and cruel?" "Is there such a thing as a greedy animal?" I replied. "Is not greed confined to the being who seeks to satisfy the unlimited wants of soul with an excess of food or of some other material good?"

"I know," I continued, "that the case against the spider seems strong. Sir John Lubbock, in speaking of a spider's rations for twenty-four hours, says: 'At a similar rate of consumption, a man would require a fat ox for breakfast, an ox and five sheep for dinner, and for supper, two bullocks, eight sheep and four hogs; and, before retiring, about four barrels of fresh fish!'" "Prodigious!" cried Mr. Gray.

"Yes," I continued, "but consider what the spider has to do on this fare. The web has to be frequently repaired; and this makes a heavy call on the spider's substance. Large flies break the web; a great wasp may destroy half of it, and then have to be cut out and allowed to go. Blow-flies have to be swathed in silk before being put into the larder. Heavy rains may damage the web, or high winds break it up. Further, the spider has not only to feed herself and provide fresh poison for her glands, but has to lay up strength for egg-bearing. Add to all this the rainy days, when no flies can be caught, and you will see that the spider that makes a good meal when it gets a chance is to be praised for its providence rather than blamed for its greed."

From man's point of view, too, the spider's great consumption of flies makes the creature a valuable ally of the insect-eating birds. One must remember, also, that while these birds claim a share of the fruit and grain harvest, the spider works without fee. Many of our most injurious moths, too, fly only by night, when birds are absent; but the snares of the spider are set by night as well as by day.

"It would seem, then," said Mr. Gray, "that with spider, as with man, a beautiful house requires, for its upkeep, a large income." "Yes," I replied, "the spiders that weave no web, but live in a simple silk-lined hole, have smaller incomes; but, on the other hand, they have smaller needs. They eat less, because they need less. If the web-spinner ate more than it really needed, it would soon become sluggish. As a matter of fact, its life is an intense one; it is always on the alert, with foot on the communication-cable, and ready to act with vigour."

"The prodigious meals recorded by Sir John Lubbock are English records," said Mr. Gray. "Have we any Australian records? As we have fewer rainy days here, and therefore a steadier supply of flies, I should expect the appetite to be less."

"An interesting suggestion," I replied. "We have no records of the kind here. We are waiting for the Australian Lubbock! How fortunate is the young Australian! So many untrodden fields! So many unexplored paths where his foot may be the first."

As to the charge of cruelty, it is true that a spider will keep in prison a fly that is still alive; but the fly soon passes into a kind of painless swoon. It is generally paralyzed by poison before it is tied up in silk. It is true, also, that the female spider often eats up the male spider, especially when smaller than herself; but does not the bee kill the drone? The truth is, that there is no room in the animal economy for drones. An animal must earn its living or die."

Mr. Gray, who had been looking with his lens at the thread of a web, cried—"There seem to be little sticky beads along the cross-threads!" "Yes," I said, "not only are the cross-threads themselves sticky, but they are studded with gluey blobs. That is why a fly that has touched a web so rarely escapes. The truth is that the spider is perhaps the best equipped of all the insects of prey. It has poison fangs, formidable claws, and its net is furnished with these sticky beads. No wonder the orb-web spider has spread over the world."

As we walked towards the house, Mr. Gray asked me about the gossamer spider. "Ah! That is an error!" I replied. "It is not a particular spider that weaves the gossamer threads, but young spiders of different families. On fine autumn days the young spider climbs to the top of the bush or fence, and throws out threads on the wind. On these threads, when matted together, the little creature sails away into the air. It seems to be one of Nature's many plans for distributing life. Meeting in the air, the threads become entangled into a mass of web, which sinks to the ground when the wind drops. Hence the gossamer on bush and grass."

"The gossamer, then," said Mr. Gray, "is the young adventurer's magic carpet for bearing it through the air to distant parts! Science, it would seem, is sometimes richer in poetry than even popular belief."

CHAPTER XXXIII.

Fish

In the course of a walk towards Heidelberg, we met some fishers returning from the Yarra. "I never understood the charms of river-fishing," said Mr. Gray, "till I watched fishers on the rivers of England. A party of us were cycling through Warwickshire. A river ran through most of the villages we stayed at; and, after the evening meal, we would spend the long twilight on the green-wooded banks watching the fishers at work, and the trout leaping at the evening flies. It was a quiet, peaceful, and often beautiful scene."

"One's thoughts," he went on, "followed the stream to the sea—the sea that runs over the earth, and that washes the long shores of Australasia. The river was a link with the great world and with Home. I realized, as never before, the charm that captivated Isaak Walton, the fisher's poet. My sympathy is usually with the fish rather than with the fisher; but, while we were passing through Hampshire, where Walton fished the rivers three centuries ago, I understood his quiet outburst of thankfulness to 'Him that made the sun and us, and gives us flowers and showers, and stomachs and meat, and content and leisure to go a-fishing.'"

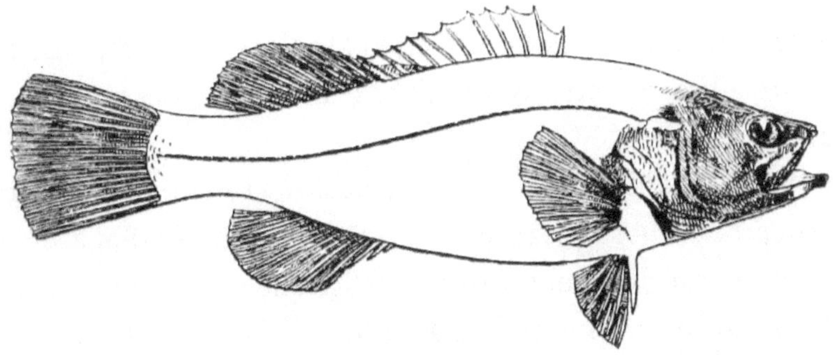

"If you knew something of sea-fish," I said, "you would find them quite as interesting as the river-fish." "Well," cried Mr. Gray, "try me! Tell me about the sea-fish!"

"First of all, then," I said, "you must think of the shore-fishes, which live on the rocks or sands near the shore, and, in most cases, never move far from the part of the coast where they are born. They must have shallow water, and the food which is to be found there. Some are tied to their little field of rocks; just as, among the fresh-water fish, some cannot live in a strange river, though the conditions may appear exactly similar."

"Then, in the second place, there are the fish like the flying-fish, sun-fish, and sword-fish, that live near the surface of the deep sea—a group of great interest." "Yes," said Mr. Gray, "I have stood for hours at the bows of the ship to watch the graceful flight of the flying-fish. They are lovers of the ocean, and I never hear of them without thinking of the eternal freshness and purity of the open sea!"

"I think of their range, too!" I said, "so different from the shore-fish tethered to reef or shoal! The common flying-fish ranges round the world!" "Ah!" cried Mr. Gray, "I feel the charm! We are all sea rovers, we English; sea-lovers at the bottom of our hearts!"

"Well," I continued, "if you will pass next in imagination to the depths of these ocean-wastes, you will find fish that are not less interesting. In depths to which light never penetrates, and where storms are never felt, a whole world of creatures lives and moves and has its being. These fish, also, may have a wide range; for the conditions of life at these great depths must be similar all over the world of waters."

"Can they see at all?" asked Mr. Gray. "Some," I replied, "at the greatest depths, are blind; having only rudimentary eyes. But most can see by the help of phosphorescence produced by their own bodies. The fish which are not thus equipped are provided with delicate feelers for groping their way in the utter darkness. As we rise to water of more moderate depth, we find fish with large eyes, capable of gathering together the few rays of light. The sunrays may reach down to a depth of 600 yards. As we go nearer to the surface than this, the eyes become smaller."

"Why don't they come to the surface sometimes?" asked Mr. Gray. "Because," I replied, "at these depths the pressure is enormous, and the fish, being fitted to resist this pressure, are unfit for surface waters. When brought up by a deep-sea dredge, they look soft and flabby, with scales standing out at right angles to the body, and eyes starting from their sockets. In their native depths, their bodies are, no doubt, firm and compact."

"I suppose that they prey on one another down there, just as on the surface," said Mr. Gray. "Yes," I replied, "one black fish of prey that was dragged up from a depth of two miles was found to contain, in a huge distended stomach, a fish twice as big as itself. Opportunities of feeding in these dim regions are, no doubt, infrequent; and so the fish lays in a store when it can."

"But they can't all live on one another!" said Mr. Gray. "There are deep-sea plants for food," I replied, "and crustaceans, and other small creatures. All the rivers of the world, too, are washing food into the ocean, and, though most of this food is eaten by the shore fish, some of it must reach the ocean-depths. Think, too, of the refuse from ten thousand ships!" "It is a pleasure," said Mr. Gray, "to know that there is no fear of man polluting the sea with his garbage."

"I can see, now," he added, "why the surface fish cannot go to the depths. They could not live under that great pressure." "No," I replied, "they could not live. Most fish sink far enough to escape storm and to get the temperature that they like best; but, to meet these needs, a short descent is sufficient."

"I suppose," said Mr. Gray, "that many kinds of fish have had to make way for superior kinds?" "Yes," I replied, "many kinds. Already, a thousand kinds of fish that have ceased to exist have been found in fossil form. We can trace in these books of stone

AUSTRALIAN SALMON.—*D* F, BACK FIN; *C* F, TAIL FIN; *A* F, ANAL FIN; *P* F, BREAST FIN; *V* F, BELLY FIN.

the rise and fall of fish types almost as clearly as we can read the rise and fall of empires in the pages of Gibbon."

"And the causes of the fall of these fish types—can they also be read?" asked Mr. Gray. "To a large extent," I replied. "The early fish had very imperfect skeletons of gristle, and had to protect themselves by a heavy armour of scales and bony plates—a kind of chain-mail, reminding one of the cumbersome body-armour worn by mediæval knights. In fishes of more modern type, the armour is replaced by light scales, and instead of a soft frame-work of gristle, we have a firm backbone."

"Fish, also," I continued, "that were adapted for special food have often died out through some accident which made that food scarce. The fish that have kept their ground best are those that have a wide range of food." "Just as," said Mr. Gray, "in the case of the birds, the sparrow flourishes because it can eat almost anything."

"Moderate size, too," I added, "has something to do with success. Many large, unwieldy fish have died out." "Ah!" cried Mr. Gray, "the dragons of the prime that tare each other in their slime! Judging from the models in museums of these extinct monsters, animals are becoming more graceful of form." "Yes," I replied, "you will see that clearly if you compare any of the extinct fishes with, say, the pilchard or the mackerel, or any of the more modern fish."

"As to the backbone," continued Mr. Gray, "I understood that all fish belonged to the order of animals that have a backbone." "So they do," I said, "but in the earliest fish the backbone is rep-resented only by a long cord of gelatine—the notochord (see fig. A). At a stage higher, a series of rings of gristle takes the place of this cord, and it is only in the advanced fish that we have the

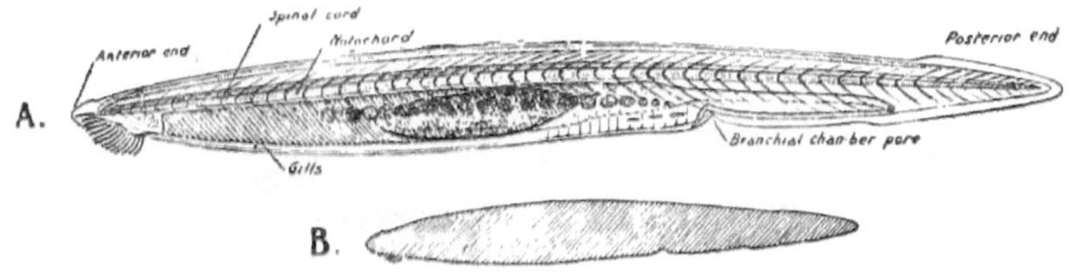

THE LANCELET.

long vertebral column which we call the backbone. Even in an advanced fish we can see the primitive form reproduced in the first stages of its growth today; and much of modern science, indeed, has been built up from the study of the early stages which animals pass through today. Even after birth there is often an entire difference between the young and the adult form. In this way history unrolls itself before our eyes."

"Another volume in the great book of history!" cried Mr. Gray. "It makes one think more highly of himself to see how the Creator takes man into His confidence in thus unveiling His plans. We have to become fellow-workers with Him, and so the Infinite Wisdom has given to us the key to the Past that we may have some guidance for the Future."

CHAPTER XXXIV

Fish

PART II

"I am much struck," said Mr. Gray, "with the beautiful adaptation of the organs of animals to their surroundings. Think of a fish breathing quite comfortably at a depth of two or three miles!" "Yes," I replied, "these adaptations are so common in Nature that one often ceases to wonder. Take the case of the lung-fish, which is found in certain rivers of Queensland. The air-bladder has been so modified that it can be used as a lung."

"The lung-fish gets its air through gills in the ordinary way, but, in consequence of the water being thick with mud, it has to rise now and then to the surface to breathe through this lung." "I have often," said Mr. Gray, "seen goldfish in an overcrowded bowl rise to the surface and try to gulp down air. The poor fish seemed to be distressed." "So they were," I replied, "and in that attempt to get oxygen direct from the air we have probably the beginning of the process which has given to this Queensland fish its lung-like air-bladder."

"What do you mean by the air-bladder?" asked Mr. Gray. "You may have seen it," I replied, "if you have ever opened a fish; the bag with silvery walls that collapse if you prick the bladder and let out the gas. The fish can fill or empty this at pleasure, and

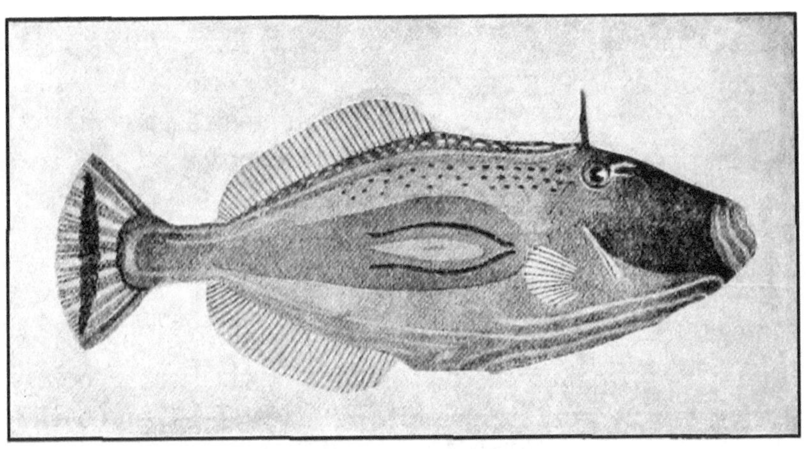

LEATHER JACKET (M'COY).

so rise or sink in the water. It is in this way that it sinks out of reach of a storm, or to get the temperature that it needs."

"You have not yet spoken of a fish's greatest charm," said Mr. Gray; "its beauty of colour. I think that no animal is more beautiful than a fish just caught. I have seen the pilchard fisher emptying his net into the boat, and can never forget the leaping, living silver." "Think, too," I said, "of the beautiful bright streakings in some of our leather-jackets, and of the lovely iridescent hues that play on the sides of our mackerel. There is the vivid green stranger, too, that is sometimes caught in Port Phillip, and a score of others. Excitement of any kind always brightens the colours of a fish, and this, no doubt, is why the colours of a dying fish are so brilliant." "Yes," said Mr. Gray, "the Roman epicure would have his red mullet brought to the table alive, so that he might watch the changing hues that mark the death-struggle."

"I suppose," continued Mr. Gray, "that with fish, as with birds, colour has always some purpose to serve in the animal's life?" "Yes," I said; "with many fish, as with many birds, the colour

HORSE MACKEREL (M'Coy).

becomes more brilliant and the spots more ornamental on the approach of the season of courtship. In both cases, also, the colour is generally protective. The pike, for example, has a dark back and a silver under-surface. Looked at from above, the fish is lost in the dark tints of the water; seen from below, the silver of the under-surface blends with the white light of the sky."

"I have noticed the same thing," said Mr. Gray, "in the case of the pilchard that boys fish for on our wharves. Seen from above, the shoals are dull-coloured, and invite notice only by an occasional gleam of silver from the under-surface." "The fish in this way," I replied, "is hidden from the sea-tern which hovers above, and from the barracouta that watches from below. Then there is the flathead, dark of colour when taken from a rocky bottom, and light of colour when taken from a sandy bottom."

Some fishes go still further, and are able to change colour to match their surroundings. The mechanism by which this is done is of great interest. In some of the sea creatures which are closely related to the fishes, the process can be studied more easily than in the fishes themselves. There is a shrimp,

Skipjack Pike (M'Coy).

for example, which can change quickly from the pale brown colour which protects it among rocks to the dark green which hides it when resting among weeds.

The colour-fluid, say green, is contained in little circular bags, which the shrimp is able to flatten out or contract at pleasure. When the bags are flattened, the colour-fluid spreads, and conceals the usual brown colour of the shrimp. Then there is a cuttle-fish which is provided with blue, yellow, and red colour-cells, and which changes hue according to the cells which it flattens. This creature can excite the colour-cells in such rapid succession that it seems to be many-coloured. It is in much the same way that fishes and frogs change colour, though, in most cases, the changes are more gradual.

"I suppose," said Mr. Gray, "that the form of a fish as well as its colour is sometimes adapted for protection?" "Yes," I replied, "there is a striking example in one of the 'sea-horses.' You know the pipe-fish with the horse-like head which is often found among the weedy reefs in Port Phillip? That is the short-snouted sea-horse. Well, there is another member of the family found in Australian waters which has many weed-like appendages

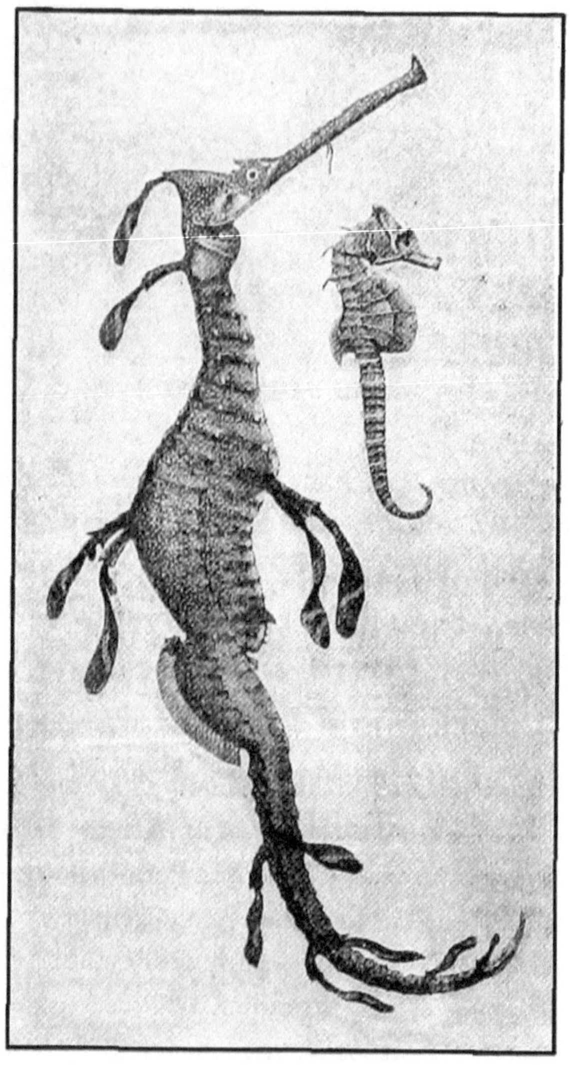

LEAFY SEA-DRAGON; SHORT-SNOUTED SEA HORSE.

streaming from its body, and giving it a remarkable resem-
blance to the seaweeds among which it lives. Especially is this
so, when the sea-horse moors itself by its tail, and then faces
the tide-current. The weed-like appendages of the fish and the

true weeds stream back in the same direction; and the sea-horse is lost to the eye."

"Are the eggs also protected by colour?" asked Mr. Gray. "In a few cases," I replied, "but, in most cases, the fish trusts rather to the great number of eggs laid than to any device for hiding them. The sharks and rays form an exception. These fish lay only a few large eggs, but they hide them carefully. You may sometimes find a wisp of seaweed moored to a stone and twisted up. If you untwine the coil, you may find a shark's egg." "I've often seen the eggs when washed ashore," said Mr. Gray.

"Some fish," I continued, "go up rivers to lay their eggs; others attach the eggs in masses to stones at the sea bottom; and others, again, lay their eggs on the surface of the sea. The eggs in this last case are exposed to many dangers. Adverse winds or currents may throw them on the beach; a change of temperature may kill them, and many fish eat them in great numbers. That the eggs, however, are not laid in a chance, purposeless way we can see from the habits of the English plaice."

The life-history of the plaice has been studied very carefully, and the facts ascertained may help to give us the key to some puzzling movements of our Australian fish. The plaice lays its eggs in the German Ocean to the east of Scotland. Borne slowly southward and landward by the prevailing currents, the eggs reach the coast when the young are hatching out. Hugging the coastline, the young fish get the food and temperature that they need. They move slowly northwards till they have reached full size, when they go out to sea to breed in their turn.

With this life-cycle may be compared the case of the herring which frequents the estuary of the Hawkesbury River in New South Wales. This fish goes to sea and lays its eggs so that the currents may bring them to the mouth of the river. The young swim upstream, and get the food and temperature that they require.

We do not yet know enough about our Australian fish to give their life-stories with confidence, and there is much work of great interest to be done in this field of science.

CHAPTER XXXV
The Frog

We had been watching the development of the jelly-like mass of frogs' eggs which we had brought from the pond. We had seen the round egg lengthen, and the black speck in it grow into a head and tail. One morning we found that the prisoner had pushed his way through the egg-skin into the water.

In this larval stage the frog was exactly like a fish at the same stage, even to the gills. Breathing took place, as in the fish larva, by gill-fringes placed, at first, outside of the head. When these external fringes disappeared, inside gills took their place, as in a full-grown fish. "Taddy," as Mr. Gray's little girl called him, was fond of attaching himself by his disc-like sucker-mouth to a water-weed, just as the young of certain fish fasten on to the sides of the glass vessel in which they are hatched.

So far, there had been no limbs, but now there appeared two buds where the hind legs were to come. As soon as these legs began to grow, the tail began to waste away. Meantime, buds had appeared which marked the beginning of the fore-legs. As the legs became perfect, and the creature passed from tadpole into frog, the tail diminished and finally disappeared.

Meantime, a large wide mouth had taken the place of the disc-sucker, prominent eyes had appeared, and the creature had to rise to the surface now and then to fill its new-grown

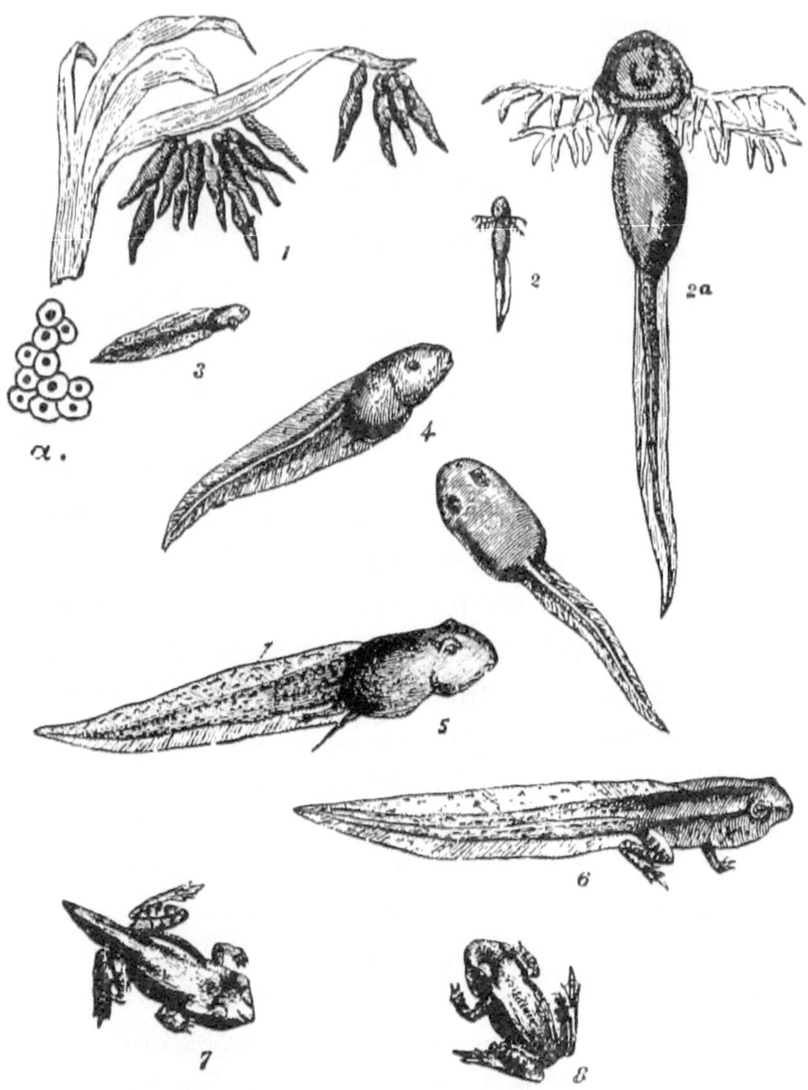

LIFE-STAGES OF FROG—NEWLY HATCHED TADPOLES TO THE YOUNG:
A, EGGS; 1, TADPOLE JUST HATCHED; 2, TADPOLE WITH EXTERNAL
GILLS; 2A, FIG. 2 MAGNIFIED; 3, SIDE VIEW OF FIG. 2; 4, TADPOLE WITH
INTERNAL GILLS; 5, TADPOLE WITH LONG HIND LEGS; 6, TADPOLE DURING
THE METAMORPHOSIS; 7, YOUNG FROG WITH TAIL ONLY PARTIALLY
ABSORBED; 8, ADULT. (AFTER PARKER AND HASWELL, 1 TO 8.)

lungs. It had passed from the tadpole to the frog; from a fish to an amphibian; from a plant-eater to a flesh-eater; from a water animal to a land animal!

"It looks," said Mr. Gray, as we walked towards the pond, "as if the progress of life were from water to land. The mosquito, when perfect, leaves the water, and so with the dragon-fly and the May-fly. Who could guess, in watching these flies, that they had ever been dwellers in water!"

"Some of the animals," I replied, "that have come out of the water still show signs of the earlier stage. The newt, for example, looks like a tadpole that has walked ashore. In Mexico there is found a newt-like creature which can continue its tadpole-life in the water, or take to a land-life, according to circumstances. If placed in a pond which shows signs of drying up, its gills shrink, and it gradually becomes an air-breathing creature, able to live ashore. Should the water supply continue abundant, it passes its whole life in the water."

"How do you explain the fact," asked Mr. Gray, "that a bird's egg produces young like the parents, while the eggs of moths, of fishes, and of frogs produce young quite unlike the mother?" "The bird's egg," I replied, "contains not only the bird-germ but a large supply of food for the growing bird. The growth of the chick is thus carried forward a long way while the bird is still in the egg. The small egg of a frog, on the other hand, contains just enough food to launch the young creature into life. Hence it has to grow up to the stage of the parent by its own efforts—that is to say, has to make its own living from the first. The simple, temporary mouth, gills, and tail are to enable it, at once, to feed and move about actively."

Some frogs flopped into the water as we came up to the

pond, and we admired the graceful ease of their swimming as they disappeared. Presently a frog came to the surface, gay in his summer dress of green and gold.

"What a beautiful creature!" cried Mr. Gray. "I suppose that the green colour is meant to match the water-weeds?" "Yes," I replied, "the power of this green frog in changing colour is remarkable. During a minute's absence of an artist who was engaged in drawing one of these frogs, the creature disappeared. A long search led to the runaway being found under the artist's chair. The frog had taken the colour of the floor! The frog needs this protection, for it has many enemies. Night-herons and waders of that class are fond of frogs; and snakes consume large numbers. That the frog fears the snake is plain from the distress shown when a stick is made to wriggle in snake-fashion within sight of a frog."

"What does it live on?" asked Mr. Gray. "On flies, beetles, grubs, slugs, and snails," I replied. "Many a mosquito leaves the pond only to be snapped up by the frogs that sit expectant on the bank. A pet frog has been seen to catch fifty mosquitoes in a minute."

The tongue of the frog is a remarkable organ. It has its root in the front of the mouth, and points backward into the throat. This enables it to throw out the full length of the tongue at a passing insect. Few observers are quick enough of eye to see the lightning flick with which the fly is caught and thrown back into the mouth. The tongue-tip is as sticky as bird-lime, so that by the slightest touch the fly is captured.

The fondness of the frog for slugs, grubs, and snails makes it useful in a garden. It feeds at night—the time when these pests are abroad. With a little kindness it may be made to return from the pond to the garden, year after year. "The same frog!" cried Mr. Gray. "Yes," I replied, "I know of a pet frog which was adorned with a red cord. It went away to the pond at breeding time, and it was absent also in the time of the winter sleep, but it always returned to the garden, wearing the faded cord."

A second frog came to the surface and began to take in the air in mouthfuls. A frog, though one of the animals with a backbone, has no ribs. Hence it cannot breathe as we do. It increases the body-cavity by lowering the skin under the chin while keeping the mouth shut, and this leads to air entering through the nostrils. Hence a frog dies if the mouth be kept forcibly open.

"How is it," asked Mr. Gray, "that a creature with such imperfect lungs can keep under water so long?" "Because," I replied, "it is a skin-breather as well as a lung-breather. So long as the skin is moist the frog is comfortable. This is why the frogs found in a garden are generally hidden away from the sun, and why they are happy on rainy days and dewy nights. The frogs that came down in showers, according to old journals, were, no doubt, bands of frogs taking advantage of a rainy day to travel." "It is curious to find," said Mr. Gray, "that even Aristotle was led astray on this point. He speaks of such frogs as creatures 'sent by Jupiter.'"

"How do they get on when water fails for years together?" asked Mr. Gray. "They are able," I replied, "to sleep through dry times, just as they are able to sleep through winter. In Central Australia, there is a frog which takes in a great store of water before a dry period. It then buries itself in the mud, and sleeps till the rain comes. When pressed by thirst, the natives search for this frog, and make use of its store."

As we walked away, the evening chorus of the frogs was beginning. *Krek, krek, krek* seemed to come to our ears from all sides, varied by an occasional *clunk*. The clunk of the frog is sometimes mistaken for the clink of the cattle-bell, when farmers, in the dusk, are seeking for their cows or horses. Now came a deeper, hoarser croak from an older frog. The cry of the frog is wonderfully varied, even among frogs of the same kind.

"No doubt," remarked Mr. Gray, "that is why the sound is rendered so differently by authors from Aristophanes downwards."

"In the days before swamps were drained," I continued, "many parts of Europe must have resounded with the noise of frogs in the breeding season." "It was the custom," said Mr. Gray, "in the castles of the French nobility, for the servants to lash the water in the ditches and moats every morning, so that my lord and lady might not be disturbed by the frogs." "Of course," I went on, "some frogs have pleasant voices. In the English fen-counties one frog is called the Cambridgeshire nightingale. That may be sarcasm, but Wallace speaks of the note of an American frog as an agreeable whistle, and Darwin tells us of a certain tree-frog that has a pleasing chirp."

Some of our Australian frogs seem to have the power of mimicking the sounds of other animals. One was heard in Queensland that gave the cry of the silver gull. This may, of course, have been a chance likeness and not a deliberate imitation; but it was close enough to deceive a practised ear. Other observers have heard or imagined a certain harmony in the varied notes uttered by frogs of different ages. Was the harmony intended?

We shall know more about this and other points when people understand that the old prejudices against the frog are unfounded. These prejudices arose at a time when frogs and toads were thought to be venomous. It was the toad that swelters venom under stones that the witches in Macbeth threw first into the charmed pot. For ages the mild toad has turned its beautiful eye on a cruel world!

"Shakespeare," said Mr. Gray, "has done justice to the toad's eye, at all events.

> *Sweet are the uses of adversity*
> *Which, like the toad, ugly and venomous,*
> *Wears yet a precious jewel in the head."*

CHAPTER XXXVI
Snakes and Lizards

To complete our study of animal types from earth-worm to bird, it was needful to turn now to the reptiles, and I arranged a visit to the Zoological Gardens.

The trees and bushes of the Gardens were alive with the songs and cries of birds on this fine summer morning. All the more striking was the silence and deadness of the reptile house. Even the land-turtles, that were moving laboriously in the peacocks' park across the way, were lively in comparison with the snakes and lizards.

"No wonder," said Mr. Gray, "that these creatures feed rarely: there can be little waste of force in their lives. One can readily believe that a water-snake can live for a year on two or three frogs." "No wonder, too," I added, "that they can sleep comfortably through the winter or a time of drought."

"I suppose," said Mr. Gray, as we looked at the water-tanks which are provided in all the cages, "that snakes must have water?" "Yes," I said, "snakes are fond of water, and drink a great deal. Their fondness for the frog too, as an article of food, points to their close relationship with the creatures of the pond and river. So, also, does their ability to stay under water for a long time. Fishers in our rivers occasionally see a snake coiled up on the sand of the river bottom. All snakes, too, swim quickly and gracefully." "You are speaking," said Mr. Gray, "of land-snakes. I suppose there are also sea-snakes?" "Yes," I replied, "in the tropical seas of Australia there are several kinds."

We were now standing opposite to the den of the tiger-snakes. One of them was having a morning bath, only the head appearing above the side of the tank. Two live frogs, beside the tank, were quietly awaiting the pleasure of the snakes. Their first paroxysms of fear may have exhausted them, and they were quite still, save for the light rise and fall of the neck-skin as they breathed.

The snake in the tank now drew its length slowly out of the water, and there was a coppery gleam from the sides and from the bands on the back. In another tiger-snake, which lay inert beside the tank, the ground colour was a light brown. Still another was dark brown. On one the dark bands were clearly marked; on another the bands could hardly be seen.

"The colour-marks are puzzling," said Mr. Gray, "but one could guess from the high-bred look of this snake that it is a fighter." "Yes," I said, "it is a creature of high courage, and its venom is the deadliest possessed by any of our snakes. One would rather study this snake behind glass than in the open field. But, like the rest, it does not attack unless provoked."

"How is it," asked Mr. Gray, "that in some cases of snake-bite the cure seems to be easy, and in others the same remedies appear to have much less effect?" "The strength of the venom," I replied, "varies with the condition of the snake. In cold weather a snake is almost lifeless; life runs low, also, when it is casting its skin. The poison-glands, too, may have been emptied by previous bites."

Here there was a movement in the next cage, where a black

snake was slowly moving forward from the rockery at the rear. As it crept down to the sandy level, the forked tongue was shot out to explore the way. Nothing is more characteristic of snakes than this quivering tongue, thrust out like the antennæ of an insect to feel the object in front.

"What!" cried Mr. Gray, "then that is not the sting of the creature?" "No," I replied, "but most people, and even many of those who have lived among snakes all their lives, still believe that the forked tongue is the sting. If people living in the country would only take the pains to read a little about snakes, they would be largely relieved from the fear that haunts many of them. The man who understands snakes has little fear. A bush-worker has been known to chop off a finger when bitten by a snake that was quite harmless. Even doctors occasionally treat patients for bites from non-venomous snakes. It is probably safe to say that snakes do less harm than does the ignorant fear of them."

"Then," said Mr. Gray, "the poison is in the teeth?" "Yes," I replied, "the fangs are modified teeth, and are so well hidden away in the mouth that they are never seen by the ordinary observer."

The black snake had now crept down to the front of the cage. This, also, is a poisonous snake, but not so pugnacious as the tiger-snake. The reptile was shedding its skin piecemeal; and it had the sluggish, untidy look of a snake in bad health. Presently another black snake, which had finished its spring slough, came gliding down with slow but graceful curves. The black of the back was fresh and handsome, and the row of red spots where back and belly met suggested the red under-surface which we could not see.

Here a voice from behind us said—"I took one of these creatures one day for a black stick, and was nearly picking it up!"

We did not see the poisonous brown snake, which is so common, nor did we see the venomous copper-head, nor the dangerous death-adder.

"Does the venom," asked Mr. Gray, "serve any other purpose besides killing the victim?" "It is believed by some," I replied, "that the poison assists digestion. It is certain that snakes have great confidence in their digestive powers. When two snakes seize the same mouse, neither will let go, and the larger snake tries to swallow its rival as well as the mouse. In such a case the larger snake has been known to digest the smaller!"

"The mouth of a snake does not seem large enough for such a feat," said Mr. Gray. "No," I replied, "but the bones of the head are so loosely knit that the jaws can be opened widely; also, there

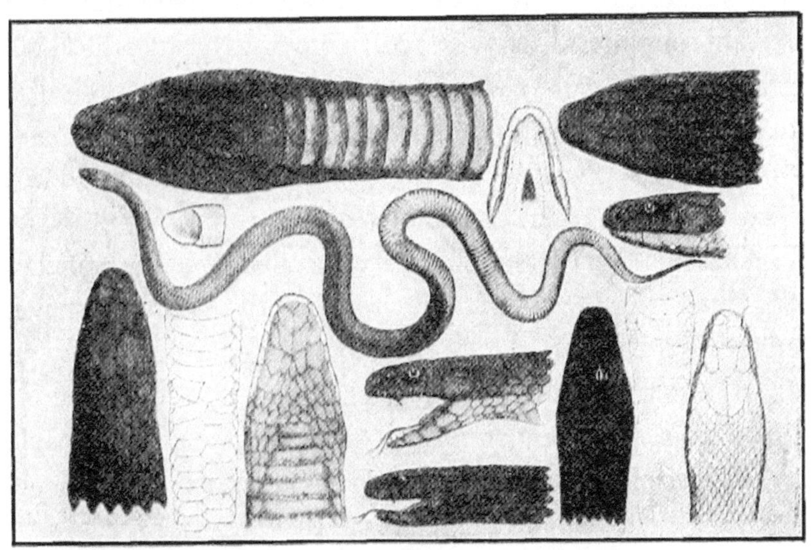

Common Brown Snake; head and scales shown in different positions (M'Coy).

is no breast-bone, and so the ribs have very free play. In this way, the snake is able to draw itself over an animal. One has been known, in this collection, to swallow its blanket, though it had the good sense to disgorge it after three weeks' trial."

"I suppose," said Mr. Gray, "that it is this free play of the ribs that enables snakes to move so easily? It seems to me remarkable that a creature which has no legs, nor wings, nor fins, should be able to move so freely. I have seen a black snake make for cover so quickly that the eye could hardly follow its movements." "Yes," I replied, "snakes, when pressed by danger, can show amazing activity. Huxley said that there was no limit to their movement except flying. A snake has many belly-plates, and each pair of ribs is attached to one of these. As each plate has a free edge pointing backwards, the animal is able, in pushing itself forward, to make use of the slightest projection in the ground. This is why snakes cannot move over a glass sheet. There must be a certain roughness in the surface. In moving through thick, tall grass, again, a snake seems to progress by movements similar to those that it uses in swimming."

I had been speaking of ground-snakes, and I now led Mr. Gray to the den of the diamond snake. This handsome snake, which is found in Eastern Victoria, was coiled about the branches of a dead tree. We noticed the great length of the tree-snake, enabling it to pass from branch to branch, even when wide apart; also the slender form, which assists it in its search for birds' eggs and their young. The belly, too, seemed to be able to shape itself to the rounded surface of a branch.

Hanging from one of the limbs of the tree was the cast skin of this snake. It had been cast whole, and showed clearly the pattern of the scales. The scales do not overlap, nor are they separable as in the case of fish-scales. The covering of the eye is shed with the rest of the skin. "Ah!" said Mr. Gray, "that explains the fixed, cold stare of the eyes. A snake, then, looks through a kind of window?" "Yes," I replied, "a window which is renewed once in every four months. It is a window without blinds. You notice that there are no eyelids, and that a snake cannot wink."

We passed now to the den of the carpet snake—a tree-snake which is found all over Australia. This creature is closely related to the diamond snake, but is a much larger member of the family. The great snake was coiled about the top limbs of its tree, with the head resting comfortably on the top coil, and its mild, fixed eye looking towards the peacocks' park, where two male birds were displaying their tails. "It looks harmless!" said Mr. Gray. "It is harmless," I replied, "and that is fortunate, because its colour and carpet-pattern conceal it so thoroughly in its forest haunts that travellers sometimes brush against it before they notice it. It kills its victim by crushing it in its folds, but it is not large enough to be dangerous to man." "Then it is a kind of python?" said Mr. Gray. "Yes," I replied, "it belongs to the same family as the boa constrictor. A point of great interest in the carpet snake is that it has the rudiments of hind legs."

Some of the peacocks were now fighting, and the air was full of their harsh cries, but the mild, steady eye of the carpet snake showed no sign. We could well believe that three or four meals a year are sufficient for this animal. As the day became warmer, there was more movement among the snakes. These animals must have heat; and, indeed, they refuse to eat except in warm weather.

We passed now to the den given up to lizards. One of them

White-streaked Earless Lizard; lowest figure, a young lizard (M'Coy).

was moving slowly forward, with forked tongue investigating the way.

"Why, this is a snake with legs," cried Mr. Gray. "Yes," I said, "the lizard has much in common with the snake; but there are differences. Do you notice that the lizard can wink, and that the eye is more friendly and human-looking than the snake's eye? Notice, too, the large ear-opening in the lizard; this is concealed in a snake. The lizard, again, has not the free play of jaw that the snake has."

"I have no feeling against the small lizards," said Mr. Gray. "I think that the common lizard is a pleasing little creature— a sun-lover which one associates with still, hot days." "Yes," I replied, "they feed mostly by night, and only come out to bask when the sun is high. They become lively only towards evening."

One of the best known of the lizards is often called the "bloodsucker," a very unsuitable name, since this small lizard is harmless; indeed it may be kept as a pet, and fed on flies. It may be seen on the stems of the ti-trees that border the coast

BLOOD-SUCKERS (M'COY).

line. Quite different in habit is the white-streaked earless lizard that keeps to the ground.

"Have the lizards any means of protecting themselves?" asked Mr. Gray. "I know, of course, that many of them are wonderfully hidden by their colours." "The lizard has the power," I replied, "of leaving the tail in the jaws of the attacking animal. It throws up the tail as if inviting the enemy to seize it. A new tail grows rapidly, and it is of interest to note that the new tail is often not quite similar to the old one, but suggests rather some ancestral form. It may be a 'throwback,' such as we see sometimes in advanced flowers which have suffered some check to their growth."

We then spent some time with those larger lizards called the agamoids, popularly called iguanas or blood-suckers. The agamoid, in its favourite pose, raises itself on its fore-feet in a listening attitude. Posed thus, it shows clearly the loose folds of skin that mark the neck like swollen veins. All the time that we remained it kept up this attitude, as if turned to stone. "It has quiet nerves," said Mr. Gray.

Still more rigid, if possible, was the alligator in a neighbouring den. It looked—this huge relation of the lizards—as if it had not moved for days. "Here," said Mr. Gray, laughing, "is a severe test for your rule that we should have sympathy for everything that has life." I did not contradict him, and, as we moved away, a sudden burst of song from a reed-ringed pond gave to us something more agreeable to talk about. It was the loud, rich, canary-like warble of the reed-warbler.

As we walked forward to look for the singer, I said—"Well, Mr. Gray, we end our Nature study as we began it—with the birds."

CHAPTER XXXVII
Method in Nature Study

The wise man is he who has observed much and reflected much. Experience is not enough—there must be added reflection. The ideal nature student is he who, after a day's holiday in the fields, reflects upon the meaning of what he has seen, and who seeks then to enrich his own thought by adding that of the best authorities on the subject. Should he add an hour's reading in White of Selborne, or Isaak Walton, or John Burroughs, and finish the day with a poem of Wordsworth, or of some other of the poets of outdoor life, he will have brought his day's study of Nature to its true flower. The fact, the meaning of the fact, and the wonder and beauty of the fact—these are the three elements in every full observation of Nature.

The student must get rid of the idea that all has been observed that is worth observing. Book knowledge, if it begets this attitude towards Nature, is a hindrance rather than a help. No doubt you will at times have the disappointment of finding that an observation, which was a discovery for you, has already been recorded. But what of that? You have had the pleasure of discovery for yourself, or, as Kepler so finely put it, of "thinking God's thoughts over again." Further, you are, in this way, becoming a trained observer, with unlimited opportunity in this new land for new work.

The records of observations given in books are often misleading to the beginner. Facts, gathered together in the course of years, may be thrown together as elements in a continuous story. This complete presentation is often necessary, but it is at first disheartening to find that Nature does not tell her story in this easy, continuous way. The fact noticed today may be meaningless until another fact is noted, months or years afterwards. In such cases, a guess at the meaning of the fact is often useful. Such a guess encourages the habit of thinking about the facts, and does much to awaken interest. An illustration may serve to make this clear.

Today, as I passed the nest of ants in the garden-path, I noticed that an ant had just left the nest, carrying something black. Now, the stones carried out of this nest by the ant-engineers are always white or yellow, and so my curiosity was aroused.

On bending over the ant, I could see, with the help of my pocket-lens, that it was carrying another ant, which was held firmly by the waist. The ant thus borne was alive and was hindering progress by clinging to the path. What could it mean? Ah! I have it: the second ant is sick. I can see that the body has been beaten in. Can there have been a fight in the nest? The ants are great fighters. Or, perhaps, a stone has fallen on the poor creature when it was helping to make a new "drive." This solution satisfies me, for the strong ant does not seem to be angry with the weak one, only anxious to remove from the nest a member who is hopelessly injured. I follow the sad journey of the two until the sick ant is set down behind a stone. The bearer departs without ceremony, and runs quickly back to the nest. The sick ant slowly follows.

The way is long, but the ant is plucky, and has accomplished half the distance when a gust of wind blows it off the track, and I lose sight of it.

A few minutes after, while watching the ants at the nest-door, I saw an ant emerge from the nest bearing an ant "egg." Strange! There was no reason why a baby should be brought to the surface at this time. Looking more closely, I thrilled with pleasure on recognizing the sick ant. The maimed body was unmistakable. What can it be doing? Have its sufferings made it light-headed, and has it seized the "egg" in delirium? My speculations were stopped by another gust of wind which blew ant and "egg" out of the field of vision.

Two minutes after I saw the sick ant coming up the hill empty-jawed. It entered the nest. In five minutes it was brought out again by a strong ant and laid on the ground—this time at a point not far from the hole. I could not tell whether the bearer was the same; if so, she acted as one who did not want another long journey for nothing. Once more the injured ant crawled back into the nest, and a third time she was carried forth and deposited at the foot of the hill. Then I had to stop my observation.

I have told you what I saw. The facts are certain: my guesses about the facts may be wrong. When I turn to Lubbock's notes on ants, I may find the incident otherwise explained. That matters little: I have had a pleasant hour in trying to read Nature's book, and my interest in ant-life has been deepened.

A mistake often made by the young Nature student is to suppose that it is necessary to go far afield in order to make serious observations. Now, while formal excursions are of high importance, and especially to the beginner, the mature naturalist knows that he has learnt more from chance observations made in his own house and garden, and on his necessary daily walks, than he has learned from all his field-work.

It must be noted, however, that the ripe naturalist has, in most cases, acquired this habit of daily skilled observation through the help of his seniors in the course of organized field-work, and the importance of such work, under good guidance, to the beginner cannot be too strongly urged.

Hardships must sometimes be faced if good work is to be done. The observer who is on the track of something new becomes oblivious to the flight of time and to the presence of many discomforts. When Dr. J. H. Fabre was investigating the power of the mason-bee to return to its nest from a strange and distant point, he found it necessary to mark each bee. In marking 30 bees, he received many stings, but he tells us that in the ardour of research he hardly noticed these. Such an observer thinks nothing of sitting up all night to watch the spinning of a cocoon or the bursting of a pupa.

The observations of others must be verified before they become really our own. It was the habit of verifying all the facts which he taught which, more than anything else, gave to Huxley's teaching its force and reality.

The occasion for observation must often be made by the student. Life is too short to wait, in every case, for Nature's chance revelations. An excellent illustration is given in Dr. Fabre's experiment, already alluded to. The bees had their nests in the eaves of Dr. Fabre's house. Having captured 30 of them, he travelled to a town some miles off—a place which was entirely strange to the bees. Having marked them, he set them free, and noted how they circled round and finally flew off. The time of release was carefully noted. Meantime his daughter was stationed at the house to note the time of the return of each marked bee that found its way home. Here, then, in a nutshell, is the experimental method applied to questions in natural history.

It is of great importance that the progress of development from the egg to the perfect animal should be studied at home or in the school; and a few hints are appended that may be of use to the beginner.

APPARATUS REQUIRED IN HOME OR SCHOOL FOR THE OBSERVATION OF DEVELOPMENT IN INSECTS, &c.

Insects.—Place the egg or caterpillar in a well-ventilated box. Supply the caterpillar with food of the same kind that it was found upon—if from a gum-tree, gum-tree leaves; if from an acacia, acacia leaves. A good house can be made by taking out the face of an old candle-box, and substituting glass. Take out also a portion of the sides, and replace with fine netting. As some insects pupate in the ground, provide the caterpillar with 3 inches of fine dry earth. Upon this place a low, flat bottle of water, and in this set a small leafy branch of the natural food, taking care to pack the mouth of the bottle loosely with cotton-wool, to prevent the insect from being drowned. A few days after a caterpillar has entered the earth it may be carefully dug up, and the pupa examined.

Mosquitoes, in their larval stage—little, brown, wriggling creatures—can be found in any stagnant water. These should be placed in an open glass bowl filled with the water in which the larvæ were found. Place in the bowl, also, a small growing water-weed, to help to keep the water well aired. From air, water, and weed the larvæ will get food. A few pieces of old stick, covered with pond slime, will also be useful in furnishing food. As the dragon-fly larva preys on the mosquito larva, these should be kept in separate bowls.

Freshwater snails and water-beetles are friendly, and may be kept in a bowl of pond-water, furnished in the same way as for

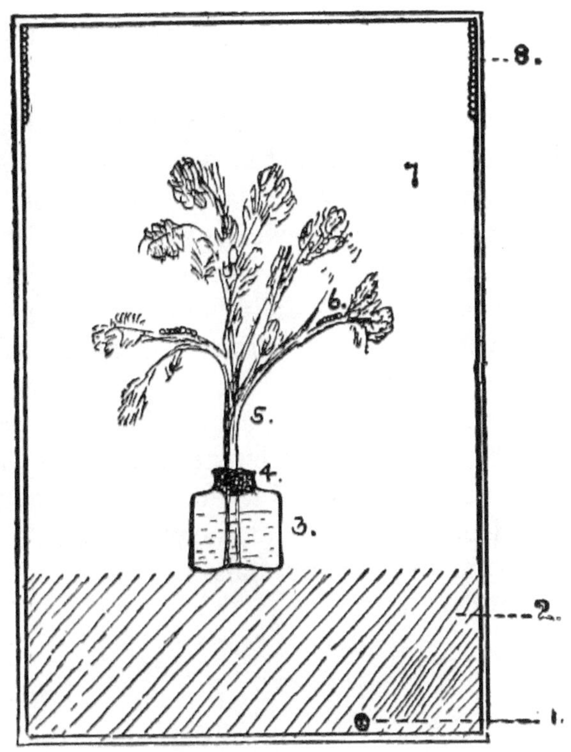

REARING-BOX FOR MOTHS.—1, GROUND-BORER AT REST IN PUPA-CASE; 2, PULVERISED EARTH, 3 IN. DEEP; 3, TUMBLER TO PREVENT GRUB'S STOPPER; 5, FOOD BRANCH; 6, CATERPILLAR FEEDING; 7, GLASS FACE; 8, VENTILATION NETTING

mosquito larvæ.

Freshwater fish, like perch, gold-fish, carp, should be kept in a vessel open at the top, but provided with cloth flaps all round the sides, to keep out an excess of light. This is Nature's method in pool or river. Water-plants, found in the creek from which the fish was taken, must be kept growing. An aquarium without water-weeds is always a failure. Without them, the fish are often at the surface, gasping for air. Supply occasionally a few insects as food.

Frog.—Pond water and growing water-plants furnish food

until the tadpole becomes a frog, when insect food must be supplied.

Lower forms of sea-life.—A simple aquarium for lower forms of sea-life may be formed as follows: Take a glass dish about the size of a wash-hand basin; place on the bottom sand and a few stones covered with sea-weed growth. Fill with sea water, and then put in the specimens which are to be kept. Complete aëration can be secured by filling and emptying a syringe of the water several times a day, injecting sharply at a distance of, say, six inches from the surface.[13] This prevents stagnation, and brings the water as nearly as possible to the condition of sea water which is freshened by the waves. The water-plants take up the carbonic acid which is given off by the water-animals; and, on the other hand, the plants release the oxygen necessary to the life of the animals.

13   Directions given in the Official Handbook to the Melbourne Aquarium.

NOTES

<u>CHAPTER I.—THE RETURN OF THE BIRDS</u>

The poet Gray: Thomas Gray (1716–1771) is famous as the author of *Elegy Written in a Country Churchyard, The Bard,* and *Ode to Eton College.*

Naturalist: One who studies Nature, and, more particularly, the lives of plants and animals.

Browning; Tennyson: The two greatest poets of the age of Queen Victoria.

Erratic: Irregular, having no fixed course or direction.

Buff: A light yellow.

Poses: Attitudes or positions.

Barbarians: Savages.

<u>CHAPTER II.—THE MIGRATION OF BIRDS</u>

Migration: Removal from one country or district to another; change of abode.

Homer: The earliest and greatest of Greek poets.

Crude: Incomplete.

Dr. Johnson was one of the most famous writers in England during the 18th century. His conversations, remarkable for their wit and good sense, were reported by his friend James Boswell.

Dogmatic: Over-sure.

Conglobulate: To form into a little round mass. Johnson was fond of using long words derived from Latin.

Gilbert White (1720–93): A fellow of Oxford, who settled at Selborne in Hampshire, and wrote *The Natural History of Selborne,* a charming book in which he records the facts of Nature as they occur in his daily walks. "How much dignity," says J. R. Lowell, "does the love of nature give to minds otherwise trivial! White's Selborne has become a classic. If he had chronicled the doings of kings and queens, he would never have emerged from oblivion. But his court journal of blackbirds and goldfinches has won him an inner nook in our memories."

Linnaeus (1707–78): A great naturalist; especially famous as a botanist.

Hibernation: State of sleep or torpor in which many animals pass the winter.

Perplexity: Doubt.

The ice age: A time when large parts of the surface of the earth were covered by an immense cap of ice.

Imperceptibly wider: Suggested by F. W. Hutton, F.R.S., in *Nature in New Zealand*, page 49. "It is supposed that, in the oversea migrations, the birds follow the old land lines. The voyages probably began when the two lands were close together, so that at no part of the journey were both of them invisible. The land gradually sank as the ages went by; but force of habit maintained the migration. The changes that took place in the land during the life of each bird would not be perceptible, and only after many generations had passed would the birds find themselves flying over a trackless ocean."

Siberian steppes: Vast, uncultivated plains in the northern parts of Asia.

CHAPTER III.—MIGRATIONS FROM AUSTRALIA

Glacial epoch: Ice age, a time when our lands were covered with an immense cap of ice.

Range: Area over which it wanders.

Ulysses of birds: Ulysses, the greatest wanderer of ancient times. He was the hero of Homer's poem, *The Odyssey*.

Tundras: Treeless plains.

CHAPTERS VI–VIII.—HOW BIRDS TALK AND SING

Sinister: Evil, unlucky.

Medley: Confusion.

Vitality: Power of life; energy.

Wordsworth: A great English poet of the end of the 18th and first half of the 19th century. In his poem beginning "O *nightingale! thou surely art*" he calls the bird "a creature of a fiery heart." *Sings darkling*, that is, in the darkness.

Darwin: The greatest naturalist of the 19th century; perhaps the greatest of modern times.

"To bathe the wing in dewy light": From a sonnet by Coleridge (1772–1834), *As when far off the warbled strains are heard.*

Varied pitch: Sometimes higher than at others.

Belated: Remaining beyond its usual time.

Weird: Ghostly, unnatural.

Mellow: Soft and musical.

Meditative: Thoughtful.

"—That tells its name to all the hills": From Tennyson's The Gardener's Daughter.

Pervasive: Having power to penetrate or travel far.

Recitative: A style of expression between speech and song.

Soliloquizing: Talking aloud to one's self.

Vesper: Evening.

Membrane: Thin layer of skin.

Vibrates: Moves quickly to and fro.

Beethoven (1770–1827): A German composer; as great among composers of music as Shakespeare among poets.

Oboe, or hautboy: A reed instrument with a mouthpiece which yields to the pressure of the lips.

John Burroughs: An American naturalist. He is a writer of authority on American birds; and perhaps no author has ever written upon birds with so much reality and charm.

Haphazard: Chance.

Fairest creations: According to Greek fable, the towers of Troy rose like a cloud to the song of Apollo, the god of music. In Celtic legend, Camelot, King Arthur's city of shadowy palaces, was "built to music, therefore never built at all, and therefore built forever." See Tennyson's *Gareth and Lynette*.

Napoleon: Napoleon Bonaparte, one of the greatest soldiers of all time, who made himself Emperor of the French. He died in 1821.

Monotone: A sound or series of sounds having only one pitch.

Recluse: One who lives alone, away from the world.

Milton: John Milton, one of the greatest English poets, lived during the 17th century. He wrote *Paradise Lost*. The quotation in the text is from his *Il Penseroso*.

"In nature there is nothing melancholy": From Coleridge's *The Nightingale*.

Vernal Chaucer: Chaucer who loved the spring-time. He was the greatest English poet of the Middle Ages, and died in 1400. His chief work is *The Canterbury Tales*. The quotation is from *Under the Willows*, by J. R. Lowell, an American poet of the 19th century. Lowell was one of the finest of men; one of the most delightful of writers.

Merle and mavis: Old names for the blackbird and the thrush respectively. They are still sometimes used in poetry.

CHAPTERS IX–X.—HOW BIRDS FEED

Shambles: Slaughter-house.

Ruskin: One of the greatest modern writers of English prose, and an intense lover of Nature. He died in 1900.

Nectar: The name given by the old Greeks to the drink of their gods, and now often used to denote the honey of plants.

The ancient Egyptians: The word ibis is of Egyptian origin.

CHAPTER XI.—HOW BIRDS FLY

Unwarranted: For which no just excuse could be made.
Undulating: Up and down and forward, in the manner of waves.
Burroughs: See note on page 279.

CHAPTERS XII–XIII.—BIRDS' NESTS

Primitive: Original. *Transition*: Passage. *Leptospermum*: A small bush of the tea-tree family, with pure white flowers.
Fledgling: A young bird almost ready for flight.
Ancestral practice: The practice of the birds from which the present-day birds are descended.
Pellet: A little ball.
Secretion: Something separated from the juices of the body.
Incubator: A contrivance for hatching eggs artificially.
Decomposing: Decaying.

CHAPTER XIV.—THE STORY OF A MAGPIE

The *white-backed magpie* is fiercer than the *black-backed bird*. The latter is the better singer.
Preen: To dress the feathers.
Rendezvous: A meeting place previously arranged.

CHAPTER XV.—THE PARTNERSHIP BETWEEN PLANTS AND BIRDS

"*Brother of the dancing leaves*": From Wordsworth's *The Green Linnet*.
Ecstasy: Rapture.
Marshalling: Arranging.
Larvæ: See footnote on the stages of an insect in The Story of the Mosquito, page 198.
The *scale-insect* is a small flat insect which exudes a sweet fluid (called *honey-dew*) upon the leaves of orange and other trees. On this honey-dew a black growth called the *sooty-mould fungus* grows up. This does much harm to the tree by clogging the breathing-holes in the leaves.

Drilled: Bored.

Pollen-bearers: See notes on self- and cross-fertilization in chapter on "Partnership of Plants and Insects," page 226.

A *parasitical plant* is one that grows and lives on another.

Glutinous: Sticky.

Germinate: Sprout.

Darwin: See note on Chapter VI-VIII.

CHAPTERS XVI–XVII.—BIRDS OF THE TOWN

Introduced birds: Skylarks, blackbirds, thrushes, Indian mynas, goldfinches, greenfinches, and starlings were brought into the colony by the Acclimatisation Society in 1864–5.

The dingo: The wild dog of Australia.

Exterminate: Put an end to.

Adaptive: Capable of fitting oneself to new conditions.

Precision: Exactness.

Intently: Attentively.

Furtive: In the manner of a thief.

Primitive: Original.

Flurried: Agitated.

Gregarious: Living in flocks.

Garrulous: Talkative, chattering.

Finches: Birds with short, stout bills; sparrows, canaries, and the like.

Lichen: A flowerless scaly plant that spreads over rocks and old rails.

Subtle: Cunningly devised. The *magpie* of Europe is not the same as the bird called the magpie in Australia.

CHAPTER XVIII.—THE SONGS OF THE TOWN-BIRDS

Burroughs: See page 269.

Macgillivray: A naturalist of last century; an authority on English birds.

Jubilant: Joyful.

Ecstasy: Rapture.

Resources: Powers.
Pervasive: Having power to penetrate or travel far.
Radius: The line drawn from the centre of a circle to the circumference.
Vehemently: Vigorously.
Most subtly: In the most insinuating way.
Babel: A confused combination of sounds.
Spendthrift: One who spends extravagantly.

CHAPTER XIX.—SEA BIRDS

Inspiration: Lofty tone of thought or feeling.
Refuse: Scum, waste matter.
Gullet: Throat, the passage for food between mouth and stomach.
Kerguelen Island: A small island in the Southern Ocean, S.W. of Australia.
Breakers: The broken water where the sea meets the land.
Poise: Balance.
Blackmail: Money paid to secure protection from violence.
Zephyr: A gentle breeze.
Garrulousness: Talkativeness.
Incredible: Unbelievable.
Flinders and Bass: Captain Matthew Flinders and Surgeon Bass, in 1798, discovered the existence of the passage now called Bass Strait.
Rookery: A gathering place for birds.

CHAPTER XX

The EARTH-WORM is one of the ring-bodied animals, which include also sea-worms and leeches.
Darwin: See note on page 282.
Microbes and bacteria: Minute creatures which live on decaying vegetable matter.
Tubal Cain: The first worker in metals.
Grader: A horse machine for levelling uneven soil.

Cocoon: See footnote to The Story of the Mosquito, page 198.

Secrete: To abstract or separate from the blood.

Zone: A girdle.

Centipede: A creature with many joints and many feet (L. centum 100 and pes, a foot).

Pulverizes: Reduces to dust.

CHAPTER XXI.—A WORD FOR THE SNAIL

The *snail* belongs to the molluscs—animals with soft bodies. These soft-bodied animals generally have a shell, but are sometimes without it, as in the *slug*.

Belly-foot: The whole of the under surface or belly is used as a foot by snails, slugs, periwinkles, limpets, &c.

Basis: Ground or guide.

The chalk counties: The counties like Kent, Sussex, &c., which have a chalky soil. The chalk under the microscope is seen to be composed of innumerable shells. Shell-back snails, therefore, are able easily on chalky soils to get the lime which they need for their shells.

Ben Jonson (1573–1637): A writer of plays, of the time of Shakespeare.

Gray: See note to Chapter I.

CHAPTER XXII.—WHAT WE SAW AT THE BEACH: PART I

The families dealt with in this and the following two chapters are:

I.—*The two-layered animals*: Anemones, corals, and sea-jellies.

II.—*The Sponges*.

III.—*The Worms*: (1) Worms with tubes of lime or sand—Serpula, spirorbis, and sand-tube worm. (2) Free worms—Sand-worm.

IV.—*Crustaceans* (L. *crusta*, a crust) or *Jointed Animals*: The acorn-barnacle, the sand-hopper, the shrimp, crabs and lobsters.

V.—*The Molluscs* (L. *mollis*, soft) or *Shell-fish*: (1) Univalves—

The warrener and other periwinkles and whelks, limpets, mutton shell-fish (or sea-ear), mail-shell. (2) Bivalves—Cockle and mussel.

VI.—*The hedgehog-skinned animals*: Star-fish, sea-urchin (Fr. oursin, a sea-hedgehog).

Secretes: Separates from the juices of the body.

Chemist: One who can break up a substance into the elements that have come together to make it up. In some cases the chemist can reverse this process.

Anemone: The wind-flower (Greek, anemos, the wind).

A *hermit crab* is one that protects its soft tail by thrusting it into the shell of a dead periwinkle. The *anemone-like creature* from which many of the sea-jellies spring is called a hydra.

Ray florets: The small flowers which form one or more circles around the heart of the daisy and other flowers of similar kind.

Germ: The egg or seed from which anything springs.

Aquarium: A vessel with glass sides for keeping sea plants and sea animals.

Slips: Small pieces cut from the parent plant. These, when planted, form roots and become separate plants.

CHAPTER XXIII.—WHAT WE SAW AT THE BEACH: PART II

Sponges: The small sponges found at Black Rock have no commercial value, but large sponges are sometimes washed ashore at Sorrento and Warrnambool.

Ship barnacles may often be seen on ships that have come in after a long voyage. They cluster sometimes so thickly on the bottom as to impede the ship's progress.

Huxley: A distinguished English naturalist of the 19th century.

Dune: A low hill of sand thrown up by the wind on a sea coast.

When man comes to his kingdom: Man has it *in him* to be the sovereign of the earth; but the extent of his rule at any moment depends on two things—(1) how much he knows, (2) how far he has learned to rule *himself*.

Homer: The most ancient of Greek poets, and the greatest. His date is uncertain; but his poems take us back 3,000 years or more to the men and women who lived on the shores of the Eastern Mediterranean. In his *Odyssey* he narrates the adventures of Ulysses while voyaging among the islands in the Aegean Sea.

CHAPTER XXIV.—WHAT WE SAW AT THE BEACH: PART III

Tyre: An ancient city on the coast of Syria. A chemical dye has now taken the place of the dye extracted by the Tyrians from a shell-fish (*murex or purpura*). The dye was got from a white vein in the neck of the shell-fish.

The *limpet's* force of adhesion is calculated to be equal to 2,000 times its own weight.

The *Oyster-catcher*: See Sea Birds, page 145.

Mussel: The large white whelk which preys on the mussel is the *Purpura succincta*.

The *mutton shell-fish* (haliotis or sea-ear) is often eaten.

Mail-shell: *Chiton*, a cuirass.

Eccentric: Uncommon.

"Did he stand," &c.: From Tennyson's Maud.

CHAPTER XXV.—THE ROSE GREEN-FLY OR APHIS

The *aphis* (plural *aphides*) belongs to the *insects* in which the mouth is formed for suction.

Antennæ: Feelers attached to the head.

The *Mallee*: The wide plains in the north of Victoria where the Mallee gum-tree grows.

Excrescence: Lump.

The *phylloxera or vine aphis* has caused enormous losses in

France and Australia. Some of our vineyards have had to be rooted out in order to check the pest.

Gall: A lump on root, branch, or leaf, caused generally by the bite of an insect.

Larval stage: See footnote to The Story of the Mosquito, page 198.

Status: Standing, social position.

CHAPTER XXVI.—POND-LIFE

The creatures found in the pond are the *amœba* (the jelly-speck that changes shape); volvox (the little round creature that rolls through the water); *vorticella* (the little bell-shaped creature that makes a small vortex in drawing in its food); whirligig beetle, great water-beetle, leech, pond-snail, dragonfly grub, tadpole, water-mite, mosquito larva.

Counterpart: Corresponding form.

Sediment: Fine matter that has settled on the bottom of the pond.

Animalcule: Minute animal.

The leech, when sucking blood, is attached so firmly that it can be detached only with difficulty. The practice of "bleeding" patients by leeches has long since been given up. *The Leech-gatherer* is a famous poem by Wordsworth. The chief figure in the poem is an old man who makes his living by gathering leeches for the doctors. "From pond to pond he roamed, from moor to moor."

Water milfoil: A common plant in stagnant water. It is readily recognized by the fine division of the leaves into numerous hair-like branches.

Sheep-fluke: A flat worm which infests the liver of sheep.

Mites belong to the same family as spiders, and, like spiders, have four pairs of legs.

Tadpole: The pond stage of the frog.

Larva: See footnote to The Story of the Mosquito, page 185.

CHAPTER XXVII.—THE STORY OF THE MOSQUITO

Development: Growth.

Mysterious transformation: A change not yet understood by science.

Gnat: The mosquito is a member of the gnat family among the flies.

Discarded: Abandoned.

Vegetarian: Vegetable feeder.

Oblivious: Forgetful.

More tolerant: Able better to bear.

Germ: Seed or egg from which something grows.

Malaria: Fever common in hot, marshy lands.

Yellow fever: A fever common in hot, marshy parts of America.

Exhilarating: Cheering.

Authorities: Men who have made a special study of a subject.

Municipality: A district governed by a town council.

Note on the emergence of the mosquito from the pupa skin: Observations made by Mr. J. A. Leach go to show that the mosquito stands on the surface of the water.

CHAPTER XXVIII.—WHAT THE SPADE TURNED UP

Compass: Travel over.

Forceps: A pair of pincers.

Millipede (mille 1,000, pes a foot): A small, many-footed creature; smaller than the centipede.

Earth-spider: See chapter on The Spider.

Cocoon: See note to The Story of the Mosquito.

The slater is one of the crustaceans, and is nearly the sole land representative of the family.

Thoreau (died 1862): An American essayist. He lived much in the open air, and was a keen observer of nature.

The *musical locust* is not a locust at all, and should be called a cicada. The cicada belongs to a different order from the grasshopper.

Scarified: The surface broken up.

A *contagious fungoid disease* is one caused by the rapid multiplication of plant-like germs. The germs of the disease are communicated by contact or by the wind.

Plague of locusts in Egypt: Exodus X. 12.

CHAPTER XXIX.—THE STORY OF A MOTH

Ovipositor: Egg-placer.

Cocoon: See note to The Story of the Mosquito.

Mummy-case: The case enveloping a dead body that has been embalmed.

The *daily miracle*: Events happening in the ordinary course of Nature, but really as wonderful as if they were supernatural.

Unearthly in its purity: Almost passing out of the region of matter into the region of spirit.

Pips: Apple or pear seeds.

Codlin moth: Other means of checking this pest can be found in the *Handbook of Destructive Insects*, by Mr. C. French, F.L.S., Government Entomologist of Victoria.

CHAPTER XXX.—ANTS, WASPS, AND BEES

Division of labour: In primitive societies every member is capable of doing any of the work required; in advanced societies each member has his special task to which his life-work is devoted.

Well organized: Well arranged.

Debris: Rubbish.

Overseer: One placed over workers to direct them.

Galleries: Side tunnels and chambers.

Pupa: See note to The Story of the Mosquito.

Pupa clothes: The outer skin within which the young ant is changed into the perfect insect.

Ameoba-jelly: See notes on Pond Life.

Caste: Society in India is divided into hereditary castes or classes which are kept strictly separate.

Hornet: A kind of wasp.

Paralyse: To make helpless.

Sheen: Brightness.

CHAPTER XXXI.—THE PARTNERSHIP BETWEEN
INSECTS AND PLANTS

Man's co-operation with Nature: When man finds out a law of Nature he is able, within certain limits, to hasten or modify Nature's course: he governs by obeying. This method is being used, for example, in order to get the wheat-plants best suited for Australia. If the plant be prolific, but too weak in the stem, we may give to it the strength it lacks by fertilizing its flowers with the pollen of a strong-stalked wheat-plant, and so on.

Fertilization: In order to make the seed-case fruitful, the stigma must be touched with pollen. When this pollen is brought from another flower, the process is called *cross-fertilization*; when from the flower's own stamens, the process is called *self-fertilization*. The seeds due to crossing are stronger than those due to the plant's own pollen. Hence all the advanced flowers have devices to secure cross-fertilization, and to prevent self-fertilization.

Anthers: The pollen cells at the end of the stamens.

Honey-track: The path, generally marked by spots or converging lines, to the store of honey.

"Many a man," &c.: Huxley was never a field botanist, and was advanced in years when he fell in love with the beautiful blue gentians of the Swiss mountains. This led him to cultivate flowers; and these became the children of his old age.

CHAPTER XXXII.—THE SPIDER

The spider does not belong to the class *Insecta*. An insect has three parts—head, thorax, abdomen; a *spider* only two parts, the head and thorax being united into one piece. An *insect* has three pairs of legs, a *spider* four pairs. We never find in the spider the compound eyes of the insect; there are eight simple eyes. The jaws are hooked, and carry a poison gland. The thread is produced by glands on the underside of the abdomen. A viscid fluid, passing through a large number of minute tubes, hardens on exposure to the air, and the threads so produced are twisted into one rope by the spinnerets. Note that the ray-threads are stouter than the cross-threads.

Cocoon: See note to The Story of the Mosquito.

Minimum: Least possible.

Trapdoor: A door, as in a floor or roof, which shuts close like a valve.

A *material good* supplies some want of the body.

Sir John Lubbock: A distinguished naturalist.

Providence: Foresight.

Drones: (1) The male bees, which are killed after the marriage-flight; (2) any members who do no work for the general good.

Animal economy: The rule of life among the lower animals.

Magic carpet: In tales of the East we often hear of a carpet endowed by magic with the power of conveying those who sat on it to distant parts.

Poetry of popular belief: As men outlive the mistaken beliefs of past times, these beliefs pass into the region of romance.

CHAPTER XXXIII.—FISH PART I

We have now come into the order of the *Vertebrates*—the animals with a backbone. The fish is the lowest member of the family. A fish can swim quickly because (1) the shape—a rounded wedge—offers the least resistance to the water; (2) the fish pours over its body a kind of slime.

The *fins* in a typical fish are: The breast-fins just behind the gills;

The belly-fins—the breast and belly fins are *paired* in order to balance and steer—a fish deprived of any of these fins loses its balance, and a dead fish floats belly upwards; The unpaired keel-fins on belly and back; The tail-fin for sculling. Fins are sometimes modified into weapons of offence.

Isaak Walton (1593-1683): Author of *The Complete Angler,* a book which interests the fisher on its practical side, and the general reader through its delightful pictures of river scenery.

The flying-fish is able, by the help of its long breast-fins, to fly 200 or 300 yards.

The sun-fish is a gigantic fish which lives on or near the surface of the deep sea.

The sword-fish is a fish of prey which spears its victim by means of its long sword-like upper jaw.

A *phosphorescent* body gives out a faint light without heat.

Deep sea dredge: An instrument for bringing to the surface objects in the ocean depths.

Crustaceans: Creatures like shrimps and crabs.

Gibbon (1737-94): A great historian. His Decline and Fall of the Roman Empire was described by Carlyle as "the splendid bridge from the old world to the new."

Medieval knights: Knights of the Middle Ages—the time between the 8th and the 15th centuries.

"Dragons of the prime," &c.: From Tennyson's In Memoriam.

Gelatine: An animal substance which can be dissolved in hot water.

Gristle: An animal substance more solid and elastic than gelatine.

<u>CHAPTER XXXIV.—FISH PART II</u>

Oxygen: A gas necessary for the support of life. Lung-breathing animals get it from the atmosphere; gill-breathing animals, like fishes, from the water.

Iridescent: Having colours like the rainbow.

Epicure: One addicted to the pleasures of the table.

Estuary of a river: The part at the mouth affected by the sea tides.

<u>CHAPTER XXXV.—THE FROG</u>

The frog belongs to the *Amphibians* (*amphi*, both; *bios*, life)—backboned animals, which can live on land or in water. The frog described is our Australian green bell-frog. A very common English amphibian, the newt, is not found in Australia.

Aristotle: A Greek philosopher (died B.C. 322), tutor of Alexander the Great. He was one of the first to attempt a history of animals.

Aristophanes (died B.C. 380): A Greek dramatist, who wrote a comedy called *The Frogs*.

Wallace, A. R.: A distinguished naturalist and traveller.

Darwin: See page 279.

English fen counties: Parts of the shires of Lincoln, Cambridge, and Norfolk have been reclaimed from swamps by draining.

Macbeth: A play by Shakespeare.

"Sweet are the uses," &c.: Shakespeare's *As You Like It*.

<u>CHAPTER XXXVI.—SNAKES AND LIZARDS</u>

The class *Reptilia* includes tortoises and turtles, snakes, lizards, crocodiles, and alligators.

Paroxysm: Convulsion, fit.

Venom: Rule for distinguishing venomous from non-venomous snakes, given by Mr. E. R. Waite, F.L.S.:—If only two punctures appear, a certain distance apart (thus

.   .), the snake is, in all probability, a venomous one. The
    wounds inflicted by a harmless snake consist of two rows
    of punctures.

Piecemeal: Bit by bit.

Huxley: See page 285.

The *boas* and *pythons* are non-venomous snakes that seize their
    prey by coiling themselves around it in numerous folds.

Rudiments: Beginning.

Throwback: When an improved kind of flower degenerates into
    the original type, it is called a "throwback."

The *iguanas*, or "blood-suckers," can give a severe bite; but
    otherwise, are harmless to man.

TREATMENT OF SNAKE-BITE[14]—Rules given by the Board of
    Health, Melbourne:—

Tie a cord (string, tape, handkerchief, bootlace, coat lining,
    shirt strips) a few inches above the wound. Screw up the
    cord very tightly with a rod, which is then to be fastened
    as shown in diagram.

Cause the part bitten to bleed freely. Pinch up the flesh and
    cut round the marks of the fangs; if no knife handy, cut
    into flesh with teeth.

Suck the wounds for the next thirty minutes. The person
    sucking must have no sores in the mouth; otherwise, he
    may be poisoned.

Get a doctor's help at once.

Minor Points:

Wash the cuts now and then with Condy's fluid, or with a
    strong solution of bleaching powder.

In case of faintness, give sal volatile or hot strong coffee.

Keep patient warm.

Do not let patient exhaust himself by walking about.

NOTE: Where a bite is on a part of the body where a cord

14   Do NOT do this. As with much medical knowledge this is now not the correct
treatment.

cannot be tied, the treatment is, in other respects, the same.

CHAPTER XXXVII.—METHOD IN NATURE-STUDY

Kepler (1571-1630): A German astronomer. He discovered that the earth, in moving round the sun, describes, not a circle, but an ellipse.

Dr. J. H. Fabre: A French naturalist; one of the best insect students of the 19th century.

Small creatures of the seashore: Acorn-shells, Serpula, &c. A good method of observation is to find a handy stone or shell with the acorn-barnacle or other creature attached, and to place this in a shallow rock-pool where a lens can be conveniently used.

Observation of birds: A fountain, a pond, or even an open trough in a garden is a great attraction to birds. Mr. Donald Macdonald makes the excellent suggestion that this should be kept in view in laying out a garden.

SUMMARIES OF THE CHAPTERS

I.—THE RETURN OF THE BIRDS

Many birds return to Victoria in summer. Among them are the house-swallow, the fairy martin, the white-shafted fantail, and the ground-lark or pipit. 2. The habits and work of these returned birds. 3. Nature requires long and sustained observation before she will unlock her secrets.

II.—MIGRATION OF BIRDS

Old beliefs with respect to the migration of birds. 2. The difficulties with which the study of bird migrations is attended. 3. The probable origin of the migratory instinct. 4. The migrations of the local and the European larks or pipits.

III.—MIGRATIONS FROM AUSTRALIA

Birds that leave Australia. The reasons for their migration. Among these birds are the bronze cuckoo, the swift, the sandpiper or sharp-tailed stint, and the sand dotterel. The lines of flight and habits of each of these birds.

IV.—BALANCE OF NATURE, Part I

Nature has a plan into which each insect, bird, beast, and plant is perfectly fitted. 2. The work done by swallows and swifts in the destruction of gnats, mosquitos, and flies. 3. Man often thoughtlessly and harmfully interferes with Nature's plan. 4. The fruit trees suffer through the destruction of the native birds. 5. The silver-eyes and tits and the aphis pest. 6. Spiders and moths. 7. The crow's evil is not unmixed with good.

NATURE STUDY CALENDAR FOR VICTORIA.

BIRDS.

JAN.

Quail rearing a second brood	S.
Young wild ducks are mostly able to fly	S.W.
Young river terns become accomplished fishers	N.W.
Swifts are going south (China to Tasmania)	N.E.
Silver-eyes teach their young to kill case-moths	E.

FEB.

The last white eggs of the season are being laid by pigeons	
Birds of prey journey away from their nesting places	S.W.
Sparrows flock, and should be destroyed	S.
Small insect-eating birds are abroad with their families	N.E.

MARCH.

Birds prepare to migrate northwards	S.
Siberian birds leave for Asia	S.W.
Many birds moult	N.W.
Swifts are returning to China and Japan	All parts
Cuckoos migrate to Queensland	E.

APRIL.

Birds migrate northwards	S.
Autumn whistle of the butcher-bird heard	S.W.
Birds donning new plumage	N.W.
Winter congregation of bower-birds	N.E.
Highland birds go to the lowlands	E.

MAY.

Grey thrush visits towns	S.

Robin appears in the open in its new red dress	S.W.
Lyre-bird vocally active	N.E.
Bird life dull	E.

JUNE.

Bush lark starts to nest	S.
Swans and geese prepare to lay eggs; bird life for the most part subdued	S.W.
Curlew and emu look for nesting sites	N.W.
Lyre-bird nesting	

JULY.

Birds still quiet if the weather is cold	S.
Robins mate and enter the bush to nest	S.W.
Magpies nest and lay eggs	N.W.
The nests of this month are mostly dome-shaped	N.E.

AUG.

Tomtits begin to be merry	S.
Plovers rear their young	S.W.
House-swallows arrive from the north	N.E.
Finches arrive from Southern Queensland	E.

SEPT.

Birds in full song	S.
Siberian birds are arriving	S.W.
Chats arrive, and will nest in October-November	N.W.
Lowland insect-eating birds start to nest	N.E.
House-swallows and cuckoos arrive from the north	E.

OCT.

Blue wren in full nuptial plumage	S.
Diamond-birds (Pardalotes) nest	S.W.
Bee-eaters are arriving from the north	N.W.
Alpine insectivorous birds start to nest; coach whip bird very active	N.E.
Pale blue eggs of perching birds (Silver-eye) laid	E.

NOV.

| Wood-swallows arrive | S. |
| Quail are abroad with their first brood of young, destroying an | |

immense quantity of noxious insects   S.W.
Black and white swallow tunnels into bank   N.W.
Parrots and cockatoos nest   N.E.
Most birds busy with their young   E.

DEC.

Babblers search for codlin moths   S.
Young birds now in a majority   S.W.
Water birds are abroad with their young   N.W.
Rails feed for the greater part on water vermin   N.E.
Young honey-eaters active among the blossoms   E.

<u>INSECTS.</u>

JAN.

Wattle goat-moth frees itself from chrysalis   S.
White ants (Termes) are particularly busy   N.W.
Cut-worm or Bugong moth (Mamestra) in
      immense quantity   N.E.
Stinging caterpillar or cup-moth (Pelora) broadly
      distributed, November-March   E.

FEB.

Pear-tree slug continues to damage foliage   S.
Manna musical locust (Cicada) (Dec.-Feb.)   S.W.
Vine-moth caterpillars are going into winter quarters   N.W.

MARCH.

Ground moth (Pielus), March-May; note empty cocoons   S.
Case-moths in the garden should be reduced   S.W.

APRIL.

Ticks travel (with sheep, &c.)   S.
Australian silk-worm moth emerges (pupated in Jan)   E., S.

MAY.

Gall-makers rearing young   N.W.

JUNE.

Mosquitoes and ants in small number; restful

JULY.

Lady-bird beetle begins to eat harmful insects   N.W.
Plant lice (Aphides) are appearing   N.W.

AUG.

Scale-insects in gardens should be destroyed   S.
White butterfly's first brood, August-September   N.W.

SEPT.

Scale-insects hatch their early young about this time   S.
Codlin moth appears with apple blossom   N.W.
Wheat-moth leaves cocoon, September-October   N.E.

OCT.

Saw-flies are leaving their cocoons in the ground   S.
Plant bugs are ready to attack soft fruits   S.W.
Processional caterpillars (Taera) appear sooner or later   N.W.

NOV.

Pear tree slug begins to appear on cherry and pear trees
Brown butterflies (Heteronympha and Xenica)
hatch out on grasses, November to March   S.
Painted lady butterfly (Pyrameis) hatches out on the plains

    S.W.

Swallow-tailed butterfly (Papilio) found near
    water-courses   N.E.
Bombardier beetle plentiful   N.W.

DEC.

Root-borer [weevil (Curculio)] in gardens is laying its
    eggs on the foliage   S.
Click beetles and wire-worms (Elaters)   S.W.
Satin-blue butterfly (November-March) feeding only on
    mistletoe   N.W.

<u>OTHER ANIMALS.</u>

JAN.

Argonaut or paper nautilus occasionally arrives   S.E., S.W.
Water-beetles and rotifers active   N.E.
River blackfish (Gadopsis) with spawn   E.

FEB.

Planarian worms with eggs — N.E., E.

MARCH.

Water rats (Hydromys) seen and their splash heard — S.
Freshwater mussel waiting in river banks
for autumn rains — N.W.
Mountain trout (Galaxias) go into hiding and develop their eggs
(March-April) — N., N.E.

APRIL.

Death-adder (Acanthophis) becomes torpid — N.W.

MAY.

Murray lobster (Astacoides) with her brilliant red eggs — N.W.
Native bear (Koala) protected by Act of Parliament — E.

JUNE.

Barracouta (Thersites) and herrings (Clupea) in the
bays during the colder months — E., S.E., S.W.
Red backed poisonous spider (Latrodectus) carries
her egg-case — N.W.
Land snail (Bulinus) — N.E.
Slugs lay eggs — E.

JULY.

Frogs' eggs (Ranoidæ) hatch; continue for months
Pouched mouse (Sminthopsis) breeds now,
and continues through spring — S.W.

AUG.

Young bandicoots (Chæropus) about to feed
upon roots and ground insects — S.W.
Blue-tongued lizard and young — N.W.
Wombat (Phascolomys) still sluggish — E.

SEPT.

Foxes rob birds' nests
Murray cod perch has its young abroad — N.W.

OCT.

Land crab (Engæus) in a colony beneath the ground — S.

NOV.

Porcupine, or echidna, a vigorous eater of ants   S.
Flying foxes (Pteropus) damage fruits   E.

DEC.

Murray tortoise (Chelymis) lays eggs   N.W.
Lizards of many species numerous   N.W.
Water snails (many genera) plentiful   S.W.
Ring tail opossum (Pseudochirus) carries young in pouch   E.

<u>PLANTS.</u>

JAN.

Prickly box (Bursaria) and honeysuckle (Banksia)   S., S.W.
Manna gum tree (Eucalyptus viminalis)   N.E.
Water-lilies seeding   N.W.
Goodenia   E.

FEB.

Sheoak (Casuarina)   S. and S.W.
Native pine (Callitris) fruits ripening most of the year   N.W.
Grasses seeding   N.E.

MAR.

Blue bell (Wahlenbergia)   All parts
Alpine plants seeding   N.E.

APRIL.

Autumn orchid (Eriochilus autumnalis)   All parts
Native raspberry (Rubus)   S

MAY.

Saltbush (Rhagodia) and Acacia retinoides   S.E.
Mushroom (Agaricus) fruits   S., S.W., E.

JUNE.

Heath (Epacris), most parts introduced furze   S.
Mosses fruiting   N.E.
Christmas tree (Prostanthera)   E.

JULY.

True sarsaparilla (Smilax), Victorian crocus (Hypoxis)   S., S.W.,
N.W. from April

| Virgin's bower (Clematis) | N. |
| Native hop (Daviesia) | E. |

AUG.

| Sundews (Drosera) Harbinger of spring (Wurmbea) | S., S.W. |
| Paper-bark tree (Tea-tree) | N.W. |

SEPT.

Tea-tree (Leptospermum)   S.; Chamasella S., N.E. (E. August)
Buttercups and crowsfoot (Ranunculus) flower on to December   S.

OCT.

Rice-flower (Pimelia), S.; acacias (wattles) going out of bloom
Heath concluding its flowering season	S.W.
Gum trees (Eucalypti), several species, flowering	N.W.
Fungi of the garden mature	S.
Supplejack (Tecoma)	E.

NOV.

Hazel (Pomaderris), trigger plant (Candollea)	S.
Buttercup and crowsfoot (Ranunculus)	
(September-December)	S.W. and S.
Grasses seeding	N.W.

DEC.

Native violet (Viola) and water plant (Chara) in fruit	S.
Boronias and daisies (Brachycome)	N.W.
Grevillea tree losing its blossoms	N.E.

Native blue-bell flowering all the year in all parts of Victoria.

The time of flowering will vary with the season, so that the month may be an earlier or a later one than that recorded.

This calendar is not to be considered as a full record of flora and fauna, but simply as an outline of how a chart might be made of particular phases of the common plants and animals. Each district should be explored and fully calendared by one or more observers.

COMMON NAMES OF AUSTRALIAN BIRDS.

BABBLER.—Chatterer, Chatty Bird, Happy Family.
BLACK DUCK.—Australian Wild Duck.
BLUE WREN.—Blue Bonnet, Blue Tit, Superb Warbler, Blue-bird.
BOOBOOK OWL.—Brown Owl.
BOTTLE SWALLOW.—Fairy Martin, Retort Swallow.
BRONZE CUCKOO.—Little Cuckoo.
BROWN TIT.—Creek Tit, Little Brown Tit, Little Thornbill.
BUSH-LARK.—Thick-billed Lark, Horsfield's Bush-Lark, Thick billed Ground-Lark.
BUTCHER-BIRD.—Whistling Jack, Derwent Jackass, Collared Crow Shrike.
COCKATOO (White).—Sulphur-crested Cockatoo.
CRANE (Blue).—White-fronted Heron.
CROW.—White-eyed Crow.
CURLEW.—Southern Stone Plover, Land Curlew.
DIAMOND-BIRD.—Wit-e-chu, Pick-it-up, Red-tipped Pardalote.
DOTTREL (BLACK-FRONTED).—Ringed Sandpiper.
FAIRY MARTIN.—Bottle Swallow, Retort Swallow.
FALCON (WHITE-FRONTED).—Little Falcon, Little Hawk.
FANTAIL (BLACK AND WHITE).—Willie Wagtail, Shepherd's Companion.
FANTAIL (WHITE-SHAFTED).—Zig-zag Fantail.
FINCH (RED-BROWED).—Red-bill.
FROGMOUTH.—Podargus, Morepork.
GRASS-BIRD.—Little Grass-bird, Stench-bird.

GRASS-PARRAKEET.—Blue-banded Grass-Parrakeet, Blue-winged Grass-Parrakeet.

GREBE.—Diver, Dabchick.

GREEN 'KEET.—Musk Lorikeet, Green Parrakeet.

GROUND-LARK.—Pipit, Meadow Pipit.

GROUND-TIT.—Speckled Tit, Chthonicola, Little Field-Wren.

HERON (WHITE-FRONTED).—Blue Crane.

HONEY-BIRD.—Meliphagidæ—Honey-eaters proper.

HOUSE-SWALLOW.—Chimney Swallow, Welcome Swallow, The Swallow.

KESTREL.—Nankeen Kestrel, Kestrel Hawk.

KINGFISHER.—Sacred Kingfisher, Wood Kingfisher, Halcyon.

LAUGHING JACKASS.—Great Brown Kingfisher, Kookaburra, Bush man's Clock.

MAGPIE LARK.—Mud Lark, Grallina, Pe wit, Pe-wee.

MAGPIE.—White-backed Crow-Shrike, Black-backed Crow-Shrike, Piping Crow-Shrike, Australian Magpie.

MISTLETOE-BIRD.—Swallow Dicæum, Flower-pecker.

MUD LARK.—Magpie Lark, Grallina, Peewit, Pe-wee.

MYNA, MINAH.—Indian Minah.

NIGHTJAR (OWLET).—Little Morepork, Little Nightjar.

PALLID CUCKOO.—Unadorned Cuckoo, Grey Mutton-bird.

PIGEON (BRONZE-WINGED).—Bronze-wing.

QUAIL (STUBBLE).—Pectoral Quail.

ROBIN (SCARLET-BREASTED).—Redbreast.

ROSELLA.—Rosehill Parrakeet.

SAND DOTTREL (DOUBLE-BANDED).

SANDPIPER.—Stint.

SCRUB-WREN (WHITE-BROWED).—White-fronted Sericornis, Scrub-Tit.

SILVER-EYE.—White-eye, Blight-bird, Spectacle-bird, Ring-eye Grey-backed Zosterops.

SONG-LARK.—Cinclorhamphus, Singing Lark.
SPARROW.—Sprig.
SPINE-BILLED HONEY-EATER.—Spine-bill, Honey-bird.
STINT.—Little Sandpiper.
THICKHEAD (WHITE-THROATED).—White-throated
   Yellow-breast.
TIT (YELLOW-RUMPED).—Yellow-tail, Tomtit, Thornbill.
TREE-CREEPER (WHITE-THROATED).—Woodpecker.
TREE-RUNNER (BLACK-CAPPED).—Nuthatch, Black-
   capped Sittella, Bark-runner.
WATTLE BIRD (RED).—Wattled Honey-eater, Wattle-bird,
   Gill-bird.